# DEAR IRENE

Irene Kelly Mysteries

*Goodnight, Irene*
*Sweet Dreams, Irene*
*Dear Irene,*

# DEAR IRENE

An Irene Kelly Mystery

Jan Burke

This edition was first published in
Great Britain in 1996 by
Judy Piatkus (Publishers) Ltd of
5 Windmill Street, London W1



*A catalogue record for this book is available
from the British Library*

ISBN 0-7499-0324-4

Printed and bound in Great Britain by
Bookcraft (Bath) Ltd

*For My Husband,*

*Timothy Burke,*

*who is one in a gazillion.*

*All my words are paupers at your door,*

*begging you to know what they cannot express.*

# ACKNOWLEDGMENTS

I AM ESPECIALLY GRATEFUL TO DAN COBURN FOR HIS HELP WITH airplanes; Ed and Kelly Dohring for once again providing help with medical questions (even during walks on Sanibel Island); Detective Dennis Payne of the LAPD Robbery-Homicide Division, for putting up with all kinds of pestering; Andy Rose and Debbie Arrington of the *Press-Telegram* for reporting insights; Robert Samoian, Deputy District Attorney for the County of Los Angeles, for help with judicial system questions; Larry Ragle, author, instructor and former Director of Forensic Sciences for Orange County; John Olguin of the Los Angeles Dodgers organization, Jack Shinar, Bill Granick, Debbie Arrington (yes, again!), and everyone else who helped with the baseball questions; Sharon Weissman for unfailing support and willingness to help; and Ken McGuire of the Los Angeles County Flood Control District, who patiently answered some strange inquiries from a mystery writer during a break in the rainy season. Special thanks are due my uncle, Robert Flynn, retired political reporter for the *Evansville Press*, whose work has always fascinated me, and undoubtedly influenced Irene's choice of a career.

No small part of the information about child care and women in the workforce during World War II was gathered from my participation as a research assistant on the "Rosie the Riveter Revisited" oral history project at California State University, Long Beach, a project funded by the Rockefeller Foundation and the National Endowment for the Humanities. I am indebted to Sherna Gluck, who designed and directed the project, for allowing me the remarkable privilege of interviewing women who worked in Southern California's aircraft factories during World War II. I am also indebted to the women themselves, whose recollections and thoughts about their lives changed my own life in ways I cannot measure.

Thanks to a great many librarians for your assistance in research and beyond, especially to those of you who work for the Long Beach Public Library, the Angelo Iacoboni Branch of the Los Angeles County Library, and the University Library of California State University, Long Beach.

As always, readers are asked to understand that while all of these individuals were of help in the research for this book, I will not allow them to take any credit for my errors.

Nancy Yost deserves thanks for so much, including insightful comments on early drafts.

My family and friends have kept me going during those times when I thought I was a goner. Tom and Marty Burke have been especially wonderful, putting up with their daughter-in-law's oddball, PST night-owl work schedule during her visits to the East Coast. Tim remained a steadfast companion and cheerleader during days when my DNA might not have tested out to be human. Robert Hahn, Heather Harkins, and members of the Flynn family who waited for me in Cincinnati deserve my special thanks for their patience.

The people who make up a company called Simon and Schuster have given me support at every level, more than I can detail here. And Laurie Bernstein will never know how much I appreciate her guidance and encouragement, because this book would cost each reader an additional ten bucks if I were allowed the time to sit here and write about it. Will "THANKS!!" do for now?

# 1

*November 28, 1990*

*Please hand deliver to:*
*Miss Irene Kelly*
*Las Piernas News Express*
*600 Broadway*
*Las Piernas, CA*

*Dear Miss Kelly,*

*I am writing to you because those guys who write the Sports Section are a bunch of jerks who won't take me seriously. My dog, Pigskin, can predict the outcome of the Super Bowl. So far, he has a perfect record. Once the playoff teams have been decided, I simply glue the team emblems to the bottoms of two dishes of dog food, put them on the floor, and whichever one Pigskin goes to, that's which team will win. I think this is pretty interesting and thought maybe you should do a story on it . . .*

I crumpled that one into a ball and spiked Pigskin right into the round file—and did it all left-handed. But after a moment, I pulled the letter back out of the trash. Setting aside my generally rotten mood that day, I decided Pigskin might be of help with this year's office football pool.

Going through my mail that Wednesday afternoon in late November, I had already sorted out the flyers on meetings and the invitations to local political wingdings. That left only the pile of the envelopes which were less easily identified. Some were handwritten, some typed, some bore computer-generated labels. Few had return addresses.

> *I. Kelly*
> *Las Piernas News Express*
>
> *Dear Bleeding Heart Kelly,*
>
> *The recent media worship of the Premier of the Soviet Union is disgusting. Presenting Mr. Gorbachev as a reformer is the most insidious communist plot yet. Not that you lily-livered leftists of the press are hard to fool, but I think it should be obvious that this is all just a charade to get us to drop our guard . . .*

I was unfazed by these unflattering descriptions of my internal organs. I admit that I was a little distracted, not paying much attention to the occasional crank among my readers' correspondence. My mail isn't always as oddball as it was that day, but the approach of certain major holidays seems to make nut cases reach for their stationery.

Most are harmless, lonely people who just need *somebody* to listen to them. Every now and again, one of them causes some trouble, like the guy who showed up in the newsroom one day with his parrot, claiming the bird was the reincarnation of Sigmund Freud. I don't know what women want, but Sigmund wanted a cracker.

*Ms. Irene Kelly*
*Las Piernas News Express*

*Dear Irene,*

*I very much enjoyed the recent commentary column in which you said that the state lottery is a tax on hope. I agree with you one hundred percent. You are the brightest, most insightful writer on the staff of the Express. Your prose is brilliant. I was greatly impressed by your grasp of the complex statistical data in the Eberhardt study of lottery purchasing patterns, as well as your ability to clearly explain the study's significance to the average reader. I would really like to meet you, but if this is not possible, would you please send me a pair of your panties?*

Lydia Ames laughed as she read that one over my shoulder. She works at the paper as an ACE, or Assistant City Editor. "Going to show that one to your fiancé?"

I gave her my best scowl. She's known me since third grade, so she wasn't much intimidated. She really delighted in that word "fiancé." Like a lot of other people I know, she's spent a number of years wondering if I would ever give her any reason to use it. I had been getting a lot of this "fiancé" stuff lately; given the way Frank Harriman had proposed, I doubt we could have managed a secret engagement.

As if thinking about the very same thing, Lydia looked down at the new cast my orthopedist had just put on my right foot that afternoon. "Did you save the 'Marry me, Irene' cast?"

"My *fiancé* has it."

She caught my tone. "I guess you're really disappointed about having to wear another one."

"Yeah, I am. I hobbled in there with visions of being free of these damned things and look how I ended up."

"Well, at least you're out of the sling, and the doctor did take the cast off your right hand."

"And replaced it with a splint."

"A removable splint."

"Terrific. He walks in and announces, 'So today we'll give you a new foot cast! This one will be easier to walk with! It's made of fiberglass!' Acting like I'd won a Rolls-Royce in a church raffle."

She didn't say anything.

I sighed, looking down at my latest orthopedic fashion accessory. Fiberglass.

I was recovering from a run-in with a group of toughs who wanted to rearrange my bones. I was healing, but my emotions could still surprise me. This was my first week back at work, and I found I had to be on guard against sudden bouts of extreme frustration.

"Sorry, Lydia. I'll cheer up in a few minutes. Things aren't going the way I planned. Thought I'd be running around, no casts, no slings, no splints. My day to be wrong. I'm also cranky because I feel useless around here."

"Just be patient with yourself, okay?"

"I'll try. But patience and I have been estranged for many years."

She laughed. "I don't think you've been introduced."

• • •

*Mr. Irene Kelly*
*Las Piernas News Express*

*Dear Mr. Kelly,*
*I am writing again to tell you that something must be done to stop the United States Government's heinous* MIND CONTROL *experiments. I am just one of* THOUSANDS *of persons who, after being* INVOLUNTARILY *incarcerated in a government mental hospital under the* PRETEXT of *being under observation, was subjected to* SURGERY *in which a computer chip was embedded under my skin. This chip is used by the government to send* MESSAGES TO MY BRAIN.
*Fortunately, I received an earlier model, so* THEY DON'T KNOW *that I'm writing to you. The newer models can tell them* EVERYTHING *you are thinking at all times.* PLEASE HELP US. *If you don't, there will be* BIG TROUBLE *for all concerned . . .*

Big trouble. Frank has complained that sometimes I seem to go around looking for trouble. Not a comforting thing to hear a homicide detective say, but maybe he's right. After all, being a reporter often involves looking for somebody's trouble. But it's not supposed to become *my* trouble. My news editor, John Walters, tries to impress this point on me every so often.

*Irene Kelly*
*Las Piernas News Express*

*Dear Irene Kelly,*

*I was dismayed to learn that Las Piernas does not have a city song. I am a songwriter (still waiting for my big break) and I know I could write a terrific song for our city. However, I would like to be fair about it, so I came up with the idea of a contest. I asked around City Hall and found little interest there until I happened to talk to a Mr. P.J. Jacobsen who said that maybe the newspaper could sponsor a contest. Mr. Jacobsen said you were just the person to contact. He said to be sure to tell you that this was the least he could do for you after that article you wrote about him last August . . .*

Poor P.J. "Sleepy" Jacobsen. What a lousy attempt at revenge. The previous August, I had brought the public's attention to the slipshod way in which Sleepy ran his office as Assistant City Treasurer. I guess he hadn't heard that old adage that says you shouldn't pick fights with people who buy ink by the barrel. The *Express* buys it by the tanker truckload.

I WASN'T CONCENTRATING AT ALL NOW, JUST FLIPPING THROUGH THE envelopes, bored silly. Among other injuries, my right shoulder had been dislocated and my right thumb had been broken, so I was slow as molasses on the keyboard. Over the last few days, I had managed to peck out a few commentary columns and a couple of obits. Lydia sent some rewriting my way, nothing that was on fire.

MY THOUGHTS DRIFTED TO FRANK, AND THE CONVERSATION WE HAD AS he drove me back to work.

"You know what you need?" he had said, glancing over at me. "You need a good story to work on. Something that will get your mind off your injuries."

"I'm not much use as a reporter right now. Besides, the most intriguing stories don't just knock on the paper's front door, looking for a reporter. You have to go out and find them. And I'm stuck at a desk."

Nobody's right all the time. As I said, it was my day to be wrong. That November afternoon, trouble came looking for me. Trouble got lucky. There was a story waiting for me on my desk. It was over two thousand years old, but it would become big news in no time.

# 2

I DIDN'T SEE IT UNTIL I MADE A second pass through my mail. It arrived in a plain blue envelope, addressed to me in care of the paper, the address on a white computer label.

*Dear Miss Kelly,*

*You will always be the first to know, because you will be my Cassandra. Who will believe you? I will.*
*The time has come for us to begin.*
*The first Olympian will fall on Thursday. The hammer of Hephaestus will strike her down and the eyes of Argus will be upon her remains.*

*Clio will be the first to die.*
*Forgive me my riddles, but it must be so. Soon you will be able to see the truth of it, Cassandra. But who will believe you?*

*Your beloved,*
*Thanatos*

Oh brother. Here was a letter from no less a figure than Thanatos, the ancient Greeks' name for Death himself. My beloved. And I was going to be his Cassandra, the prophetess who spoke the truth but was never believed. Charming. I looked through the rest of my mail. Little of worth.

Having nothing better to do, I read the Thanatos letter again. It had been years since I had read anything about ancient Greek stories or mythology. I couldn't remember Hephaestus or Argus. Thursday—tomorrow. My brows furrowed for a moment over that.

Clio would be the first to die. Clio was one of the Greek Muses, the nine daughters of Zeus who presided over the arts. I was trying to remember which one she was when the phone rang.

"Kelly," I answered.

"Hello, Irene. It's Jack. I told Frank I'd give you a ride home from work. He's going to be tied up for a while. What time should I pick you up?"

"Jack! Just the person I need to talk to." Jack Fremont was our next-door neighbor. "Didn't you once mention that your mom used to tell you stories from Greek mythology instead of nursery rhymes?"

"You've got a good memory. Yes, I did. She loved mythology, especially Greek and Roman."

"Well, which Muse was Clio?"

"History. Why?"

"Nothing important—just satisfying my curiosity. I got a letter from a kook today and it's full of references to Greek mythology. What about Argus?"

"Argus. The giant with a hundred eyes. You know who Zeus was, right?"

"The Olympian head honcho."

"Right. He wasn't known for being faithful to his wife, Hera. One of the women he went after was Io. Hera got miffed about it and turned Io into a heifer. She gave Argus the task of guarding her."

"I suppose a guy with a hundred eyes could make one hell of a cowherd."

"Tough to sneak up on him. He could sleep with some eyes while the other eyes stayed awake. So Zeus sent Hermes, the messenger god, to kill Argus. Hermes was clever; he told Argus one boring story after another, until finally Argus fell completely asleep. Hermes killed him, but Hera took the one hundred eyes and put them in the tail of her favorite bird, the peacock."

I smiled to myself. "Thanks, Jack. The letter doesn't make any more sense, but at least I know more about the names he mentions in them."

"Read it to me."

I did. There was silence on the other end of the line. "Am I boring you, Jack? Have you fallen asleep like Argus?"

"Maybe you should show the letter to Frank, Irene. This letter writer sounds like the Zodiac killer or something. He calls himself Death, you know."

"Yes, I remembered Thanatos was Death." I thought about it. "If my editor doesn't mind, I guess it wouldn't hurt. But I get weird stuff like this all the time."

"Really? Like this one?"

"Well, no," I had to admit. "The Greek mythology is a new twist. And it is a little unusual in tone, a little more grim than most. Talks more about death. Okay, Jack, if John doesn't object, I'll show it to Frank."

"Now, before I forget—what time should I pick you up?"

"Any time. I thought there might be something here for me to do, but Lydia's just making work for me."

"You want me to come by now?"

"If you can, sure."

He told me he would be on his way.

I stumped over to John Walters' office. He's a bear of a man, and he was growling over a sheaf of copy when I entered his lair.

"Okay if I go home early?"

"I thought you just got here," he snarled.

I'm used to him. "I did," I said evenly, "but we both know it's a slow day. Too slow to force you and Lydia to think up things for me to do—no, don't protest, John. I went through my mail and there's nothing left for me to work on. It wasn't even good mail. Take a look." I showed him the letter.

"You attract these types like flies, you know it?"

"Thanks, John. Lovely thing to say."

"I mean it. I don't think Wrigley himself gets more of these, and they figure they've reached the top dog when they write to him."

"Okay if I show it to Frank?"

He shot a questioning look at me, then gave the letter another reading. "Is there something more to this?"

"Not that I know of. I had to have Jack tell me who Argus was and which Muse was Clio. I forgot to ask him about Hephaestus."

John went over to a dictionary. He thumbed through some pages and came to a stop in the Hs. He ran his finger down a column, then paused and read the entry. " 'Associated with fire and the forge. Blacksmith and armorer of the gods. Son of Zeus and Hera. Identified with Roman god Vulcan.' "

"Well, it all makes sense now, doesn't it?"

He made a copy of the letter and handed me the original. "Probably just another nut. But go ahead and show it to Frank." I saw him glance at the cast. His brows drew together. "Go on home," he said, setting his large frame back down in his chair. He went back to frowning over news copy.

JACK TOOK ME HOME, WHERE I WAS GREETED WITH LOUD YOWLS OF welcome by Wild Bill Cody, my twenty-pound gray tomcat. I managed to feed Cody, fix a sandwich, and take off my shoes by myself—all much easier to do with the new splint. Frank called and said he'd be late, then asked if he should call Lydia and ask her to come over and help me out. I told him not to bother, bragged on my accomplishments, and told him I had a letter from a lunatic to show him.

We said good-bye, and I settled in to watch a Kings hockey game. Frank still wasn't home when it ended in a tie. I was able to get undressed by myself, although my shoulder protested now and again. I was too happy about being so self-sufficient to care.

I crawled under the covers and fell asleep listening to Cody purr. I half-woke when Frank came into bed, just enough to give him a kiss and curl up next to him. His skin was chilled, but I fell back to sleep as he warmed beneath me.

I was having a dream about a giant with one hundred eyes when the phone rang.

# 3

FRANK REACHED OVER AND ANswered "Harriman" while I tried to focus on the alarm clock. Five in the morning.

"The zoo?" he said, then paused to listen, taking notes. "Okay, I'm on my way."

"The zoo? What's going on at the zoo?" I asked sleepily.

"Someone found a body there. Woman had her skull bashed in. Somebody tossed her into the peacock enclosure."

"Peacocks?" I was suddenly fully awake.

His back was to me as he started to get dressed. "Yes, peacocks. God knows why."

"Argus."

"What?"

"I think someone tried to tell me this was going to happen."

He turned around, stared at me.

"I'm not certain about it, Frank. But let me show you that letter before you go."

I got up and fished it out of my purse. He read it and then listened as I gave him a quick rundown on the mythology references.

He ran a hand through his hair. "So you think whoever sent this was telling you that someone was going to die in front of the peacocks at the Las Piernas Zoo today?"

"Like I said, I don't know what to think. But this is too much of a coincidence to just dismiss it."

"I agree. Thanks, I'll take this with me. I don't suppose you saved the envelope?"

"Sorry. It was a light blue one, with a computer label and no return address. I didn't pay attention to the postmark. I might be able to dig it out of the recycling bin at work."

"I've got to get going, but I'll probably need to talk to you more about this later. Okay if you get into work late?"

"I'll see if Lydia can give me a ride if you're held up. But I'll either be here or at the paper."

He kissed me good-bye and headed out the door.

I was wide awake by then and couldn't get back to sleep. I waited until 6:30, then gave Lydia a call. She agreed to come by and pick me up. I figured that even if Frank got back sometime that morning, he'd want to get some sleep—although the first hours are the most important ones on a homicide case, so I doubted he would be back home until much later.

At work, things were humming. Mark Baker was out on the story at the zoo. John Walters saw me limp in and waved me over to his office.

"You hear about the body at the zoo?" he asked.

"A little. Frank was called out on it early this morning. I didn't learn much from him before he left, but he said something about the peacock enclosure. He said he might need to talk to me more about the letter."

John looked disgruntled, and I figured I knew what was eating at him. I used to cover crime stories, but getting together with Frank put me beyond the pale as far as the *Express* was concerned. Reporters are discouraged from dating cops; the potential for a conflict of interest led Wrigley to forbid me to work on any story involving the police. Frank and I each took some flak over our relationship at our respective workplaces. Mark Baker had taken over most of the stories I used to handle.

As I watched John brooding at his desk, I wondered how they were going to keep me out of this one. Then I told myself not to jump to conclusions. The letter might not have anything to do with what happened at the zoo.

"Let me tell you what we know," he said after a moment. "The victim is Dr. Edna Blaylock, a professor of history at Las Piernas College. Current theory is that she was killed elsewhere, then the killer or killers took her body to the zoo. Death was apparently from a number of crushing blows to her skull."

"Clio, the history Muse," I said softly, unable to deny the connection now.

John picked up his copy of the letter and read it over. "Let me see if I've got this straight. He calls you Cassandra, who is the woman who foretold things accurately, but whom no one would believe. He tells you that you will always be the first one to know, and calls you his beloved."

I felt a knot forming in the pit of my stomach. John went on.

"He calls himself Thanatos, or Death. He says the first murder will take place on a Thursday. The weapon is a hammer. He writes that the eyes of Argus, which are in a peacock's tail, 'will be upon her.' He tells us Clio, the Muse of history, will be the first to die." John looked up from the letter. "In other words, if he didn't kill Professor Blaylock and put her body in the peacock exhibit at the zoo, he sure as hell knows who did, and knew about it long before it happened."

Somehow having it all laid out this way made me stop thinking of it as a story and start thinking of it as personal contact with a killer.

"You look like you just swallowed a dose of castor oil," he said.

"I guess some part of me kept hoping it was just another harmless nut. I'm not ready for this now." I shook my head, trying to clear it of the kinds of thoughts I was still prey to; the fear that had been haunting me since I had been hurt.

"Sit down before you pass out, Kelly."

I obeyed. I took a few deep breaths and felt better.

"Maybe you've come back too soon."

"No!" John's a big man and it's hard to make him jump, but I apparently startled him with my vehemence. "Not on your life, John. I'm tired of giving up." He started to interrupt, but I held up my splinted right hand in protest.

"I've moved out of my house. I've given up my sleep. I've had nightmares on a regular basis for weeks. And there are other problems. I'm often afraid to be alone. I'm scared every time I venture outside of Frank's house. If a stranger walks up to me, I find myself bracing for a blow. Well, hell if I'm going to just give in to all of that. I'm sure as shit not going to abandon my career. Coming back—even part-time and as useless as I am—is important to me, John. I have to try to get back to some kind of normal life."

He sighed. "I just don't like the looks of this. Oh sure, it's great for the *Express*. Wrigley will be beside himself with joy. We'll sell a lot of papers. But you, I worry about. Those days you were gone were tough on a lot of people, Kelly, not just your boyfriend."

Coming from John, that was the sentimental equivalent of an orphan's choir. I tried to lighten things up. "You know I hate the word 'boyfriend.'"

"Oh, excuse me, your *fiancé*. Pardon me, Miss Priss. Look, the point I'm trying to make is that—oh hell. Forget it."

He started stabbing his blotter with his ballpoint pen.

"What's wrong?"

"In that list of things you've given up? You haven't given up being bullheaded. I don't pretend to understand it, but I ought to see it coming. I know when I'm wasting my breath. Go on, get out. Get back to work."

"I'm sorry you're worried about me, John."

"Out."

There was no use trying to mollify him.

I WENT OVER TO THE LARGE RECYCLING BIN THAT SITS IN THE NEWSROOM and slowly started emptying it, looking for the blue envelope. The bin is about three feet tall, and an amazing amount of paper had accrued in it during the last twenty-four hours. I was bending deep into it when I heard a familiar voice behind me.

"Stuart Angert sent me over. He's concerned about your loss of dignity."

I turned to see Lydia regarding me with amusement. Stuart is a friend and veteran columnist on the paper. He writes a regular feature on the lighter side of life in Las Piernas. I glanced over at him. Judging from his grin as he waved from his desk, being on the phone was the only thing that had kept him from getting a staff photographer to capture the rather unflattering view I had presented to the newsroom. I could just imagine what a nice contribution that would have made to the office Christmas party.

"What are you doing?" Lydia asked.

"Trying to find the envelope my love letter arrived in yesterday."

"Let me help." She made sure the City Editor could handle the desk alone for a while, then started lifting papers out by the stackful. "What does it look like?"

I described it. It took some rummaging, but eventually we found it. We were able to make out the zip code on its blurred Las Piernas postmark. Lydia looked it up. It was the zip code for the college post office.

The phone on my desk rang. I limped over and sat down as I picked it up left-handed.

"Kelly."

"Good morning, Cassandra."

I froze. The voice was not human. The caller was using some sort of device that masked or synthesized his own voice into an unearthly, low-pitched sound. Clearly understandable, totally unrecognizable.

"Thanatos?" I asked it as calmly as I could. I stood up and tried waving my right arm in an attempt to get Lydia's attention. It hurt like hell.

"You will believe me next time, won't you?" he said. His voice was almost whisper-soft, mechanical.

"I believed you this time," I fibbed, stalling, trying now to get anyone to look at me. For once, everyone in the newsroom was minding his or her own business.

"You failed me. There wasn't anything in the newspaper about it."

"I've been away from work for a while."

"Yes. You were hurt. Your foot is in a new cast. And although you're out of the sling, there's something wrong with your arm."

"Sweet Jesus," I whispered. I tried tapping the splint on the top of my computer monitor to try to get someone to look my way.

"What?" he asked.

"I didn't have time to get anything written up," I said, hoping he wouldn't figure out what I was trying to do.

"Well, you'll know better next time."

He hung up. Just then, three different people took notice, Lydia among them. Their expressions plainly said they thought I was having some kind of fit.

I swore as I hung up the phone.

"What's wrong?" Lydia asked.

"That was him!"

"Who?"

"Thanatos. The letter writer."

"Are you sure?"

"Yes." I sat down and shook my head. Fought down nausea. The phone rang again and I just stared at it. Lydia picked it up.

"Irene Kelly's desk . . . No, she's right here, Frank." She handed the phone to me.

"Frank? Frank, he just called me. He's seen me. He knows I'm wearing a cast and that my arm is hurt—"

"Whoa, slow down. Who called you?"

"Thanatos. The letter writer. The killer."

"He called you at the paper?"

"Yes."

He was quiet for a moment, then asked, "Did he threaten you?"

"No. He just kept talking about next time—"

"Tell me exactly what he said."

I repeated the conversation. This time, there was a long silence.

"I don't like it," he said at last.

"I'm not so hot about it myself. We found the envelope, by the way. He mailed it from the college post office."

"Are you okay? You sound upset. I can understand why—"

"I'll be all right. Just shook me up."

"How about if I come by in a few minutes? I need to talk to John anyway."

I felt some of my tension ease. "I'll warn him you're on your way."

We said good-bye and I went off in search of John. He was talking to Stuart but broke off when he saw me hobbling in his direction. He met me halfway. I told him what had happened. He was scowling when I said, "Frank's on his way over. He said he needed to talk to you."

"Yeah, well, I need to talk to him, too."

I didn't know what to make of that.

I spent the twenty minutes or so that I waited for Frank trying to figure out why the letter writer had contacted me. I logged on to the computer and called up an index of stories I had written in the past six months. Nothing seemed to fit; no stories on ancient or modern Greece, nothing on mythology, nothing on the college or its professors. My stories mainly focused on local politics and government; outside of some implausible connection to ancient Greek city-states, it didn't make sense that I should be the person he contacted. Why write to me? I wasn't even well-versed in mythology.

I made a note to ask Jack for recommendations on mythology books.

I searched the computer for stories that might have appeared in the *Express* about Professor Edna Blaylock. Zilch. "Peacocks" didn't pan out, either. There had been a few stories about the zoo itself, but unless Thanatos was upset about the zoo changing its hours or getting a new bear, I couldn't find the connection.

Although this first round of inquiries didn't prove fruitful, it did have the effect of helping me to calm down. I was still unnerved by the idea that Thanatos had watched me, but by the time Frank arrived, I had stopped feeling like my knees were made of gelatin.

Geoff, the security guard for the building, must have let John know that Frank was on his way to the newsroom, because he stepped out of his office just as Frank entered the room.

"So, when's the wedding?" he boomed.

"It's up to Irene," Frank answered, making his way to my desk. John met him there with an extended hand.

"I haven't had a chance to offer my congratulations, Frank."

Frank thanked him and shook his hand. At the same time, he studied me.

"I'm okay," I said, answering the unspoken question.

He didn't seem convinced, but asked his other questions aloud.

The first was, "Did the call come through the switchboard, or directly to you?"

I felt like an idiot for not checking that myself, and started to call the switchboard operator when John said, "Never mind, Kelly. I already called Doris. She hasn't transferred any calls to you today. Must have come through direct."

"Then it's most likely someone you've met, perhaps given your business card to, right?" Frank asked.

"Maybe," John said, before I could answer. "But it's not that hard to learn someone's direct dial number. There are a number of ways to do it. You could ask the switchboard operator for the number; she'll usually give it out for anyone who's not in upper management. If you wanted to be a little more sneaky about it, you could call another department, say, 'Oops, I was trying to reach Irene Kelly. The operator must have transferred me to you by mistake. Could you tell me Irene's extension?' "

"Even if it's someone with a card—I've given out a lot of them," I said. "I had a new direct dial number when I came back to the paper, so I had to let people know how to reach me. I had to re-establish contact with a lot of old sources, and I had to meet some new ones. And on almost every story, I end up giving a card to someone."

"Well, it's something to think about," Frank said. "Maybe you'll recall someone who mentioned this history professor to you, or who seemed interested in you in some unusual way—or who just seemed odd."

" 'Odd' will not narrow the list much."

"Probably not. You said you found the envelope?"

I nodded, and handed it to him.

"Lydia!" John shouted, startling me. "Find something to keep Miss Kelly busy for a while."

"Wait a minute—" I protested.

"You can live without him for five more minutes, can't you, Kelly? You haven't gone *that* soft on me, have you?"

I could sense something was up and that John was in a conspiratorial mood. But I couldn't figure out a way to object before they walked off into John's office, Frank turning at the last moment to give me a shrug of feigned helplessness.

I practiced breaking pencils with one hand while Lydia tried to find something for me to do.

# 4

"IF HE DIDN'T KILL HER IN HER office, he made a damned good start there."

Pete Baird, Frank's partner, had accepted our invitation to join us for dinner that night. While Frank acted as chef, Pete was filling me in on the progress they had made in the Blaylock case. "There was blood splattered everywhere—over her desk, the windows, her books, the floor, her papers. The guy went nuts. Really sprayed the place. I doubt she walked out of there, anyway. We'll know more when the lab and coroner's reports come in."

You get two homicide detectives together, you have to be prepared not to let much of anything ruin your appetite.

"She was killed there," Frank said, coating some orange roughy fillets with a mixture of herbs and a small amount of olive oil. "All the blows were to her skull. He was hitting her hard."

"He?" I asked.

"Figure of speech," Pete said. "But didn't you say the voice on the phone was a man's voice?"

"It was synthesized. No telling. But I admit the letter made me think the writer is a man. Thanatos is a male character in mythology, for starters. Clio is female, a woman was killed. Cassandra was a woman. But maybe the killer is a woman who wants us to think she's a man, to throw us off her trail."

"If the killer's a woman," Frank said, "she's very a strong woman."

"Why strong? You told me that you thought the professor was sitting at her desk, bent over some papers ..."

"Right. Her desk faces some windows. It was late at night. If she had been looking up, she might have seen his reflection in the windows. Might not have made a difference if she had seen him, but in any case, there was no sign of a struggle on her part. I think he got her with the first blow."

"Exactly," I said. "One good blow to the head and she wouldn't have put up much of a struggle. So the killer wouldn't need to be strong."

"If the body had been left there, I'd agree," Pete said. "But after making all that mess, the killer was very neat. Must have bagged her—or at least wrapped her head up, because there wasn't so much as a drop of blood out in the hallway. My guess is that he was wearing something over his own clothing—coveralls, maybe—because he couldn't have been in that room or picked her up and carried her out without getting anything on himself. The professor wasn't a very big woman, but even if she only weighed about a hundred pounds, that's a lot to lug around. He carried her downstairs, took her to a vehicle, drove to the zoo, and then dumped her over a fence and in with the birds. Leaves her wallet and all her identification on her, so that we know exactly who we've got."

"He's damned sure of himself," Frank said, putting the fish under the broiler. "No question about that."

"Yeah, and not just because he left her ID," Pete said. "You ever been around peacocks? They're noisy suckers. He had to know that someone was going to hear all that racket."

"Zookeepers might be used to it," I said.

"The birds were raising Cain. They're beautiful, but not pleasant, if you know what I mean. In fact, they—" Pete halted when he caught Frank shaking his head. "Sorry. We shouldn't be talking about this before dinner."

If it was something that bad, I wasn't going to challenge him.

"You said the chair of the history department let you into Dr. Blaylock's office," I said. "Was it locked?"

Pete nodded. "Yeah. But the killer probably just locked the door after he left. Hiding the mess for a while."

"He didn't need a key to lock it?"

"No, the history offices are in one of the older buildings. Some of the buildings on campus, especially the ones where they keep a lot of equipment—art studios, science buildings, the gym—those buildings have electronic locks that open with key cards. They lock automatically when the door shuts. But the college couldn't afford to put them everywhere, so lots of the classrooms and faculty offices are standard type locks. Use a key to get in, but once you're in, you have to push a button lock on the other side to lock yourself in."

"And you don't think she locked herself in?"

"No, probably not. She taught a class on Wednesday nights, and had a habit of working late in her office after the class. She usually had the door open or unlocked, from what the other faculty and her students say."

"So we've got one of two possibilities," I said. "Either she invited the killer in or he entered without her knowing he was there."

"You ask me, she didn't know he was there. Probably never knew what hit her—BAM!—and she's out. He keeps going at her, but not 'cause she's fighting him."

Throughout dinner, I picked up other details.

No one at the college or the zoo reported seeing anything suspicious before the body was found, but it would not have been difficult to move around unnoticed at either place during the hours in question, sometime between midnight and four in the morning.

The professor was fifty-four years old. Her colleagues described her as a vivacious woman who wore her years well. She lived alone. She seemed quite devoted to her students; she often held meetings of her graduate seminars in her home, and willingly gave of her time to students who needed extra help. She taught a seminar in twentieth-century U.S. history on Wednesday nights, and was doing some research on the Truman administration. It was not uncommon for her to work late in her office on her research and writing. When she was killed she had been working on an article she hoped to submit to the *Journal of American History.*

After Pete left, Frank and I sat together in the living room. I asked him about his meeting with John. At first he claimed that they were just talking about cooperation between the newspaper and the police on the Blaylock case.

"No sale," I said. "You wouldn't need to exclude me from that conversation."

"Okay, so maybe we talked about you. What of it?"

"What of it? I'll tell you what of it. Shall I go into Captain Bredloe's office and have a nice long talk with him about you?"

"Be my guest."

"You wouldn't like it."

He was quiet for a moment then said, "No, I guess not. Look, John's just concerned about you."

"Concerned how?"

"Well, in a fatherly kind of way, I guess."

"Fatherly? You mean as in *Father Knows Best?* As in 'Well, son, we menfolk need to protect our little gals'?"

"I don't mean that at all ..."

"I got scared today," I went on, ignoring his protest. "*Anybody* would have been scared, I think. But because of this damned splint and cast, my being scared looks different to him. John doesn't think I'm ready to come back to work."

There was a long pause before he said, "Well, yes. That came up in the conversation."

I stood up. "You know what I want?"

"Irene ..."

"Faith. Faith in my ability to function. Less help. Less control by well-meaning but—"

"No one is trying to control you—"

"Bullshit. Oh, it's all in the name of taking care of me, mind you. Friends. People who just want to make sure I'm all right. I'm all right!"

He was silent.

"He had no business talking to you about my ability to do my job!"

"You're right."

"Absolutely none."

"None whatsoever."

"You're not even a relative."

A pause. "No."

"You're just ... you're just ..." I was losing steam. I sat down next to him. "Why am I yelling at you? It's not your fault."

"No, it's not." He said it without looking at me.

"Sorry."

He didn't say anything. It was then I realized it wasn't anger that was keeping him quiet.

"You're better than a relative," I tried. "Much better."

Still nothing. For a few awful seconds, I felt like I might start crying or something.

*Don't do it,* I told myself.

He finally looked over at me. When he did, his expression changed. "Irene? Hey ..."

My turn not to answer.

"It's okay," he said, putting an arm around me and pulling me closer. "Go ahead and cry."

"No way," I said stubbornly.

He started laughing. "You are one of a kind."

"Thanks, I guess."

"John said that to me today. 'Kelly's one of a kind.' "

I had to smile at his imitation of John's gruff voice.

"That's what I meant by 'fatherly,' " he went on. "I think with your dad and O'Connor gone, John felt like it was his duty to check me out. He was trying to figure out if I was going to be a suitable husband. He mentioned the divorce rate for cops more than once."

"Of all the damned nerve!"

"Take it easy. It didn't really bother me. He's right. From the outside, it probably looks dicey. Look at it from his perspective. A cop and a reporter. Who would think it could work?"

"The people on the inside. The only people who count."

He smiled. "I move that the people who count call it a night."

Motion carried unanimously.

LIFE LEVELED OUT AGAIN DURING THOSE FIRST WEEKS IN DECEMBER. There were no more letters from Thanatos. True to John's prediction, the story about the murder and Thanatos' contact with me had sold a lot of papers. In spite of earlier prohibitions, I had been allowed to cowrite the first few stories on the case with Mark Baker.

I did a lot of reading on the subject of Greek mythology. Jack loaned me books by Edith Hamilton and Robert Graves, along with translations of Ovid, Aeschylus, Sophocles, Euripides, and Homer. He was kind enough to spend several evenings talking with me about what I read. I also spent hours searching the newspaper's computer files from every different angle I could think of, looking for something that would have connected my writing to someone who wanted to kill a history professor and leave her body at the zoo. I started reading stories by other reporters, thinking I might find the connection to the paper, if not to me personally. I reviewed anything in the *Express* files about the college, as well as stories about any of its professors. Nothing, except Frank growing tired of me saying things like, "This is a Sisyphean task."

He had his own problems. As the investigation of the Blaylock murder went on, it focused primarily on the professor herself. It became clear that Edna Blaylock had enjoyed the extra-curricular company of several of her male graduate students. Six of them eventually admitted to sexual liaisons with her. The professor had been a little more devoted to her students than others had imagined.

But the six lover boys were all able to account for their whereabouts on that Wednesday night, which was during the last week before finals, and Thanatos remained undiscovered.

I GOT A FEW PHONE CALLS FROM MEN PRETENDING TO BE THANATOS, but they were not the synthesized voice. At the request of the police, we had left that detail out of news reports. Two other factors helped to identify them as crank calls. They contained more references to sex acts than to Greek mythology. And they all came through the switchboard.

But three times, just as I returned from lunch, someone called me through the direct dial then hung up without speaking. Those three silent calls bothered me more than the obscene ones.

They occurred on what I started to refer to as my "paranoid days." These paranoid days had a pattern of their own. Lydia and I would leave the building to walk to lunch; as I hobbled down the street, I would become convinced that someone was watching us. I started looking over my shoulder. During a downtown lunch hour, there are plenty of people walking around, so inevitably I would see some man walking behind us. Never the same man. Never anyone who showed more than passing interest in us.

*You look odd,* I told myself. *People are going to watch someone who is limping along in a cast and wearing a splint. Stop acting crazy.*

Sometimes I could talk myself out of it.

FRANK PUT IN LONG HOURS ON THE BLAYLOCK CASE, AS DID EVERYONE else assigned to it. He made sure someone—usually Jack or Pete—was with me if he couldn't be. I had mixed feelings about the protection, but didn't protest.

As the days went on and Thanatos' trail grew colder, I gradually felt more relaxed. I put any anxious energy I felt into my physical therapy. I was bound and determined to put the days of injury behind me as quickly as the healing process would allow. I could tell that my shoulder was greatly improved, but my right hand seemed hopelessly weak. I was told again and again not to be discouraged. By people with two good hands.

But as it turned out, the cast and the splint came off early, a little more than a week before Christmas. I felt like someone had freed me from chains. I still had to spend a lot of time squeezing a rubber ball with my right hand, but that exercise was a small price to pay.

Frank and I celebrated that Friday night by going out to an evening at Banyon's, a local watering hole shared by the police and the press. There were lots of familiar faces on hand. The band was on a break, so it was relatively quiet, which meant you could still hear yourself think over the rumbling mixture of boisterous conversations and a distant jukebox speaker.

"Well, look who's here!" a voice called out over the din. I looked across the room to see a sandy-haired man with boyish good looks grinning at us. Kevin Malloy, an old friend, waved us toward him. Not long after I was injured, he had stopped by the house to cheer me up, and now he seemed happy to see me out and about. Kevin was the Malloy in Malloy & Marlowe, a public relations firm, and had been my employer for a time. He had also shared a friendship with my later mentor, O'Connor. I hadn't been to Banyon's since the night before O'Connor was killed, but I pushed that thought from my mind as we made our way toward Kevin.

"Well, lass," Kevin said, hoisting a pint of Guinness, "we haven't seen you in here for an age. And look at you! No sling, no cast . . . Liam!" he called to the bartender. "A round for the house. We'll celebrate our lost lamb's return to the fold."

That brought a cheer, but for a free drink, most of them would have cheered anything short of the words "last call." One of the reporters bent close to Kevin and whispered something to him. Kevin turned to us in surprise. "What's this? Engaged?"

"It's true," I said.

"And how many times did you have to beg him on bended knee before he said 'yes'?"

I laughed and answered, "Believe it or not, he asked me."

"Well, now, listen up!" he called in his carrying voice, then stepped up on a chair, so that he towered above the crowded bar. As the buyer of the aforesaid round, he had their grateful attention. The bar was so quiet, you could actually hear what was playing on the jukebox. Kevin glanced at Liam, who promptly unplugged it.

"There's a nasty kind of rumor going around," Kevin began, then paused, turning to Frank.

"Tell us!" A cooperative crowd. They'd heard him before. Frank looked a little uneasy.

Kevin looked back to the crowd. "It's said that the men in the Las Piernas Police Department have lost their courage!"

"No!" This chorus from the cop contingent, all of them grinning as they looked at Frank.

"'Courage among our policemen?' they say, 'Why, it's easier to find a politician who wants to make a good Act of Contrition.'"

"No!" the chorus supplied.

"Yes, that's what's being said. I'm told the police so lack courage, they've become as useless as a snake's glovemaker!"

"No!" Again the chorus, but through laughter.

"Nearly as useless as reporters," Kevin said, causing an outbreak of shouts and laughter.

"Impossible," more than one voice called.

"I'm here to tell you that the rumor is *false*—absolutely false—and I can prove it," Kevin said. He pointed to Frank. "This man, Frank Harriman—*Detective* Frank Harriman—is employed by our very own Las Piernas Police Department. And I'm telling you, he has more courage than any man among you. He's the bravest, most stouthearted, brass-balled sonofabitch I know! Do you know what he's done?"

Eager silence.

"He's asked Irene Kelly to marry him!"

There was a great deal of shouting and cheering at that point.

"Fools rush in!" remarked one of my coworkers.

A series of more picturesque comments followed.

Kevin motioned the crowd to silence by simply lifting his pint of stout.

"Here's to Frank Harriman, who's had the courage to take our treasure from us! May he and Irene Kelly share a long and happy life together!"

Finally able to drink, the crowd was especially lively in joining this part of the toast.

After accepting the congratulations of a number of the patrons, we settled down into a couple of chairs at Kevin's table. It felt so comfortable, this pub and all its memories. It was where O'Connor had most often held court. On Friday and Saturday nights, when they had live music, he would sit and watch the dancers. I thought of nights when Kevin, O'Connor, and I would argue and laugh and generally carry on until closing. Somehow all those memories brought back an old sense of myself. An Irene who was less afraid. I was free of more than a fiberglass cast.

I ordered a Tom and Jerry to warm my bones. As the waiter brought it, I looked up to see Frank quietly regarding me. We smiled and lifted our glasses to one another.

"So when will this wedding take place?" Kevin asked, watching us.

"She refuses to set a date," Frank told him.

"What? Irene! The man has proposed. What more do you need?"

I just shook my head.

"What makes you hesitate?" he persisted.

"I just need time to heal, Kevin."

Frank reached over and took my hand. "She can take as long as she likes, Kevin. She said 'yes' and she knows she's not getting out of it."

Kevin gentled his tone, needing no further explanation of my meaning. "Well, Irene, here's to healing quickly. Don't begrudge your company to those of us who would salve your wounds."

"I don't. Being here, I feel better already."

We talked for a long time, reminiscing about Kevin's days with the paper, where he worked before starting his PR firm. Taking an off chance, I asked, "Kevin, can you remember any work I did for you that might tie into the college or the zoo or Greek mythology?"

"You're speaking of the case of the history professor?"

"Yes."

"Wouldn't you remember writing a publicity campaign for the college or the zoo?" Frank asked.

"I know I didn't do anything on the zoo or the college directly. But Kevin knows the clients better than I do."

"If the connection is through us, it's very subtle," Kevin said. "You don't have any particular client in mind?"

I shrugged. "No. I don't even remember half of them, to tell the truth."

"Let's see. Greek mythology is a complete dead end, I'm afraid. The only person I've known who could quote the Greeks was O'Connor. You know how he was. He also quoted the works of Shakespeare, Eleanor Roosevelt, Yeats, Marx—Groucho, that is—the Bible, the Tao, and anyone and anything else that happened to interest him. No, it must be something else. Perhaps one of the people you dealt with is a big donor to the Alumni Foundation or to the Zoological Society . . . Hmmm." He thought for a while longer then said, "I'll go through the computer files on your work for us. If I see any names that look like they might have some connection, I'll let you know."

FRANK AND I ENDED UP TAKING A CAB HOME. INSIDE THE HOUSE WE were greeted by Cody, the old reprobate, who bit my newly uncovered ankle. I yelped as he ran off in a gray streak.

"Cody's waited more than six weeks to have a chance to do that," Frank said, grinning in a way that made me forget all about my ankle.

I reached around him. "God, it feels good to hold you with both arms."

He kissed me, slow and easy; a kiss that had more hello than good night in it. He took me to bed, where I got a chance to try out some of the things *I* had been waiting more than six weeks to do.

# 5

I HAD MY HEAD INSIDE THE LIBERTY Bell and someone was striking it repeatedly with a large mallet. I groaned and woke up to hear Frank's simultaneous groan. The phone was ringing. I fumbled for that instrument of torture and looked at the clock and scowled. Seven o'clock. Who the hell was calling us at this ungodly hour?

"Irene?" the voice on the other end asked from a distance. I flipped the receiver around so that I was no longer holding it upside down.

"Barbara," I said to my sister, "the next time you call me this early on a Saturday, I will attach you to a twenty-foot bungee cord and push you from a nineteen-foot overpass."

Frank groaned again and put his pillow over his eyes.

"You're hungover!" she scolded loudly. I moved the receiver a good six inches from my ear while she prattled incessantly about how ashamed my mother would have been had she lived to see me behaving like this. (I am convinced that Barbara, given a choice between dropping a neutron bomb and invoking my mother's memory, would still find the latter a more potent weapon.)

Frank groaned louder and rolled onto his stomach. I reached down and unplugged the phone, wondering as I fell back to sleep how long it would take Barbara to realize all her bitching was failing to do more than sear some phone lines.

Sometime around noon, as I lay watching him, Frank pulled the pillow off his head. "I don't know how you do that without suffocating," I said.

He managed a smile. "I'm going to tell your sister that we are moving to the Himalayas and can't be reached by phone."

"Sooner or later she'll see my byline in the *Express* and know she can start calling again."

"You'll have to make up a pen name." The smile broadened to a grin. "How about—"

"Never mind. I can tell from the look on your face that it doesn't belong in a family newspaper."

"What did Barbara want?"

"I don't know. I unplugged her."

He laughed and pulled me close. "Let's stay in bed all day."

"Are you kidding? I just got my cast off. I want to get some exercise."

"Who said you won't be getting exercise?"

There was a loud banging at the front door. I heard my name being screeched by a fishwife. The bedroom is at the back of the house, but we could hear her "I know you're in there!" quite plainly.

"Barbara says I won't be getting exercise."

Frank groaned for the fourth time that morning and reached for his jeans. I hurriedly got into a bathrobe, amused briefly by the realization that I could now do something like pull on a bathrobe and run to the front door.

"Hell's bells, Barbara," I called out as I made my way down the hallway, "keep your pantyhose on!"

I opened the door and she shot into the house like she had been launched from a catapult.

"Of all the despicable tricks! I can't believe you were so rude! I had hoped Frank would teach you a few manners but I can see . . ."

What she could see just then was Frank, coming down the hallway as he buttoned a shirt. It stopped her mid-tirade.

"Good afternoon, Barbara," he said.

She took in his bare feet and sleep-tousled hair and began to stammer. "Fr-Fr-Frank. I . . . I only saw Irene's car. I didn't know you were home."

"My car is at Banyon's. We took a cab home last night because your sister and I forgot to draw straws for designated driver. We were celebrating the removal of her cast and splint."

"Oh." She looked more than a little disconcerted.

"Were you yelling at me on the phone all this time?" I asked.

That brought back some of her ire, but Frank's chuckle cooled it right back down into embarrassment. "Never mind," she said.

"Come on in and make yourself comfortable," Frank said. "I'll make some coffee."

Barbara looked down at my hand and, seeing the puffiness around my thumb and forefinger, said, "It still looks funny."

"Thank you." I walked back to the kitchen, leaving her to follow or stand there.

She chose to follow and soon the pleasant aroma of coffee allowed me to become a little more human.

"Anything I can do to help?" she asked.

"Not a thing," Frank said, getting some cups and saucers.

"I'd be happy to help," she tried again.

"Just relax and enjoy yourself," Frank said easily.

As I watched her take a seat at the kitchen table, I mused to myself that Barbara had probably never in her life "relaxed and enjoyed herself." She's bird-nervous by nature.

I put a couple of pieces of nine-grain bread in the toaster on the table and studied my sister while I waited for them to pop. For the most part, Barbara and I don't look or behave as if we could be related. She has my mother's red hair and green eyes; she's tall and willowy. Her delicate features are very similar to our mother's. Her skin is soft and white.

I'm only a little bit shorter than Barbara, but I'm built differently. She has always seemed more fragile to me; even though she's the older sister, I've been the one she runs to with her problems. Unlike her, my hair is dark, my eyes blue. I look more like my father's side of the family. I am, I admit, much less feminine than my sister—always have been. I was climbing trees while she played with dolls. I felt great when I hit my first home run, she felt wonderful when she learned to put on nail-polish. I got tremendous satisfaction out of digging a hole in the backyard and filling it with water and then bombing it with dirt clods. Barbara was in the house, trying on my mother's high heels. I still haven't learned to walk gracefully in heels.

She married O'Connor's son, Kenny, and divorced him when he turned forty and went thorough man-o-pause. He was brutal in his verbal abuse of her in that period. I couldn't stand him before that, and afterwards was unwilling to try for polite. She got back together with him, much to my dismay. I was praying they wouldn't remarry. But it's her life. Barbara and I have never been great pals; in fact, we usually drive one another crazy.

The toast popped.

"Your hair is growing," she said to me, as Frank filled our coffee cups. It made me reverse some of my thinking of the last few minutes. We *are* sisters, and woven over our differences is a fabric of kindnesses paid out to one another in times of trouble. After my captors had cut my hair into odd-shaped clumps, it was Barbara who came by and patiently reshaped my hair out of its bizarre styling into the cut I wore now. Having my shoulder-length hair lopped off by those men had been demeaning and extremely upsetting; Barbara's efforts had made it much easier to look at my reflection in the days following that ordeal.

"Yes," I answered. "Thanks again for the haircut."

"I should trim it for you."

"No thanks. I want to let it grow out again."

"You can't go around with the same hairstyle you had in ninth grade, Irene. You're a grown woman."

I was determined to keep my cool. "Like I said, I appreciate what you did for me, but I'm going to let it grow out."

"Honestly. You'd think you'd act your age."

Frank was looking between us, not trying very hard to hide his amusement. To hell with him, I thought. I'm still not going to be drawn into a fight with her. My head hurt.

"Was there something you wanted this morning?" I asked.

"It's afternoon."

I shifted in my chair a little but said, "This afternoon, then."

"Well. Yes." She took a dainty sip of coffee and glanced nervously toward Frank. He looked toward me with a silent question and I answered with a look that asked him to please stay put.

"Don't drum your fingers, Irene," she said.

"You came by this afternoon to ask me not to drum my fingers?" I took a deep breath. "I have to drum my fingers. It's part of my physical therapy."

Frank made a sputtering noise in his coffee, but she either didn't pick up on it or was still too intimidated by him to comment. "Oh," she said, "I'm sorry. I didn't know."

"I'll stop doing it. Now, you were saying?"

Once again she looked over at Frank, who seemed to have himself back under control. "Well," she said.

We waited. When she got it out, it was all in a rush.

"How can I make any of the wedding arrangements if you won't set a date? Of course I didn't tell him you were living together, but Father Hennessey is willing to give Frank instruction and said he would set aside a date for the wedding if we would just name one."

Two sounds broke the brief second's total silence which followed this announcement. One was Frank's coffee cup clattering onto its saucer, and the other was a rushing noise I heard in my ears. I began to realize that the latter was the sound of my blood boiling.

"Of all the unmitigated gall!" I shouted. "Barbara, who asked you to make any arrangements? Who asked you to talk to Father Hennessey? Who in the hell do you think you are, talking to him about Frank converting when I've never even said to you that we would be married in the Church?"

"Not get married in the Church!" she shouted back. She looked between us as if I had just said we planned to go live naked in the woods.

"The point is, my dear sister, that you are once again butting your nose in where it doesn't belong!"

"I'm your *older* sister. I have an obligation to take our mother's place in situations like these! If Mother were alive—"

"Don't start! If Mother were alive, she'd respect my wishes. But she's dead, Barbara. She's been dead for over twenty years. And you won't *ever* take her place in *any* situation!"

"You are being mean and selfish!"

"*I'm* being selfish? Look at you!"

Our shouting match came to a sudden halt when Frank stood up and looked between us. He shook his head, then walked out of the room. Not much later, I heard him going out the front door.

"Now look what you've done," Barbara said, but I had already decided to honor Frank's unspoken request—to grow up—so I didn't rise to the bait. She went on for about another thirty seconds, but conversations with Barbara, like earthquakes and dental appointments, always seem to last longer than they actually do. When she finally wound down, I even managed to hold back the 486 really spectacular comebacks I had been considering, and simply said, "I need to find Frank. You need to go home. We need to talk about this later."

"What do I tell Father Hennessey?" she whined.

"That there has been a misunderstanding and that I'll call him if I need him." *To administer Last Rites to my sister,* I added silently. Okay, so I was only pretending to have grown up.

"And Bettina Anderson wants to do the flowers! She's going to be so upset with you."

"Who the hell is Bettina Anderson?"

"You don't remember her? You went to high school with her."

"I'm not just trying to irritate you, Barbara. I swear I didn't go to high school with anyone named Bettina."

"Betty Zanowyk."

"Betty Zanowyk? Lizzy Zanowyk's sister, maybe? I went to school with Lizzy Zanowyk. What does that have to do with this Bettina person?"

"Bettina Anderson *is* Elizabeth Zanowyk. Or should that be the other way around? You know her, Irene. She called herself Betty Zanowyk after high school. Lizzy, Betty, and Bettina are all names that come from Elizabeth. She's been Bettina Anderson for about five years now."

My head was aching again. "Let me guess. She's not a Zanowyk because she got married to someone named Anderson?"

"No, she got tired of being a 'Z.' She says she was subjected to alphabetic discrimination all her life."

"Barbara . . . please, go home."

"I don't know if you should marry Frank. It's not healthy to deal with anger by going off and pouting," she said.

"Barbara." I said it very softly, with my teeth closed. She knows that when I say her name like that, she has gone too far. This has been instilled in her since childhood, when she learned about it the hard way. I use it sparingly.

"He isn't used to us yet, I suppose," she mumbled.

"What does that mean?"

"We bicker. We fight. But we stick up for each other, too. Don't you remember? Dad used to say it was because we're Irish."

"I don't know if it's being Irish," I said. "But it's true that Frank's quiet, for the most part. I can get him to shout, but most people can't."

She smiled knowingly. "That's how you know he loves you. I read about this in a magazine at the place where I get my nails done. If he's willing to shout when he's around you, it means he trusts you enough to get angry with you."

"Well then, Jesus Christ, Barbara, I must trust you to the depths of my soul. Go home. Let me get dressed and go after him."

She stood up, then asked, "How do you know he didn't just drive off?"

"His Volvo's at Banyon's, he's too tall for the Karmann Ghia, and I didn't hear him call for a cab. There's a beautiful beach about a block away. Where do *you* suppose he went?"

I FOUND HIM LEANING AGAINST THE RAILING AT THE TOP OF THE CLIFF, near the steps that lead from our street down to the beach.

"Sure you want to go through with this wedding, Harriman? Barbara as a sister-in-law? Think it over."

"She's not as bad as all that."

I didn't reply. Why start another argument?

"She's just excited about our getting married," he said. "She's just trying to be helpful."

"I've told you how I feel about all the help I've been getting lately."

He smiled. "You've mentioned it."

We stood there for a moment, just watching the waves below.

"Want to go for a walk on the beach?" he asked.

I hadn't been able to do that in weeks. He saw me brighten at the suggestion and led the way down the stairs.

We hadn't walked far when he said, "You were right the other night. There *are* people who try to do too much for you."

"I shouldn't let it get to me. What happened with Barbara happens to all engaged couples, I suppose. There's going to be a lot of pressure on us now."

"I can't wait to find out what Episcopalian minister in Bakersfield my mother has set up for us. But she's probably gone further than Barbara. Watch out. If we don't set a date, she will."

"Just promise me you won't ever get the two of them together. God knows what they'd plan for our lives."

He shuddered and I laughed.

He took my hand as we made our way down the beach. In spite of the run-in with Barbara, I was feeling good. Gradually, something was reawakening within me. It might have been my courage.

# 6

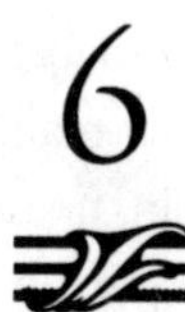

MONDAY WAS A COOL BUT SUNNY day, my first day driving myself to work. In celebration of that new-found independence, I put the top down on the Karmann Ghia and took to the streets of Las Piernas at a speed that created a biting windchill factor inside the car. Well worth it.

Even downtown morning traffic didn't dampen my spirits. I parked the car, put the top up, and went into work.

When I got to my desk, the phone rang. I answered.

Nothing. Not even breathing.

"Sorry, wrong number," I said, and hung up.

I took off my coat and started sorting my mail. There's always a lot of mail to deal with on a Monday, but with the approach of

Christmas, the usual onslaught tripled. A large percentage of it arrived in colored envelopes.

Since receiving the letter from Thanatos, I had developed a daily postal ritual. First, I carefully separated out all mail in colored envelopes. Then I sorted the colored envelopes. As I went through them, I made a special stack for those without return addresses, addressed to me on white computer labels. This would be the last stack I opened. I started in on my other mail.

The phone rang again. Again, no one on the line. I hung up and called Doris, the switchboard operator. No, she hadn't put any calls through to me that morning.

I shrugged it off. The calls weren't being made after lunch time, so they probably weren't being made by the watcher. And there was no watcher anyway, I reminded myself. None. No one. Think about something else. At this rate, someday I would be the one writing letters about dogs picking Super Bowl winners.

Still, it made me feel a little spooky about the last stack of mail. I got a cup of coffee, logged on to my computer, checked my calendar. Told myself to get it over with, picked up the stack, shuffled them, counted them. Thirteen. Thirteen? Better check the count, I thought, then became so angry with myself that I ripped the first one open. A coupon for a discount on carpet cleaning. I was more careful in handling the others, but that coupon turned out to be the most spectacular item in the group. So much for my frightening mail.

I went to work on a story that would run near New Year's Day, our annual standard story on new laws and programs going into effect January 1st. Said, "Yes, it's great to have the cast off," to at least two dozen well-wishers.

I ate lunch in the building, telling myself I stayed in because I was so busy, not because of the phone calls. I kept distracted by my work and coworkers for the rest of the afternoon. It was dark when I left the building, but as I stepped out the door and glanced toward my car, I came to a halt.

My parking lights were on.

For a brief moment, I was simply confused by it. Had I turned the parking lights on? No, I was certain I hadn't.

The next thought: *Two phone calls.*

Lydia came out the door and said cheerfully, "It must be great to be able to drive again."

"Walk me to my car, would you, Lydia?"

She followed my gaze and said, "Uh-oh. Worried about your battery? No problem. I've got jumper cables in my car. Why did you turn your lights on this morning?"

"I didn't."

"Then how—"

"He's trying to scare me."

"Who? Who's trying to scare you?"

I hesitated. Lydia had been dealing with my unfounded fears on a daily basis. *Thanatos* suddenly seemed like a crazy answer to her question. I forced a smile. "No one, no one. Sorry. I was just thinking about something else. I don't know why I turned the lights on. Haven't driven for a while, so I guess I was out of practice."

"With the Karmann Ghia?" she asked. "You've driven it since college." She was watching me carefully now, giving me the same look she might have given a strange dog that came trotting toward her, wagging its tail and growling at the same time.

By then we had reached the car. There was no one lurking in the small interior. The doors were locked. The windows were up. No visible damage to the ragtop. I tried not to shake as I opened the door and got inside.

The car started right up.

Lydia smiled.

"I guess I won't be needing those jumper cables," I said. "Thanks for waiting."

"Any time." She started to walk off, then turned back. "Are you all right?"

*I don't know,* I wanted to answer. But I nodded and waved, then drove off.

As I drove, I tried to tell myself that maybe I *did* accidentally turn them on. I looked at the switch for the lights. No. Not something anyone would do "accidentally." And not something I did and then forgot. It had been a sunny morning. If it had been foggy or dark, I would have turned the headlights on, not the parking lights—in California, it's illegal to drive around with only your parking lights on. And I would have noticed that the parking lights were on when I pulled the top back up.

At home, I debated with myself about telling Frank about the lights. He had so much on his mind—did he need this? But what if Thanatos *had* been near my car?

The issue was decided for me when Frank came in the front door.

"What a day," he said. "Okay if I go for a run before dinner? I need to do something to get my mind off lunatics and assholes."

Not wanting to fall into either category, I told him dinner could wait and stayed silent on the subject of parking lights.

On Tuesday, Kevin called to say he had searched his files but hadn't found anyone that he could connect to the Thanatos letter. The people I had worked for had no strong ties to the college or the zoo, even if some of them belonged in the latter.

I pestered Mark Baker into giving me the phone numbers for the professor's old boyfriends. The one I most wanted to talk to was a man by the name of Steven Kincaid, who appeared to be Dr. Blaylock's most recent conquest. But Kincaid was either out or didn't answer his phone. That was further than I got with four of the remaining five, who had disconnected the numbers Mark had for them. Fleeing media attention, I thought, until I reached a fellow by the name of Henry Taylor.

"A few more minutes and you would have missed me," he said in a pleasant voice. "Does the paper want to interview me again?"

"I just had a few more questions," I said. "Could we meet somewhere?"

"Gee, no, I'm sorry, that's what I was trying to say. The semester's over. My girlfriend will be here any minute now. We're going to be flying back to Michigan, to her parents' house. I'm going to pop the question at Christmas."

"Pop the question?"

"You know, ask her to marry me."

"Excuse me, Mr. Taylor, if I sound a little confused. It's just that your name has been associated with—"

"Edna, yeah, I know. Really sad. Oh, you mean, is Connie upset about that? No, hell, she knows it was years ago."

"Years ago?"

"Yeah. Edna and I had a brief little fling about two years ago. My senior year, before I started the MBA program."

"You're not a history major?"

"Hell no. History major? No money in it. All undergraduates have to take a semester of U.S. history. I took a history class from Edna to satisfy the bachelor's degree requirements. I was expecting to be totally bored, but she made it interesting. And something about the lady attracted me, I guess, but nothing came of it then. I was seeing somebody else. But then I broke up with that girl, and the next semester, I saw Edna in local club one night . . . and I don't know, I guess we just decided to go for it."

"How old were you then?"

"Twenty-six." He paused then added, "I work and go to school, so it's taking me a little longer."

He sounded embarrassed about it, so I told him I had taken more than four years, and not just because I worked. "But listen—about Dr. Blaylock—can you tell me if she ever mentioned anything about Greek mythology, or the zoo?"

He laughed. "We didn't really do a whole lot of talking when we got together, if you know what I mean. It was just a brief affair. Nothing very involved. I think we both realized that it wasn't for the best—not for either of us."

"Did she ever mention anyone who might be angry with her, or seeking revenge?"

"The cops and the other reporters asked me about this kind of stuff," he said easily. "I've got nothing to say, really."

"I won't quote you. I just need to get a lead on this."

"You're a little late on the story, aren't you?"

"I'm the one he mailed the letter to."

"Oh." The chipper attitude seemed to drop away.

I waited.

"I guess I can understand why you're still looking into it, then."

"Can you help me out?"

"Look, Miss . . ."

"Kelly. Irene Kelly."

"Okay, Irene Kelly. I don't like to be so blunt about it, especially talking to a woman, but I can't see any other way to get this across before Connie comes walking in here—at which point I will definitely not discuss it any further. Edna Blaylock and I got together for sex. That's all. Just sex. That's all either of us wanted at the time."

"But if she talked to you . . ."

"I don't think you could type up more than ten sentences if you quoted every word we said to each other that wasn't just small talk. We'd go out to a bar, drink, dance and then go home and have terrific sex. At least, it was terrific at first. I guess I felt sort of turned on by the idea of having sex with this sophisticated older woman. A professor, for godsakes. But the thrill wore off pretty quickly, for her as well as for me. I didn't learn her secrets, and she didn't learn mine. I was sort of on the rebound, I guess you'd say. Some clown from school remembered seeing Edna and me together once, and told the cops I was her boyfriend."

I heard noise in the background, and he excused himself then covered the phone. I could hear him say, "In here. I'm on the phone.

No, some reporter. Aw, Connie, for Godsakes, she's dead. Give it a rest, would you?" He came back to me. "That's Connie. I've got to go."

"Look, Mr. Taylor, I need to talk to you a little more. Is there a number where I can reach you?"

"I don't think that would be such a good idea."

"How about when you get back?"

"Maybe. But I'm pretty busy. Gotta go."

He hung up. Connie didn't sound so forgiving. But there was no chance of talking to Henry Taylor or Connie until they came back from Michigan. I wondered if she would say yes to his proposal.

I tried Steven Kincaid again. No luck.

John came by my desk and talked me into going down to City Hall to cover the first reading of a zoning proposal. So much for Thanatos. But I agreed with John that the proposal might turn out to be more than the routine issue it appeared to be. I learned long ago that sometimes the most important issues in the city were decided in the most boring meetings.

Sure enough, by Wednesday morning there was a story on the front page of the *Express* that would guarantee a handsome turnout for the second reading of the proposal. It was my first story on page A-1 since the Thanatos letter, and I was working very hard at not showing how pleased I was by it.

The proposal would have changed the extent and type of building that could take place on the site of a Las Piernas landmark that had been destroyed by a fire. The council was already reneging on promises made in the last election. My phone was ringing off the hook. I felt like a kid who had just aimed a water hose at a hornet's nest. Better yet, I felt like I was back to being a reporter. At times, the two sensations are not unalike.

In between calls, I cheerfully went through my mail sorting routine, opening Christmas cards and humming "Jingle Bells" to myself. All the same, when I was down to the final group, I opened them carefully, using the letter opener to pull them out, so that I didn't touch the contents with my hands. Four flyers for meetings I would not attend. One more to open. Did it really matter that I was careful? I stopped humming when I unfolded it on my desk.

*Dear Cassandra,*

*Have you missed me? You must be patient.*
*Thalia is next. It has already begun.*
*You tell me you need time to prepare. I will give you the time you need. Wait for Janus.*
*Enjoy the Saturnalia, Cassandra.*
*Thalia will learn the agony of Tantalus and more. Who helped Psyche to sort the seeds that Venus placed before her?*

*Your beloved,*
*Thanatos*

My phone was ringing again, but I didn't answer it. As soon as it stopped, I called Doris, and in as calm a voice as I could manage, asked her to hold all my calls.

"I don't think John will like it," she began. "We're getting a big reaction to your story."

"Yes, well, I'll talk to John."

I called John on the intercom, asked for a moment of his time, used a folded strip of paper to cover my fingers when I gingerly picked the letter up by a corner, grabbed a mythology book, and somehow made it to John's office without dropping anything.

He looked up from reading copy and raised an eyebrow as I dangled the letter forward and dropped it on his desk.

"Is it going to bite?" he asked sarcastically. But his face set into a frown and he swore under his breath when he saw what it was. He read it, then said, "Since we hadn't heard any more from him, I was hoping this creep had been run over by a car or something."

"Are you going to turn it over to the police?"

"You know how I feel about that, Kelly. I'm not going to let the Las Piernas Police Department tell me what we can and cannot publish, but I'm not going to impede a homicide investigation. Have you already called Frank about this?"

I was dismayed by the question. "Of course not."

"Just wondering how far all this nooky-nooky stuff had addled your reporter's sensibilities. So what does this letter mean?"

"Thalia is one of the Graces. She represents Good Cheer. Not much of a clue as to the identity of the next victim, I'm afraid."

" 'Enjoy the Saturnalia,' " John read. "Does he mean Saturday?"

"Maybe, but I would guess he means Christmas, because he tells me to wait for Janus. January is named after the god Janus."

"That's Roman, not Greek, right?" he asked.

"Right. Thanatos mixes in some Roman references in this letter. Saturnalia was a Roman winter festival in honor of the god Saturn. It was held in late December and there was feasting and exchanging of gifts. Someone once told me that's why Christmas is celebrated in December, because the early Roman Church made use of a pagan holiday for their own—converting it, you might say."

" 'Thalia will learn the agony of Tantalus and more,' " John read aloud.

"Tantalus—his name gave us the word 'tantalizing.' He's in Hades, and stands in a pool of water that shrinks away from him whenever he bends to drink from it. When he stands up, it fills up again. And over his head, there's a fruit tree with wonderful fruits that are always just beyond his grasp. He's always hungry and thirsty, with relief within sight, but out of reach."

"Not short on cruelty in those stories, were they?"

"No. But Tantalus had it coming. He killed his own son and boiled him in a cauldron, then invited the gods to a banquet with his son as the soup du jour."

"Cripes." He was looking at me as if I had authored the tale.

"That's really the way the story goes," I protested. "Tantalus thought he could show that the gods were fools, but they knew what was on the menu and decided to skip a meal and punish him. They restored his son to life. Cannibalism was frowned upon by the gods. They didn't like measly little mortals trying to outwit them, either."

He shook his head. "What about Psyche and the seeds?"

"Oh, that's a great story—Cupid and Psyche." I started to thumb through the book.

"Just give me the part about the seeds," John said, looking like he wasn't ready to hear too much more about the Greeks and Romans before lunch. "It's not gory, is it?"

"No, no, it's a love story," I said, reading over it quickly. "It's told in Latin by Apuleius."

"Never mind that. What happens in the story?"

"Psyche was a beautiful woman. Venus was jealous of her. It was actually being claimed that she was more beautiful than the goddess, which offended Venus to no end. So Venus sent her son, Cupid, on a mission to make Psyche fall in love with the most vile creature on earth. But once he saw Psyche, Cupid ended up falling in love with her instead."

"What about the seeds?" John groused.

"The middle part of the story is really very—"

"Look, get to the seeds. Someday when I'm in a better mood, you can tell me all of it."

"You, in a better mood? I suspect we'll be sitting by a very, very warm fire. Our host will have horns, but we'll have lots of time on our hands—"

"Kelly, I swear to God—"

"Okay, okay. Condensed version. Psyche and Cupid loved each other, but as things happened, they were separated. Psyche decided to search for him, but Venus put a few obstacles in her way. Venus gathered a huge pile of the tiniest seeds—poppy seeds, millet, things like that—and told Psyche to sort them by nightfall. As Venus knew, it would have been impossible."

"So who helped her?" John said through gritted teeth.

"Pardon?"

"The question in the letter! Who the hell helped her?" he shouted.

"Ants."

"Ants."

"Yes, the ants took pity on Psyche and an army of them helped her. Venus came back to find the seeds sorted. There's another story about ants—"

"Never mind," John said. "This guy Thanatos doesn't make a lot of sense. Some Muse of Good Cheer—"

"Grace of Good Cheer."

"Okay. Some Grace of Good Cheer will know the agony of Tantalus, he wishes you a Merry Christmas—or happy Saturnalia—wants you to wait until January, and puts something in here about ants."

"I agree it doesn't make much sense. The last one didn't make much sense either, until after the professor was murdered. Are we going to run it?" I asked.

"Of course." He used the intercom to call Lydia into his office.

"What about Frank?" I asked.

He thought for a moment, then said, "He can have the original." He picked up the letter and walked over to the copier with it before I could protest about fingerprints. I didn't say anything about it, knowing it was unlikely that the forensics lab could lift a good print from the paper, even if Thanatos had not used gloves.

Lydia came into the office, and John handed her a copy of the letter. The minute she saw what it was, she looked over to me. I tried for nonchalance. I could see she didn't buy it.

"Tell Mark Baker to get on this right away," John was saying.

"Kelly can fill him in on the translation. And tell Design I want to run the letter on A-1 tomorrow—anybody has any objections, see me. I don't see how they can argue. For all we know, someone out there may be able to foresee that they're in danger if they read this."

A passage in the letter came to mind. " 'It has already begun,' " I quoted, suddenly feeling a little shaky. "I think we may be too late to warn the victim."

"You don't know that!" John said vehemently. Seeing my surprise at it, he added, "Besides, I hate all the dull stuff we've been running lately. I hate the holidays."

"Bah, humbug!" I said.

"Go ahead and laugh. You and your snookums will be having a great time, Kelly, while I slave away."

He was trying to make me believe that he hadn't forgiven me for asking for a few days off around Christmas.

"What *are* you doing over Christmas?" Lydia asked.

I hesitated. I wasn't completely comfortable with the plans Frank and I had made, but in a moment of testing myself I had agreed to them.

"We're going up to his cabin in the mountains."

"The mountains! Where—"

"No. Different place—not where they held me. According to Frank, his place is more like a house than a cabin."

"But it will be near there, won't it?" she asked, then saw I didn't like the question.

John, in the meantime, had dialed Frank's number. He told him about the letter and after a pause said, "She's fine. You want to talk to her?" and handed the phone to me.

Frank told me he'd be down to pick up the letter and asked if the three of us wanted to join him for lunch. John begged off but Lydia was agreeable.

• • •

## DEAR IRENE,

FRANK HAD SPENT THE MORNING DOWN AT THE COUNTY BUILDINGS, taking care of some business at the courthouse. He was happy to get a change of pace. We had lunch at a little hamburger joint a few doors down from the paper. It's had about five different names in about as many years, but the same people seem to own it—or cook in it, anyway. They make good old-fashioned burgers, so risking arteries that will probably look like pinholes, I ordered up a cheeseburger, fries, and a strawberry shake. Frank followed suit but Lydia behaved herself with a chicken sandwich and a salad.

"So what are your plans for the holidays?" I asked her.

"Guy is going to spend them with me and my mom. You know that Rachel is coming out to spend Christmas with Pete, right?"

I nodded. Guy St. Germain had been dating Lydia since the summer, and Frank's partner had been seeing as much of Rachel Giocopazzi, a Phoenix homicide detective, as he could manage between their work schedules and his fear of flying.

"Well, Rachel and I got this idea to do up a real Italian Christmas dinner," Lydia went on. "It's a two-day affair. You get everybody together on Christmas Eve and eat nothing but meatless dishes—fish is okay, but no meat. Like Fridays used to be. Then on Christmas you go for broke. I'm doing Christmas Eve, Rachel's doing Christmas, and my mom will do all the breads and desserts—*oro corona pane, dodoni,* rum tortes, things like that. We'll eat both meals at my place. We've invited Jack Fremont to join us."

Thank God our food came. Lydia is a fantastic cook, and I was working up an appetite listening to her. So our friends would be together. I became aware of Frank watching me. Lydia kept describing her culinary plans until she suddenly she noticed his silent study as well. She looked between us. "I wanted to invite you two, but Pete said you already had plans, Frank. Irene tells me you're going to the mountains."

I concentrated on eating my lunch.

"Yes," he said. "That's been the plan. But I'm not sure we'll do it. We may stay down here."

"What?" I said, putting my cheeseburger back on the plate.

"I've given it a lot of thought, Irene. I know you agreed to go, but are you really pleased with the idea of going to the mountains, or are you just trying to make me happy?"

"I used to love the mountains."

"That's what I mean. Used to. Maybe we should stay home."

"I don't want to wimp out, Frank. I've got to keep facing the things I've become afraid of, get back into life."

"There's such a thing as pushing yourself too hard."

Lydia has been a friend of mine since grade school, and she has seen me at high and low tide, but nevertheless there are some conversations I'd rather not have in front of her. I noticed her interest in this debate. I guess Frank saw me glancing over at her, because he said, "Let's talk about it later tonight, okay?"

I nodded. I was a little quieter at lunch that day than usual, I suppose, but I had a lot of things to think through. As I swirled the same cold french fry in the same puddle of catsup half a dozen times, I wished that I could just think them through one at a time.

# 7

I SAW THANATOS' LATEST MISSIVE as a declaration of war, so I spent the first part of that afternoon studying my enemy. I went over all the stories about the first murder, and I read the copies of the two letters again and again. I was pretty sure I knew what he was going to do and when. I just didn't know who he was going to do it to, or why.

Lydia stopped by my desk and interrupted my musings. "You're pulling on your lower lip," she said. "What's up?"

I put my hand down quickly. Beyond being chums for years, Lydia and I were roommates in college, so she knows most of my little idiosyncrasies. I don't see this as a big plus.

"I was thinking about how it would feel to be very hungry and within sight of a bountiful feast, and yet unable to eat any of it."

"Are you writing a Christmas piece on the homeless?"

I didn't register what she meant for a moment. "No, no. I'm talking about Thanatos. I think he plans to kill someone by starving them to death within the sight of food."

She gave me a look that was one part skepticism and two parts revulsion.

"I do, Lydia. What else could the reference to Tantalus mean? Nothing else in the letter lends itself to a method of murder."

She shuddered. "It would be such a slow way to die. Not very practical as a means of murder, is it?"

"How practical is it to take someone's body from a college campus and toss it into a pen full of peacocks? Besides, he's hinted that it's going to be a slow death. He says it's already started and will come to an end in January."

"Good Lord."

"I wish to hell I could figure out who Thalia represents. Grace of Good Cheer. Who could that be? I've been pouring over the stuff on Edna Blaylock, trying to learn something from it. It's maddening."

"You think there's a *reason* for these killings?"

"Yeah. You and I might not think his way of choosing his victims is rational, but I'll bet he believes it's perfectly logical."

"But a history professor? Why? Do you think she had a secret past or something?"

"Hard to imagine. She fooled around with some students, so she wasn't an angel. But other than that, she's as solid as bedrock." I read from my notes. "She was born in L.A., lived here in Las Piernas since she was about eight or nine years old. Her mother raised her; her father died in World War II. She went to Las Piernas College, then went on for a doctorate at UCLA. She wasn't the most spectacular contributor to American historical scholarship, but she had been published in a few minor history journals. The article she was working on for the *Journal of American History* would have been an important feather in her cap."

Lydia looked toward the City Desk, where Morry, the City Editor, was beckoning. "I've got to get back over there," she said. She took a couple of hurried steps toward the City Desk, then stopped and turned back to me. "Do you think he might be a student or some other man she turned down?"

"Maybe."

I watched her walk off. I thought about the first letter and the fact that whoever had killed Edna Blaylock not only knew her schedule, but knew how to sneak a body off campus. Maybe it was a former student or a faculty member. After all, the first letter had been mailed from the campus.

On the other hand, we had checked out the second envelope and figured out that it had been mailed from the downtown post office, not far from the *Express*.

Had Thanatos been down this way to find his next victim? Or had he been near the newspaper, watching me again?

I PICKED UP THE PHONE AND TRIED CALLING THE ONE PERSON LEFT ON my list of Dr. Blaylock's former lovers: Steven Kincaid. As far as I knew, Kincaid had been Dr. Blaylock's last lover; he was the only one who admitted still being involved with her at the time of her death.

The phone rang about five times before he picked it up.

"Hello?"

"Mr. Kincaid?"

"Yes."

"This is Irene Kelly with the *Las Piernas News Express*."

He hung up in my ear.

I took it in stride. Certainly wasn't the first time it had ever happened to me. Angry sources come with the territory. Before I could decide on my next move, the phone rang. It was Kincaid.

"I called to apologize, Miss Kelly. That was very rude of me. I don't usually hang up on people. This has been a very difficult time for me. I'm not sure why I . . ." His voice faltered.

"It's okay, Mr. Kincaid. I understand."

"I'm not sure you do. The newspapers—I wasn't very happy with what they said."

"Let me assure you right off the bat that I'm not interested in adding anything more to what Mr. Baker has written about your relationship with Dr. Blaylock. I just thought you might be interested in trying to help out. I received another letter from Thanatos today."

There was about a full minute's silence. I knew he hadn't hung up on me again, because I could hear him breathing. It was the kind of breathing you hear when someone is trying to bring themselves back under emotional control.

"I don't know how I could possibly be of help," he said, "but go ahead."

I had already decided to try to meet him face-to-face. It's much harder to walk away from a person than to hang up on a voice. "Look, why don't we meet for a cup of coffee? I'll buy."

There was another pause before he asked, "Where?"

"You live near campus?"

"Yes."

"You have classes today?"

"No, winter break is just starting. Finals just ended."

"Hmm. How about the Garden Cafe—is it still around?"

"Yes. That sounds fine."

I described what I was wearing and arranged to meet him at this old college haunt in half an hour. I hung up and wondered at the differences between this man and Henry Taylor. Taylor had seemed no more personally affected by Edna Blaylock's death than a man reading about a flood in a distant country. Kincaid, on the other hand, sounded as if he was just keeping his head above water.

Just before I left, I stopped in to see John, and told him of my plan to meet with Kincaid.

"Watch out, Kelly. For all we know, he could be the one who killed her."

"He had an alibi, John."

"You've covered trials. I don't need to tell you that sometimes an alibi can be pretty easy to come by."

I shrugged. "Maybe so. But then again, maybe this kid is innocent and will end up telling me things he wouldn't tell the cops."

"And if he gives you any information? Is this going straight to Frank's ears?"

"That's why I came in to talk to you. I won't talk to Frank if you tell me not to. I just need to know where the paper stands on all of this."

"You've got an obligation to Kincaid. He can't act as a source and not be made aware of what you plan to do with the information. If he asks for confidentiality, he should get it.

"On the other hand, I'm not overlooking our obligation to the community. Had a long talk with Frank about this, and later with his lieutenant—what's his name?"

"Carlson."

"Yeah, well, we're all on thin ice here. And if Wrigley gets word of this, we could both end up sending out our résumés. For now, I'd prefer you talk things over with me before you say a word to anyone connected to the police—*anyone.* The only exception would be if you were fairly sure that someone might be physically harmed if you didn't contact the police immediately. Can you live with that?"

"Sure. I'm going to be pestering you a lot, but I don't mind if you don't mind."

"Well, let's just play it this way for now. Now scram. You're going to miss Kincaid and deadline both if you don't get a move on."

• • •

The Garden Cafe hadn't changed much since the 1970s, other than the clothing and hairstyles of the clientele, and even some of those were the same. It was a college hangout when Lydia and I were students, as it had been twenty years before we started school. The walls were covered with photos of Las Piernas from about 1910 up to the present day. There was no particular theme, except that after the cafe's founding in the 1950s, photos of alumni who had made good decorated portions of the wall behind the old fashioned cash register. I wasn't up there.

The "garden" was a small enclosure behind glass that featured a couple of ficus trees, a few ferns, and a small fountain. They used to have finches in there, but every once in a while they'd bang up against the glass and kill themselves, which didn't do much for the appetites of the customers who saw it happen. So the birds had been gone for some time.

I stood by the door, catching snippets of conversations that ranged from the Lakers' chances to go all the way this year to whether or not the Stanford-Binet tests were a valid measure of intelligence. There were one or two people who looked like they might be faculty members, but I was definitely an oldster in this crowd.

A few people turned my way when I walked in, but nobody seemed to take special notice. I was a few minutes early, but wondered if Kincaid was already there. I looked to see if anyone might be trying to attract my attention. I saw a self-conscious young man peering up at me over the rim of his glasses. He studied me for a while, and I figured him to be Kincaid. He was skinny and had that archival pallor that scholars develop. I decided that he looked to be the type that would take his fifty-four-year-old professor to bed with him.

"Miss Kelly?"

I jumped and turned to look behind me, where the voice had come from. I was almost nose-to-nose with one of the most gorgeous men I have ever laid eyes on. And he knew my name.

"Sorry, I didn't mean to startle you." He extended a hand. "I'm Steven Kincaid."

I decided to close my gaping mouth before I gave him enough time to examine my dental work, and reached out with my right hand. He glanced down and noticed the swelling, and gave me a gentle but warm handshake. I was still speechless.

He grinned. Goddamn. No wonder old Edna hadn't been able to keep her mitts off him. I tried to imagine having this stone fox stare at my podium for an hour or two a day. I would have been sorely tried.

"You're not what I expected," he said, and led the way toward the back of the cafe. With his back to me, I was able to shake myself out of the daze I was in and follow him. I thought of Frank and felt a wave of guilt, then smiled to myself. I could enjoy looking at Frank for a hundred years, go blind, and still want to be next to him for another hundred. More than just another bonny lad, Frank Harriman.

Feeling my equilibrium return, I sat down across from Steven Kincaid in the last booth outside the kitchen. It was only then that I realized that conversations had been dropping off in volume or halting all together, and that some people were openly staring at us. Kincaid saw me looking around and said, "I'm afraid I've become notorious, at least around campus." He swallowed hard. "Some of them probably think I killed E.J."

"E.J.?"

"Professor Blaylock. Her name was Edna Juliana Blaylock. She was E.J. to her friends."

"If you're uncomfortable here, we can go somewhere else."

He shook his head. "Might as well face up to it. I have nothing to be ashamed of. People think E.J. and I were trying to be clandestine. We were only trying to be discreet. There is a difference."

A waiter came over and brought menus. I wasn't hungry, so I used the opportunity to study the man across the table. I guessed him to be in his mid-to-late twenties. He had easy-to-look-at masculine features: a strong jaw, high cheekbones, and cobalt blue eyes with dark lashes. His hair was almost jet black. His skin had the kind of tan a person has in December only if they regularly enjoy some kind of outdoor activity. He wore blue jeans and a light blue shirt, and filled both of them out just fine. He had a broad-shouldered, narrow-hipped, athletic build. Probably could win an election for "defines handsome" without going into a runoff.

But there were dark circles under his eyes, and a kind of tiredness in his face that showed he had been under a strain lately. I noticed then that those eyes were avoiding my own, that he was pretending to be fascinated with a menu he had probably memorized. I realized that I might be making him nervous. People often are jittery around reporters, but I had been so dumbstruck by his appearance that I hadn't made any small talk or other efforts to get him to relax a little.

"What were you expecting?" I asked.

"What?" He was startled into looking at me.

"You said I wasn't what you were expecting."

He looked down at the menu again. "Oh. I guess I was expecting someone—I don't know—hard-boiled? Tougher?"

I laughed. "Don't let my appearance deceive you."

He looked chagrined.

"I'm afraid I'm not doing a very good job of putting you at ease, Mr. Kincaid. As I said, my main interest is in trying to learn enough about Dr. Blaylock to be able to make more sense out of this man who calls himself Thanatos. I'd like to try to figure out who his next victim might be—before it's too late."

The waiter reappeared. Kincaid ordered a piece of carrot cake, and it sounded so good I ordered one, too. I was going to have to get back to my running routine soon, or eating like this would become a real liability.

"You said he sent another letter?" Kincaid asked.

"Yes. It arrived at the paper today." I hesitated. "I've got to ask if you would mind my sharing any of the information you give me with the police. I wouldn't have to disclose your identity; you could be anonymous as far as they're concerned. And if you don't want me to tell them anything at all, then I won't."

He sighed. His eyes suddenly reddened and he looked away for a moment. He took a deep breath and said quietly, "I don't care who you tell. Like I said, I have nothing to be ashamed of. I want her killer to be caught, but I'd rather not have any more encounters with the police myself. You can tell them whatever I'm telling you. The police—well, some of them were quite considerate, others weren't at all. Nothing has been easy."

I waited while he worked to pull himself together. Our coffee and carrot cake arrived, and we spent a few moments fiddling around with cream and sugar as a distraction.

"Let's get something clear from the start," he said, surprising me with the sudden fierceness of his expression. "I was not in a relationship with E.J. while I was her student. I want it made clear that there was no 'A for a lay' or any of the other kinds of sordid, unethical behaviors that some people have been hinting at. It just isn't true."

"Listen, Mr. Kincaid, if someone from the paper—"

He went on as if I hadn't spoken. "Yes, I took a graduate seminar from her. But nothing happened then. I found myself very attracted to E.J., and I restructured my whole master's thesis committee and the classes on my program just so that I could be with her without there ever being a cloud over our relationship."

"You don't have to defend anything to me."

"I know, I know. But let's face it. Most people just don't understand why a man my age would get involved with a woman her age. They figure I must have received some kind of special consideration as a student or that I was after something—her money or her house, I suppose. Well, she didn't make all that much, and she had willed everything to the American Lung Association years ago—and I knew that. I didn't need anything like that from her, anyway."

"Why *were* you attracted to her?"

He drew a deep breath and lowered his gaze. I found myself silently urging him to confide in me. When he looked back up, he gave me a fleeting smile. "You know, I think you're the first person who has asked me that recently who might actually believe the answer. I was with E.J. because she was wise and full of life and witty and strong and intelligent. She made me laugh. I could talk to her. And I found her beautiful. There was something very sensual about her. At first, I suppose it was a sort of animal magnetism. But it became much more. Much, much more."

"And how did she feel about you? I mean, there seem to have been other men."

"No one else for the past year. None of the men mentioned in the paper were involved with her recently. You can check that out pretty easily. No one since we got together."

"You're a handsome man. Were there other women in your life?"

"No. No one else. You look like you find that hard to believe, but it's true."

"I don't find it hard to believe that you were devoted to her. I find it hard to believe that no one else expressed an interest in you."

He waved a hand in dismissal. "So what? Most of them are a nuisance, if you ask me. At the risk of sounding like I've got a gargantuan ego, I'll be straightforward with you, Miss Kelly. Many women find me attractive. They hit on me. They seek my attention. Why? Because of my face. I suppose a lot of men would say I have nothing to complain about, that they would love to have that problem. But they don't know what it's like. These women don't give a damn about what I think or who I am—not really. It's as if I'd be some kind of trophy. If all I wanted was a string of one-night stands, I'd be happy. I happen to want more."

"And Dr. Blaylock was different."

"Yes, she was. She took time to get to know me. She was very good to me. We wanted a future together . . . but now . . . God, now I'm just lost."

He was starting to lose control again. I didn't want to gratify the base curiosity of the people around us by having him break down in the restaurant, so I told him about the second letter from Thanatos. He knew all of the mythology, so at least I didn't have to cover that again. It was a good distraction. For a few moments he thought about the letter more than about the loss of E.J. Blaylock.

His brows furrowed. "It sounds like he's starving someone to death."

"My theory exactly," I said, noticing the carrot cake was no longer appealing.

"But you have no clues as to who Thalia represents?"

"None. But maybe if you tell me about Dr. Blaylock, I can begin to get an idea or two."

"What do you want to know?"

"What do you know of her past?"

"Starting when?"

"As early as possible. Whatever you know."

"Well, let's see. She was born in Los Angeles in about 1936. She never really knew her dad; he was a sailor who was killed in the attack on Pearl Harbor. That was at the end of 1941, so she would have been about five years old when he died.

"Her mother got a job in an aircraft factory—Mercury Aircraft. She was sort of a Rosie the Riveter, I guess. She got transferred down here near the end of the war. Mercury had two factories in Southern California then. Now it just has the original plant, the one in Las Piernas."

I made notes, not sure any of what he told me would help. I found myself circling the word "Mercury." After receiving the letters from Thanatos, names and words associated with mythology often caught my attention. They were everywhere. Among other things, Mercury had lent his name to a planet, an element, an automaker, and a dime. I reminded myself that at this rate, if E.J. Blaylock had ever eaten a Mars bar, laughed at Mickey Mouse's dog, suffered insomnia, or used a mnemonic device, it was all going to be Greek (or Roman) to me.

"That's how E.J. first came to Las Piernas," Steven was saying. "I don't know too much more about her childhood, just that she was always good in school. She loved history. She got straight A's in every history class she took, even through college and grad school. She got into Las Piernas College on a scholarship. She went on to UCLA for her doctorate. She met a man there and married him."

"Hold on a minute—she was married?"

"Briefly. It lasted less than a year. James, I think his name was. She went back to her maiden name, and has—had—used it ever since."

"She ever tell you why the marriage broke up?"

"Not really, just said it had been a case of two people doing what was expected of them and then learning it was a mistake. No details. To be honest, she never talked much about the men in her past, which was fine with me."

"She didn't stay in Los Angeles?"

"No. After she graduated, she had several offers to teach, but she took a job here in Las Piernas so that she could take care of her mother. Her mother was ill by that time. Some kind of lung disease. She had been a heavy smoker and worked around some toxic chemicals, but there was no way to know which gave her the problem, which was . . . let's see . . ." He thought about it for a moment, then shook his head. "Emphysema, maybe? I'm sorry, I've forgotten. Anyway, they lived together for about fifteen years. E.J. took care of her the whole time. Her mother died about ten years ago."

"So, in about 1980?"

"Somewhere around there. I guess E.J. sort of came alive then. I don't mean to say she had never dated or was some kind of shrinking violet under her mother's thumb. She loved teaching and enjoyed being with students; she was a very popular instructor. She really went out of her way to try to get students excited about history."

"So how did she 'come alive'?"

"E.J. just had less of a load to carry. She told me that for several years before her mother died, she had felt helpless to ease her mother's pain. She had watched her suffer and waste away. She hadn't realized what a toll it was taking on her until after her mother died. But she was lonely without her mom around."

"So she put time into her teaching and writing."

"Exactly. And yes, she went through a time of involving herself sexually with some of her graduate students. The *Express* has made quite a big deal out of that," he said bitterly.

I held up my hands. "Wait a minute. I've told you. I'm not here to dig up dirt on her. Quite frankly, I don't blame the other reporter for mentioning it, but it's old news at this point. I just thought you'd like to help me discover who had something against her, or what she might share in common with whoever this Thalia may turn out to be. I'm just trying to find the link between Thanatos, Thalia, and Dr. Blaylock."

"I'm sorry. Mr. Baker, the other reporter, wasn't rude to me or anything. It's just that afterward, I felt angry. I guess I was just upset about some of the coverage."

"I can understand that," I said gently. "It's an upsetting time for you anyway."

It was either the wrong thing to say or the wrong tone to use. He was better off a little angry. To keep him from getting all choked up on that teaspoon of sympathy, I said, "When I was in college, it seemed to me that professors who were very popular with students were distinctly unpopular with most other faculty members."

He spread his fingers on the table top and pressed down on them. "Yes, there was some of that. But there has been for years."

"Anyone in particular?"

He shook his head. "You should talk to other faculty members. It would be hard to find a faculty group in any academic institution that didn't suffer some in-fighting. But I don't know of anyone who was especially upset with E.J. She didn't have any sworn enemies, if that's what you mean."

"Is anyone else on the history faculty very popular with students? Someone who is very cheerful all the time, perhaps?"

His brows knitted. "You think someone has a grudge against the history department?"

"Stranger things have happened."

He relaxed his hands. "Well, let's see. To be honest, I can't think of anyone who would fit that description. They're not a somber lot, but no one is a really happy-go-lucky type."

"I'm trying to come up with someone who might fit Thalia. How about someone in another department on campus? Drama? Communications? Theater? Anyone else who's very popular?"

He thought for a moment, then said, "I hate to admit this, but I'm not a very good person to ask about this. I'm a graduate student—all my classes are in history now. And the reason I'm a graduate student in history is because all my favorite classes as an undergraduate were in that department. I'm sorry."

"What about this ex-husband? Was there a lot of bitterness? Or something that might have become important between them?"

He shook his head. "Highly doubtful. Like I said, I don't even remember his last name. There was never any rancor in her voice when she spoke of him, which wasn't often."

I was stewing over this when a young woman strolled up to our table. The hem of her black leather skirt just made it past her skinny behind. She had long, straight blond hair and saucer-like brown eyes. Her cherry red lips formed a moue, and she cocked her head to one side in an affected way. On Sunset Boulevard, it could have earned her an hour's work.

"Steven," she said on a sigh that made it a much longer name. She reached over and put a hand on his shoulder. He looked at it like it was a leech, and she removed it.

"Hello, Lindsey," he said then. She eyed me but he didn't introduce us. She looked back at him.

"Are you okay, Steven? Is there *anything* I can do for you?"

"I'm doing fine, Lindsey. Thank you."

She swayed her weight from high heel to high heel, then said, "Well, I've got to go. But I just wanted you to know I'm here for you."

"Thanks."

Seeing that she wasn't going to get any more out of him than that, she turned and walked away.

"See what I mean?" he said with exasperation. I nodded. He didn't have to say anything more.

"Look, I've got a deadline to make, so I'd better scoot. I appreciate your meeting with me." I gave him a business card. I added my home phone number, hoping he didn't think that meant I was hitting on him, too. I paid up and we left.

Out on the sidewalk, he seemed to relax a little more.

"This is the first time I've felt like someone really wanted to know about her. The others—well, maybe it was just that I was so upset. I still can't believe it happened. She didn't deserve this. No matter what she may have done, she didn't deserve this. No one does."

"I agree. By the way—are you familiar with her research and writing?"

"Yes."

"Let's talk more about that sometime soon—if you don't mind?"

"No, no, not at all. Her research was very important to her."

He seemed distant for a few moments, obviously remembering E.J. Blaylock. I wished there was something I could say to comfort him. I watched him struggling to learn that trick of functioning with grief—that trick of remembering and forgetting all at once, of letting the ghost walk at your side, but not block your way. I was learning it myself. A close friend of mine had died a little more than six months earlier, and Kincaid's grief was almost too clear a reminder of that loss.

But before I could think of anything to say, he came back from whatever world he had mentally wandered into, and we shook hands and said good-bye.

I thought of Lindsey and how repulsed he had seemed to be by her attentions. I wondered, as I climbed into the Karmann Ghia, if Steven Kincaid's good looks would make him into a bitter and lonely man.

I sighed and started the car. The windshield wipers came on.

# 8

"MAYBE WE SHOULD GET A DOG. You like dogs, don't you?"

We were sitting in front of a fire that evening, one of our rare evenings at home together, drinking hot chocolate laced with peppermint schnapps, when Frank came up with this idea. We had been talking about our plans for Christmas, which somehow led to talking about my feeling safe when I was home alone in the evenings. Perhaps, after calling him from the Garden Cafe earlier in the day, I seemed more fearful. Whoever had turned on the windshield wipers hadn't left any prints. Frank had been a little angry with me for not mentioning the parking-light incident, but I couldn't tell if he thought someone was trying to frighten me, or if he was just convinced I was going over the edge. Now he was suggesting things like new locks, self-defense classes, and dogs.

"I love dogs," I said. "And you like them, right?"

"Yeah, although I haven't had one since I was a kid. I used to have this great mutt who was some kind of lab/retriever mix. Trouble."

"The dog caused problems?"

"No. Trouble was her name. My dad named all of our pets. When he watched this pup follow me home, he said, 'Here comes trouble.' The name stuck. We also used to have a rabbit named Stu."

"So *that's* where you get your sense of humor."

"Trouble was great. I swear that dog could understand English. I could say, 'Go to my closet and bring back my blue tennis shoes.' She'd do it."

"*Blue* tennis shoes? I thought dogs were color-blind."

Frank shrugged. "She would have known which ones I meant."

It sounded like classic dog-owner bragging to me, but I didn't want to further impugn the memory of Trouble.

"I used to have a dog," I said. "She was mostly a beagle—named Blanche."

"Blanche?"

"Blanche Du Bois."

He smiled. "Blanche Du Bois? A *Streetcar Named Desire?*"

"You *are* a detective. My dad named our pets, too. Blanche was a stray, and Dad said she had survived because she had 'always depended on the kindness of strangers.' "

"Were your other pets named Stanley and Stella?"

"No, Blanche was he only one that took her name from Tennessee Williams. Dad was being a little dramatic himself. It was a protest of sorts. He wanted us to get rid of her."

"Your dad didn't like dogs?"

"He was just exercising his authority. You know how this goes. He grumbled that he didn't want a dog, told us to take Blanche to the pound, but then he ended up being the one who fed the dog from the table—he'd even let Blanche sneak up onto the couch when my mother was in the other room. Blanche was crazy about him. She was only my dog until my dad came home from work, then she shadowed him."

"Trouble used to follow me everywhere I'd go," Frank said.

I laughed. "Sorry. It still sounds funny."

"I had the same problem talking about her as a kid."

"I used to take Blanche hunting for hot dogs."

"Had a lot of wild hot dogs burrowing around in Las Piernas back then?"

"Given the opportunity, I *will* explain. I'd steal a hot dog out of the refrigerator, drag it around on the ground, and hide it somewhere in the yard. Then I'd put her on a leash, and she would follow the trail and track it down. She'd find it every time."

"Poor mutt. Reduced to stalking Oscar Meyer."

"At least she got to eat the hot dog. I never asked her to fetch my stinky old tennis shoes."

He laughed. We sat there for a moment, remembering our dearly departed canines, listening to a blues program on KLON. The wood popped and crackled in the fireplace. We began softly touching each other. The caresses weren't so much sexual as tender; small gifts of affection. I traced the ridge of his eyebrows, ran the back of my nails beneath his chin; he stroked the back of my arm above my elbow, found that place along my left shoulder blade that loves to be lightly scratched.

"About the mountains," he said. "Let's wait. We can go up for the weekend sometime in January or February."

"Frank, really, I don't need to be babied about this."

"Neither do I. Could you stand to pass up all that food Lydia was talking about?"

"First you practically hypnotize me with whatever that wonderful thing is that you're doing to my ear. Then you bring up Lydia's cooking. Do you use these same methods at work?"

"You get all kinds of special privileges."

"Keep it that way, Harriman."

We watched Cody trot in through his new cat door and head straight for the fire. He gave us a look that said we should have called him to let him know there was a fire in here for a cat to enjoy.

"Think Cody would run away if we had a dog?" Frank asked.

"No, he knows who owns the can opener. Oh, I shouldn't insult him. Cody's a handful, but he's loyal. He'd probably sulk for a few days, then he'd adjust. We'd just have to give him extra attention."

I got up and refilled our hot chocolates. Cody noticed the mint smell, of which he is enamored, and made a pest out of himself trying to get a taste of it.

Frank gently pulled me back over to him, encircling me with his arms. "You haven't had so many nightmares lately."

"No. At least, not the really intense ones. I might wake up, but I'm not screaming bloody murder."

"So you *are* still having them." I could hear the worry in his voice.

"Not as often as before. I'm almost used to it now."

"These letters and pranks getting to you?"

No use lying. "A little."

I felt him tense. "I guess they worry me, too. Especially because I know you won't be able to resist trying to track him down."

"It's in my nature, Frank. A strong sense of curiosity is one of the things we have in common. You know I can't ignore these letters. I don't know why you find that hard to understand."

"It isn't hard to understand. There's just a difference between what I understand and what I feel happy about."

"I'll be careful."

Lots of silence. Finally, he sighed and relaxed a little.

"You worry too much, Frank. Besides, I'm not his target."

"Not yet," he said, and the tension returned.

I reached up and started massaging his neck. He murmured something about it feeling good.

DEAR IRENE,

"You know what, Frank? I'm really enjoying having two hands."

"Wrong. I'm the one who's enjoying it."

THE NEXT MORNING, I WAS SITTING AT MY DESK, DAYDREAMING ABOUT my old friend O'Connor. The desk used to be his, and it took a while for me to learn to say "my desk" when referring to it. It would always be his, of course, and I often felt especially near to him when I sat there. O'Connor was fond of quoting things he had read here and there; he was a walking book of proverbs, old saws, and words of wisdom. He had one for any occasion, but you were especially likely to hear them from him when he had a skinful.

One night at Banyon's he had been holding forth on the role of the press, and he asked me if I had ever heard of the Greek historian Herodotus. O'Connor was just short of being knee-walking drunk, so I wasn't even sure I had heard the name right, and said no, I didn't know about Herodotus.

"Well, my darling," he said, trying to look me straight in the eye, "Herodotus said a thing or two worth remembering, but my favorite is this: 'Of all men's miseries the bitterest is this, to know so much and to have control over nothing.' "

How he could pull these things out of his memory when he was soused I'll never know, but he did it again and again. And he'd remember he had said them the next day and give me a follow-up lesson if my own hangover would allow for it.

That's how I happened to be thinking of Herodotus when Frank called.

"I think I know who Thalia is," he said. "A good candidate, anyway."

"Who?"

"A woman by the name of Thayer. Rosie Thayer. Owner of Rosie's Bar and Grill down on Broadway—about six blocks from the paper."

"I know the place. I've never been in there, but I've walked past it. How did you come up with her?"

"I asked Missing Persons for a list of everyone reported to them since the day Edna Blaylock was killed. Thayer seems to be a good candidate."

"Good Cheer—a bar owner?"

"Yes, and a couple of other things. Thayer sounds a little bit like Thalia, and she's the same age as the Blaylock woman."

"What?"

"Yeah, she's fifty-four. I don't know what to make of that; in fact, I don't have the complete file on her yet. But I wanted you to know. If it checks out, do you think John would let you run something on her, help us try to find out if anybody has seen her?"

"I'll ask him."

"If he says yes, give me a call back. I should have the rest of the file by then. Oh—have you asked Lydia about Christmas?"

"Not yet. I'll try to ask her on my way out of John's office."

But John was busy and I had to wait until a copy editor had finished talking to him. In the meantime, I told Lydia that we were staying in town and ready to invite ourselves to Christmas dinner. She was more than pleased with the news.

"Fantastic! We'll all be together!"

"You'll be able to feed two more people?"

"Both nights, without any trouble. Never worry about having enough to eat when a bunch of Italians are doing the cooking."

Stuart Angert walked over and we started exchanging stories about oddball letters. "I've got a fish advocate now," he said.

"Someone who promotes eating seafood?"

"No, just the opposite. Every time a photo of someone standing next to a big catch appears in the sports section, this woman writes in to say that fishing is cruel and immoral and that printing a photo of a fish carcass is demeaning to the fish."

A couple of general assignment reporters gathered around us, and one of them urged Stuart to tell me about someone they referred to as Zucchini Man.

But before Stuart could reply, John yelled out, "Kelly? You want to see me?"

I went into his office and told him about Rosie Thayer and my conversation with Kincaid. He thought things over for a few minutes then decided he didn't have a problem with my writing a story on Thayer. He also said I could go ahead and tell Frank what I learned from Kincaid.

I had just walked back out into the newsroom and was looking for Stuart when Mark Baker called out to me, telling me I had a phone call. I forgot all about Zucchini Man and hurried over to my desk and took the receiver from Mark.

"Miss Kelly? Steven Kincaid."

"Hold on a minute." I gave Mark a "get lost" look but he ignored it. I covered the phone and said, "Thank you very much, Mark, you can go back to whatever it is you do around here."

"You're starting to sound like John Walters," he said, but moved away.

"Hello," I said into the phone, "I'm back with you again. What can I do for you?"

"You mentioned wanting to talk about E.J.'s research. I stayed up last night and made a list of the things she had written and worked on. I thought you might want to have it as soon as possible and, well, I couldn't sleep anyway. Would you like for me to bring it by?"

"Sure. Listen, did Dr. Blaylock know someone named Rosie Thayer?"

He thought it over before answering. "I can't remember her ever mentioning anyone by that name."

"Did she ever go to a place called Rosie's Bar and Grill down on Broadway?"

"No, at least not with me. Why?"

"Nothing important—I was just thinking of trying it out for lunch, wondered if you'd heard of it. In fact, why don't you let me buy you lunch, Mr. Kincaid? You're doing me a real favor by gathering information on Dr. Blaylock's research."

"Sure, I'd like to have lunch with you. And please call me Steven."

"Then I'm Irene, not Miss Kelly, okay?"

"Okay."

I called Frank back.

"Hi. Christmas is all set. Tell me about Rosie Thayer."

"First of all, turns out Rosie was a nickname. Her real name was Thelma. Thelma Thayer. Thalia from either one, I guess."

"Any connection to Edna Blaylock?"

"None we've been able to uncover. In fact, they only share one or two similar traits. I mentioned the age business. Both longtime residents of Las Piernas. Both unmarried."

"Blaylock was married and divorced."

"What?"

"Didn't the police find out about that? According to my source, she was married for about a year when she was at UCLA, during or immediately after grad school."

"*Your source?*"

"That will have to do for now, I'm afraid." It wasn't the first time one of us had been forced to say something like that; I didn't think he'd mind. We had agreed early on in our relationship to respect certain job-related boundaries.

"Who did she marry?"

"Don't know. Think your guys could find something out? All I have is a first name—James. Apparently it was long ago and no ill-will remaining, at least not on Blaylock's part."

"I'll check it out."

"I'm thinking of going down to Rosie's Bar and Grill for lunch," I said.

"I've got to get down there myself. Want to have lunch together?"

"Uh—no, not really. In fact, could you be out of there by eleven?"

Dead silence.

"Let me rephrase that, Frank. I'm going to be having lunch with someone who won't be comfortable talking to me in front of a cop. I'd love to have lunch with you, but I think this guy will speak more openly to me if there isn't a third party involved."

"Who is 'this guy'?"

"Can't tell you. Not yet."

"A suspect in this case?"

"Frank, I said *I can't tell you.*" I emphasized each word, wondering if my growing irritation would make any impression.

"Look, Irene, I know we've agreed to some limits, but just about anyone who has information about this case is potentially a murder suspect. And I don't trust anyone who tells you they don't want the police around. It's a homicide investigation, for Christsakes. What if you're meeting Thanatos for lunch?"

That really steamed me. The man clearly thought I was an idiot.

"Never mind who I'm going to lunch with," I hissed from between clenched teeth.

"Who the hell is it, Irene?"

"Goddamn it, Frank, it's none of your business. I'm not required to report every contact I have with any other male in Las Piernas to the local police department. Or to you personally, for that matter."

"Just tell me."

"Just drop it."

"Are you near your period?"

"No, Frank. Is someone pinching your balls?"

"Don't be ridiculous!"

"Don't be an asshole!"

He hung up. I slammed the phone down so hard, the casing cracked. I looked up to see Mark Baker a few feet away, trying desperately to stifle laughter. I stomped out of the newsroom, stringing swear words together under my breath. I went downstairs.

"Geoff, you know where I'll be if anyone comes looking for me," I said on my way past the security desk. I went down into the basement.

Geoff is a skinny old gem of a man, and he often looks out for me when I'm in hot water. He has known me for a dozen years, and that means he knows that when I need a break from the *Express* staff, I often go down to the basement to watch the presses run.

Danny Coburn, one of the press operators, smiled when he saw me, but quickly figured out that I needed to be given a wide berth. He let me go past him without doing more than handing me some ear protectors and saying, "Go on, just about to start them up."

I knew my way through the maze of presses. I stood somewhere out in the middle of that web of machinery and wires and paper and ink. Just as Danny had said, they were starting up. Of course, the fact that I wasn't really supposed to be there made it more enjoyable.

The growling start-up built into a roar, and I put the ear protectors on. Within a few minutes, the rumbling could be felt in the floor beneath my feet. The newsprint was moving faster now, flying past the place where I stood and weaving over, under, and between rollers. It came back up out of the presses in a blur, was cut and rolled and turned and folded. Knowing I'd never be heard over the presses, I hollered half a dozen obscenities at the top of my lungs. I breathed in the smell of the ink and the paper and felt better for it. I was at home there.

I have a fierce temper but I don't usually stay mad for long. I know myself well enough to realize that one of my challenges in life is to keep it under control, to accept the fact that most of the things that make me angry aren't worth the effort. It's usually a matter of perspective.

But being engaged to be married does strange things to one's perspective. Everything gets filtered through a sieve labeled "the rest of your life." As I stood there watching the intricate network of paper and machinery do its work, I wondered if Frank and I could possibly overcome this particular obstacle.

There was an important principle being tested here, I told myself. As a reporter, I needed to be able to move among a wide variety of people—including unsavory characters. I didn't believe I should be obliged to get Frank's approval to talk to them. Frank's protectiveness, so welcomed when I was injured, would suffocate me if it went too far where reporting was concerned. I needed him to trust me.

"No use asking anyone to trust you, Irene," O'Connor once told me. "It's like asking someone to love you. He either does or he doesn't. The request doesn't change a thing."

The love I was sure of. The trust? Only a maybe. No matter what my sister had read while getting her nails done.

I looked up and saw Coburn waving me out from my hiding place. I took a deep breath and walked out to see why I was being summoned.

"Geoff says there's someone here to see you," Coburn shouted. I nodded and handed back the ear protectors. I glanced at my watch as I walked up the basement stairs. 9:30. Way too early for Kincaid. I reached the top of the stairs and Geoff motioned to me. I didn't see anyone in the lobby.

"What is it, Geoff?"

"Detective Harriman is waiting to talk to you."

"Look, Geoff—"

"I asked him to wait outside. Now, I ain't so old I don't see you two must have had a scrap or something—he don't leave his police work to come down here all of a sudden-like just on a whim. It's none of my business, but I've never seen you be a coward, Miss Kelly, so you better get on out there and talk to the man, or you'll disappoint me."

I had to grin. "Lord knows, Geoff, I can't afford to do that."

I went out the front doors and saw Frank leaning against the building, looking at the toe of one of his shoes like it held the secret of life.

"Crime on a coffee break in this town?" I asked.

"Hi." He stood up straight, but didn't come closer. Wise man.

"I'm under strict orders from Geoff to listen to what you have to say. Have you been bribing that old geezer?"

"No, but it's a thought. I came down here to apologize. They told me your phone is out of order."

I reddened a little, but held my ground. "I was just thinking about why you made me so angry."

"Well, besides the fact that I insulted you, you probably think I don't trust you."

That floored me. I don't know exactly why. He has this knack for getting to the heart of things that has unnerved me more than once. It's a little disquieting to be with someone who can read you like a large-type book. I didn't say anything.

He sighed. "I'm sorry I lost my temper. And I do trust you."

"Do you? I could have sworn otherwise from the conversation we just had on the phone."

He leaned back against the wall and went back to studying his shoe.

"Look," I said, "I accept your apology. I owe you one, too. As for the trust issue, I guess we need to talk. What time will you be getting home tonight?"

"Late," he said quietly.

He was unhappy and I knew it, but I fought the urge to say something just to make him feel better. This was too important. I repeated that to myself a couple of times.

"If you aren't too tired when you come home," I said, "let's talk. I'll try to stay up. Or wake me when you get in."

"Okay, I'll see you at home then." He turned and walked off without saying another word.

Well, I had stood up for myself all right. Why did I feel so shitty?

# 9

I TRIED TO CRAWL UP OUT OF MY foul mood before Steven Kincaid arrived. He showed up a little early; I was still working on some notes, but I asked Geoff to send him up. I glanced up as he entered the newsroom, and noticed that every female within shouting distance was looking him over.

Then I noticed the men. Hostile doesn't quite describe it. I expected to hear the cry of Tarzan any minute. It was apparently stuck in some newsman's throat.

"Hello, Steven," I said with a smile that was as much amusement at the general consternation he had caused as it was a welcome.

"Hi, Irene. I'm a little early."

"O'Connor once quoted someone as saying that 'the trouble with being punctual is that nobody's there to appreciate it.' "

He shrugged and gave me a fleeting, disarming grin. "Evelyn Waugh said punctuality is the virtue of the bored."

"I think I like that one better. But you don't strike me as being bored."

"No. Restless, I suppose. Who's O'Connor?"

"I'll tell you about him on the way to lunch. Do you mind a walk of about six blocks?"

He didn't. I used the time to talk on and on about my old friend and mentor. It made me smile, but when I looked over at my companion, his brows were knitted in concern.

"You say O'Connor was killed?"

"Yes. He was murdered."

"So you know what it's like."

I stopped walking. "Do you mean, I know what *you* feel like? I don't. He wasn't my lover, but he was a beloved friend. But if you mean, I know what it's like to lose someone suddenly, violently . . . well, yes, I guess I do."

He looked like he might break down right out there on the sidewalk, so I took hold of his hand and pulled him forward. "Come on, keep moving. It's good for you."

"I'm sorry," he said, following me. "I can't seem to control my emotions these days. It's humiliating. I'm not used to it at all."

Well, the Banshee of the Press Room had no trouble understanding what that was like. I let go of his hand but kept walking at a brisk pace. He was forced to keep up with me. "You need to get some sleep, Steven. Your batteries are too run down to cope with everything that's happened."

Just then I noticed one of my shoelaces was untied. I stopped and bent to tie it, and became aware of someone watching us. From a car. A familiar car.

"Excuse me a moment, Steven. I need to embarrass someone." I left him standing dumbfounded on the sidewalk and ran over to the car, just as the red-faced driver tried to start it up. I pounded on the window and he rolled it down.

"Pete Baird. What a surprise."

"How're you doing, Irene?"

"Pissed off, as a matter of fact. Since you're willing to do your partner's dirty work, I don't suppose you'd mind being an errand boy. So here's a message: you can tell your pal Frank that if he's going to send his partner downtown to follow me around, he can—"

"Whoa! Wait a minute! Frank didn't send me down here to watch you. It was my own idea. I swear it. He doesn't know I'm here. And you damned well better hope I don't tell him I saw you holding hands with young Studley Do-Right over there."

"In the first place, you know I wasn't 'holding hands,' not in the way you imply I was. In the second place, buzz off. This doesn't concern you or Frank—and no, don't give me a lot of bull about it. I'll call Bredloe and tell him his boys are harassing me."

"That would be a laugh. The Captain knows what a pain in the ass you can be."

"Are you on assignment right now?"

He turned red again.

"I thought so. Have you ever done this before?"

"Tailed people? Sure . . ."

"No, I mean, watched me walk to lunch."

His brows drew together. "What?"

But I had already reconsidered the question. Pete was working with Frank in other parts of town on the other days I thought I had been followed.

"You've gotta believe me, Irene," he was saying. "It was my idea. Frank would kill me if he knew."

I didn't doubt that Pete would come up with something like this on his own. He was as loyal as an old hound to Frank, and notorious for sticking his nose where it didn't belong. A fight between Frank and me would be all the excuse he needed. "I'm very fond of you, Pete, but sometimes you are a true butt itch. I'll just stand here until you get yourself gone."

He muttered something and pulled away. I waited until he had driven out of sight before I went back over to Steven, who was clearly puzzled.

"Who was that?"

"A secret admirer. Are you hungry?"

He nodded.

WE WALKED ABOUT THREE DOORS DOWN AND ENTERED THE WORLD OF Rosie's Bar and Grill. Up until the moment we walked through the door, all I was hoping for was a chance to find out a little more about Rosie Thayer. I'll admit that I was bringing Kincaid along to see if anyone there acted like they recognized him, although I was fairly sure he would have balked at having lunch there if he had been lying to me about not knowing Rosie Thayer. He was not the kind of man who went unnoticed.

But as soon as my eyes adjusted to the dark interior, I made the connection between E.J. Blaylock and Rosie Thayer. The place was empty, so it wasn't the patrons that provided the clue. It was the decor. Rosie's Bar and Grill was something of a shrine.

"Rosie the Riveter," I said.

Steven apparently had the same thought. "Will you look at this place?" he whispered, as if he were in a church, not a bar.

The walls were covered with pictures of World War II vintage airplanes, of fighter pilots in leather jackets, of bomber crews standing alongside their planes. Interspersed were dozens of photos of aircraft factories taken in the 1940s, and lots of pictures of women workers in coveralls and scarves. Behind the bar was a poster-sized print of Norman Rockwell's painting "Rosie the Riveter." There were other posters of the same era here and there—"Loose lips sink ships" and other slogans abounding.

I remembered what Steven had told me the day before. Maybe Rosie Thayer and E.J. Blaylock's mother both worked for the same aircraft company. But the photographs were from the war years, and Rosie Thayer was E.J.'s age. Too young to have worked during World War II.

"Most of the photographs come from Mercury Aircraft," Steven said, moving closer to a cluster of them. "That's the company E.J.'s mom worked for. E.J. was really proud of her mother's war work. That's one of the topics she wanted to write about—women war workers."

I looked at a note written below a photograph of a woman making part of an aircraft wing: *Bertha Thayer (Mom) working on aileron.*

"Her mother . . ." I said. "Rosie Thayer is as proud of her mother as E.J. was of hers."

Steven looked over at me, comprehension dawning. "Do these photographs have something to do with E.J.? With why she was killed?"

"I don't know."

"But you were asking about this bar when I called this morning. Now you tell me their mothers worked together. What's going on? Are we here to talk to this Rosie Thayer?"

Before I could answer, we heard a man yell, "Be right with you," from a back room. He made it sound as if it was a damned shame that we were going to make him wait on somebody.

"Calm down, Steven," I said in a low voice. "I'll tell you more later. But for now, just roll with it, okay?"

He didn't act like it was the easiest thing in the world for him to do, but he nodded and followed me to a booth near the bar and sat down. A skinny old sad sack came shuffling over to us like he was on the fourth day of a forced march.

"What'll it be?" he made himself ask.

I had checked out the "on tap" signs and knew I wouldn't find it disagreeable. "A couple of your draught beers and menus, please."

"Sure," he said, as if it broke his heart. He shuffled off.

"So?" Steven said, as soon as the other man was out of earshot.

"I'm just following up on a lead."

"You won't tell me? I'll give you a start, then. *Mercury Aircraft*. Mercury, Roman version of the Greek god Hermes. Messenger of the gods—"

"The god of commerce, manual skill, cleverness, and travel," I finished for him. "I looked him up in my mythology books after you mentioned Mercury Aircraft yesterday. He's also the god of thievery."

"Maybe Thanatos worked there, too."

"*Maybe*, Steven. That's what I'm trying to say. Let's see where it leads. I don't want to play some guessing game, and I don't want to talk about my theories in here. I want to ask the guy who works here a few questions. If you don't think you can sit there calmly while I do that, tell me now and we'll leave."

He was quiet then. "Sorry. I'm just anxious to see her killer caught. You'll let me know what you learn?"

"Sure."

Old Happy Pants came back with the beers and tossed a couple of menus on the table.

"Before you walk off," I said, "I wondered if you could talk to me for a few minutes about Rosie."

He eyed us suspiciously. "You with the cops?"

"No, newspaper. This is Mr. Kincaid. My name's Kelly. I'm with the *Express*."

"Kelly—Irene Kelly?" For the first time, he smiled. "You the one who wrote about the witches?"

"The same."

"I thought a couple of guys beat the crap out of you." He seemed so happy about it.

"They did. But I'm okay now. Thanks for the concern." I could see that Steven was taken aback by this last exchange, but he didn't say anything. I did catch him looking at my right hand again.

"Yeah, well, you gonna put me in the paper?" Happy asked.

"Depends. For starters, what's your name?"

"Just remember to spell it right," he laughed.

Lots of people think we've never heard that old line. I pulled out a notebook. "Okay, so spell it for me."

"J-O-H-N-N-Y—you got that?"

"I'm still with you."

"S-M-I-T-H." He started guffawing. He was full of appreciation for his own humor, which made him a party of one. I smiled anyway, since I needed his cooperation.

"Wait a minute," he said, suddenly sobering. "You the one who wrote about that gal who got her brains bashed in down at the zoo?"

Steven turned chalk white, but caught my warning glance and stayed silent.

"Yeah, I'm the one who wrote about it. And I hate to say it, but I'm afraid this same guy might have something against Rosie."

"Rosie? Naw. Naw, I don't believe it. She never had an enemy in her life." But he didn't look so sure of it. He pulled a chair over and straddled its back. I noticed he was holding on to that chair pretty tightly.

"How long have you known Rosie, Mr. Smith?"

"Aw, call me Johnny. I've known her almost all my life. Since high school, leastways."

"How long has she been missing?"

"Since early last Thursday."

Almost a week ago. "That's when you noticed she was gone?"

"That was when she *was* gone. We had a quick drink after closing on Wednesday night—Thursday morning—and she left at about two-thirty. She didn't show up that afternoon—Thursday afternoon. I had to take care of the lunch crowd all by myself. Not like her to miss coming in. She's never been sick a day in her life. I called, wasn't nobody home. I called the cops. They wait for a while before they'll say someone is missing. That kinda made me mad."

"She's never gone missing before?"

"Never. She never missed a day here. This is her pride and joy. She says it shows the American way still pays off."

"American way?" Steven asked.

"Yeah, you know, democracy. She wasn't born rich. She never even finished high school—flunked out. Too busy chasing boys, to be honest. But she's just like her ma—worked hard and made something of herself. She was always real proud of everything those women did for the war effort. She was real proud of her ma. She never has liked to be called Thelma. She's been calling herself Rosie for years."

"Is her mother living?"

"Naw, old Bertha kicked off about five years ago."

"Do you have a picture of Rosie?"

"I did have, but the damned cops took it. Maybe they can give you one."

"She have many friends around here?"

"Me. Unless you want to call that bunch of lushes that tries to get credit off her 'friends.' We got our regulars, and Rosie's a real cheerful, friendly type. But this place is her life. She doesn't have time to pay social calls on people."

"Are you involved with her?"

He laughed. "You mean, are we shacking up? No. That's why we stayed friends."

"Did she have a boyfriend?"

"There have been guys here and there, but nobody for some time. She told me she's worn out on men. Said we weren't nothing but children, always needing something from somebody. I told her she was wrong, but I gotta say, she seems happier now that she stopped chasing after men."

"Anybody been through here lately with a special interest in her?"

"Naw. Nobody even asks where she's gone. Makes me mad. Except for you and a cop that was in here earlier, nobody's even showed an interest."

I pulled out a business card and wrote my home number on the back. "Here. If you hear from her or from anyone who might know more about her, let me know, okay?"

He studied it at arm's length. I suspected he wore bifocals, but was too vain to put them on.

"You want something to eat?" he asked, tucking the card in a shirt pocket.

We ordered a couple of sandwiches. As soon as Johnny walked off to make them, Steven whispered, "It *has* to be Mercury Aircraft. Other than that, Rosie and E.J. couldn't be more different. Maybe their mothers knew something about Mercury, or maybe—"

"Slow down. We have a lot of ground to cover. But I agree, it seems to be one of the few things they had in common. But it could be a coincidence; thousands of women worked for Mercury during those years. We don't even know for a certainty that Rosie is Thalia, but if she is, Thanatos may be choosing these women because of their ages, and because they're single."

"Do you think she's dead? Rosie, I mean?"

"I don't know." That, of course, was stretching the truth. If Rosie was Thalia, I figured the chances that Thanatos had delayed his plans were slim to none; I just didn't know if they had reached their conclusion.

"What did Mr. Smith mean about someone hurting you?"

I shook my head. "You don't need to hear it right now, and I don't need to tell it." At his look of chagrin, I added, "Don't worry that you've offended me. I'll tell you someday."

"I didn't mean to pry."

"It isn't prying, really. Now, you had some research to show me?"

He pulled out the list of E.J.'s research papers and articles and interests. Most were about the U.S. in the postwar era, particularly about two topics: women war workers and the Truman presidency.

"She was really interested in the role of women in the workforce in the postwar era," Steven said. "But she couldn't get published back when she first wrote about it, in the late fifties and early sixties. So she started to delve into the Truman administration."

Johnny brought the sandwiches, which were surprisingly good, given his lack of enthusiasm over being of service. He didn't linger at the table, just set the plates down and ambled back to the kitchen. As we ate, I thought about E.J. Blaylock and Rosie Thayer. I looked across the table. The professor certainly hadn't given up on men.

"Do you have family in this area, Steven?"

"No, why do you ask?"

"Friends?"

He shrugged. "Not really. The two or three people I could call friends have gone home for the holidays." It didn't seem to bother him much.

"What about you?" I asked. "Will you be going home for the holidays?"

He shook his head. "My folks are in Florida. I can't afford to go back there. And I wouldn't even if I could."

"Why not?"

After a long sigh he said, "They didn't approve of my relationship with E.J. I haven't had much to say to them for the last year."

"Sorry. You see? *That's* prying."

"It's okay. I appreciate the concern."

"I just wonder if this sleeplessness and isolation is healthy for you."

"What should I do? Start bedding women like Lindsey? Hardly any solace in that. I'd rather be alone. Or with you." He blushed. "I mean, working on this with you."

"That's fine as far as it goes, but you probably need more than a research project to settle your nerves. And no, I'm not talking about indiscriminate sex as a remedy for insomnia. But why not make an effort to get to know some people? People you could respect."

Whatever reply Steven might have made was forestalled when Johnny walked up and gave us the check. I paid it and left him a handsome tip, hoping it would help to keep me in his good graces. We said good-bye to him and started the walk back to the newspaper.

Although I had expected a lot of questions about E.J. and Rosie once we were outside, Steven was quiet as we walked. When we reached the Wrigley Building, he stopped and said, "I guess I'd better be going. I promised Dr. Ferguson—he's the department chair—that I would have all of E.J.'s things out of her office today."

"What?"

"Well, the police have taken what they need. The dean asked the campus police to keep it sealed, but I guess they finally convinced him that it . . . it wouldn't serve any purpose. The department wants to use her office."

"But why you?"

"She doesn't have any relatives. And even though Dr. Ferguson was upset by the articles in the *Express*, he's quite sympathetic. He knew about my relationship with E.J. I guess he doesn't know who else to ask to take care of it."

"Steven, do me a favor. Let me go with you when you go over to Dr. Blaylock's office—"

"It isn't necessary—"

"Give me the benefit of a doubt, okay? Give me time to write up my story. Just hang loose for a couple of hours and I'll help you. It won't hurt to have someone with you—I don't know if you've thought much about it, but it isn't going to be easy on you."

"I know that gathering her things together will be painful but—"

"Have you been in her office since she died?"

"No."

"Have you seen it at all since then?"

"No."

I sighed. "Well, let's just say the cops don't get into janitorial work."

He caught my meaning. "Oh."

"So you'll wait for me to go with you?"

He nodded. "I'll wait at home until I hear from you."

He left and I ran upstairs. I had a lot of writing to do. I also needed to call Frank and pick up the photo of Rosie Thayer. And to start rebuilding a bridge I had damaged that morning.

# 10

I WAS ABLE TO WRITE UP THE PIECE on Rosie Thayer fairly quickly. My adrenaline was flowing and it felt good to move at the fast pace that afternoon demanded. I found I wasn't feeling as moody as I had that morning. Maybe thinking about Thayer being starved to death somewhere changed my outlook on my own troubles.

I discussed my progress with John Walters, then called the Las Piernas Police Department and asked for Robbery-Homicide. Frank was on another line, so I left a message that I was on my way over.

When I got there, he was talking to Pete about something. Pete saw me and gave me a pleading look, but then excused himself. Frank didn't look overjoyed to see me. I couldn't blame him.

"What can I do for you?" he asked. You would think I had walked into a shoe store.

"Unless you'd rather wait and read about it in tomorrow's *Express*, I have some information that might interest you."

He motioned for me to sit down, then sat up straighter in his own chair. His desk was neat and clutter-free. Next to it, Pete's desk was covered with an Everest of paper, coffee cups, and file folders. Frank pulled out his notebook and looked over at me. "Go ahead."

He ruffled my feathers a little with his show of detachment, but I figured he was still smarting from this morning. I shrugged and started to tell him about my conversations with Steven Kincaid. He listened attentively and made notes, and gradually his interest in what I was telling him started to lower the tension level.

"You were over at Rosie's Bar and Grill this morning, right?" I asked.

He nodded.

"Well, there are lots of photos from Mercury Aircraft. Turns out both Rosie Thayer and Edna Blaylock were daughters of 'Rosie the Riveters.' Their mothers both worked for Mercury. I'm not sure that's the only connection, since a hell of a lot of women worked there in the 1940s. But it's hard to come up with much of anything else. Have you had any luck trying to find out what might have become of Thayer?"

"No, but we haven't been at it for very long, just a few hours."

"Missing Persons didn't have anything on her?"

"No, but they have a heavy case load. They've asked a few people a few questions, but there wasn't any sign of a struggle at her apartment, nor were there any other indications that she had been abducted." He paused a moment then added, "Your story will probably help. Maybe someone saw her taken somewhere."

"I hope so. Johnny Smith said you had a photo of her?"

"You've saved me having to drop this by the paper," he said, opening a desk drawer and pulling out a file folder. He removed a 4 x 5 print from a small stack of photos, and handed it over to me. I was relieved to see that whoever had taken the picture had known how to focus a camera; sometimes the paper is asked to run a photo that is so blurred, studying it for hours will allow you to conclude only that the missing person is basically shaped like a human being.

In this photo, Rosie Thayer was smiling. The years hadn't been as kind to her as they were to Edna Blaylock, but there was a sparkle in Rosie Thayer's eyes that gave her image a warmth that hadn't come through in any photos I had seen of the professor.

Pete walked back in the room and came over to his desk. He searched through the chaos on it for a moment, then turned to Frank.

"Call me."

Frank smiled. "You've lost it again, haven't you?"

Pete looked exasperated. "Just call me, damn it."

Frank picked up his phone and punched a few buttons. We heard a muffled ringing sound. Pete went toward it, and suddenly it stopped. He turned to give Frank a dark scowl, causing Frank to start laughing.

Frank moved his thumb off the cradle and punched in the numbers once again. The odd ringing returned. Papers were flying everywhere as Pete tried to track it down. Suddenly he yanked the bottom desk drawer open, then threw some file folders onto the floor. He reached in and held up the phone in triumph.

"I forgot I put it in there for safekeeping," he said.

Much to Pete's dismay, I lost my struggle not to laugh. I looked over and saw that Frank was grinning. It was one of those moments when I felt so attracted to him I stopped breathing for a while. I exhaled and decided that I wasn't going to wait to make amends. "Could we go somewhere to talk for a minute?"

He lost the grin, but said, "Sure."

I followed him into a small interview room. "There aren't any hidden mirrors or cameras in here, are there?" I asked.

"Not in this one," he said.

"No recording devices?"

"Not at the moment."

What the hell? I thought. I pushed him up against the door and then reached up and pulled his head down toward me for a kiss. He was surprised for about one-tenth of a second, then reached around me and kept it going. You'd think one of us had been overseas for six months.

"Does this mean you're not mad at me anymore?" he asked, keeping his arms around me. "Or do we need to make up now that we've kissed?"

"Sorry about this morning. I just felt hemmed in. I thought you were being a little overprotective."

"I guess I'm not quite over being afraid for you. I don't ever want to have to go through another night of not knowing where you are or worrying about what someone may have done to you."

I leaned my head against his shoulder. "I'll never walk around believing 'it will never happen to me'—those days are over. But I can't just crawl into a cocoon with you, Frank, and you know it. You would grow tired of it. You'd resent my helplessness."

I felt him shaking beneath me. He was laughing. I couldn't believe it.

"Irene, if there is one word I'll never use to describe you, it's 'helpless.' "

Well, that made me feel better. "Thanks. But do you understand why I was upset this morning?"

"I think so." He sighed. "I guess this means you're getting back to being your old self."

"Don't sound so disappointed."

That started him laughing again, which somehow led to kissing again.

"Damn," I said. "If we don't stop now, I'm going to risk being the first person to be arrested for lewd conduct while visiting the Las Piernas Police Department."

"Plead entrapment."

"So you won't be home until late, huh?"

He shook his head. "Believe me, I'll be there as soon as I can. By the way—Saturday night there's an office Christmas party. Want to be my date?"

"Sure. Are you still off this weekend?" I asked.

"Depends on what comes up, but it looks like it. Why?"

"Well, I have to work a day shift Saturday, and we'll be with our friends on Christmas Eve and Christmas Day. I just wondered if I'd get you all to myself on Sunday. It's Christmas Adam."

"Christmas Adam?"

"The day before Christmas Eve."

"Of course. You are one weird broad." There was tenderness in that, so I didn't challenge him.

I WAS WHISTLING AS I DROVE OFF, AT LEAST, I WAS UNTIL I REMEMBERED what was up next on the agenda. I pulled over and called Steven from a pay phone. We agreed to meet at the college. I dropped by the paper to turn in the photo of Rosie Thayer, then found Lydia and quickly gave her the rundown on Steven Kincaid.

"You're concerned about him being alone for the holidays," she said.

"Right."

"Invite him to join us, of course. What did I just tell you this morning?"

• • •

WHEN I REACHED THE BUILDING THAT HOUSED THE HISTORY FACULTY offices, Steven was waiting outside the doors. He seemed agitated.

"Are you okay?" I asked.

He nodded. "It's just—I've been thinking about what you said."

"I guess that wasn't very kind of me."

"No, I'm grateful. At least I'm a little better prepared."

"Has the college done anything at all in the way of clean-up?"

"No." His face was set in a tense frown. "Dr. Ferguson told me that after all the rumors about her, he wanted me to have a chance to remove her belongings, especially personal things, before the cleaning crew worked on the room. I assumed he was being respectful of her memory."

To change the subject for a few minutes, and because I didn't know what kind of shape he'd be in later, I asked him about coming over to Lydia's for Christmas Eve and Christmas. He brightened and thanked me, and agreed to join us.

His spirits dampened again as we made our way up the stairs to the office. The place was deserted: a few days before Christmas and grades already turned in. There was a spooky silence in the building. When we reached the third floor, he stopped and turned through a door leading out into a hallway. I saw that he had already stacked about three dozen cardboard boxes near one of the office doors. He must have spent most of the time he waited for my call by hauling boxes.

"Think you've got enough of these?"

He shrugged. "I'm not sure. But I hope so."

His hand shook as he put the key in the door and unlocked it. He pushed the door open and took one step in. He froze for a moment, then swayed and whirled around. He pushed past me, a horrified look on his face. He rushed down the hall to the men's room. Standing in the doorway, I could see why he had felt sick. It was all I could do not to follow suit.

Edna Blaylock's office was small and narrow. There was a couch against one wall, a desk facing out toward some windows. There was a small bookcase between the couch and the desk. The other wall was covered by a large set of bookcases that were absolutely full. But there was no sense of the tranquil academic life that might have normally gone on in that office.

The room had been closed up and smelled sickeningly of old blood. And plenty of it. It was sprayed all over the walls, windows and bookcase, and large pools of it had dried in black cakes on the desk and floor. Papers on the desk were matted with it. Only the couch and the part of the bookcase nearest the door were free from the dark stains. Throughout the room, there were small signs here and there of the work of the forensics team. The room was silent, but not at all peaceful.

Steven Kincaid was wrong. Nothing I had said to him could have prepared him for this.

I felt a surge of anger. Ferguson should have at least had someone in to do some preliminary cleanup. I held my breath and went over to the windows and opened them as wide as I could. Cold air came flooding in, but it was fresh air. I looked around, then pulled a large calendar with Ansel Adams photos on it off the wall. I used it to cover up the blood stain on the desk, apologizing mentally to Mr. Adams and to the stately El Capitan of Yosemite—the photo for November. That was all I had time to do before Steven returned.

"I'm sorry," he said. His eyes were red. He still looked shaken.

"Nothing to be ashamed of, Steven. This is worse than I thought it would be. Why don't you sit down for a minute? I'll bring in some boxes and you can work on the far end of the bookcase until you feel better."

"It's not fair to you," he said, but sank down onto the couch, his eyes averted from the desk. "You didn't even know her."

"That's exactly why it will be easier for me to deal with the worst of it. I won't throw anything away, I'll just box it up. Then you can deal with it a little at a time, as you're able to."

If you're ever able to, I thought. And I wouldn't blame him if that day never came. I got him started on his part of the task, then went to the other end of the room. I moved the calendar off the desk and set it aside. I figured the desk was the worst place in the office, and I wanted to spare Steven as much as possible.

Blood-soaked papers were stuck to the desktop. Once I had gingerly peeled them off, the surface of the desk was not so bad. A neatly clipped stack of phone message slips caught my attention. At first I thought they might be recent calls, but then I saw that some of them were quite faded. The slips were in alphabetical order, and dates on them ranged over several years.

"It was her informal system," Steven said, seeing me reading them. "They aren't personal friends or people she contacted often—those names and numbers are in her Rolodex." He glanced over the desktop, then turned away from it. "I guess the police took that," he said, not very steadily. "The message slips are resource people. Librarians and reseachers, archivists and curators that helped her with specialized research."

"Such as her research on war workers?" I asked, concentrating now on the notes Edna Blaylock had written on the bottom half of each slip.

"Maybe," he said. He was sitting on the couch again, looking pale.

"Mind if I keep any that look interesting?"

He shook his head.

"Are you all right?"

He managed an unconvincing smile. "I will be in a minute, I think."

One of the slips was for a man named Hobson Devoe. The name itself drew my attention, but after I read the words *Knew Mom* at the bottom, I pocketed it.

I looked over at Steven. He had gone back to work at his end of the room, the worst apparently having passed.

I stuffed all of the contents of the desktop into one box, then closed and labeled it with a black marking pen I found in a pencil jar. For a moment, I registered surprise that there was no picture of Steven on the desk or on any of the nearby shelves, but then I remembered that theirs was a very private relationship.

That thought led to the decision to let him be the one to go through the desk drawers; despite a niggling curiosity, somehow, I didn't want to invade Edna Blaylock's privacy in that way. I figured Frank's crew had probably already been over it with a fine-tooth comb anyway. I started grabbing books from the shelves that had the worst staining.

As much to keep my mind off this grisly task as anything, I asked Steven about his family, his childhood, his interests in history. We were almost finished by the time I had learned his life story. Talking seemed to relax him a little. He even started working on the desk drawers. He asked me about how I got started in journalism, and my work. He shyly ventured to ask if I was seeing anyone, and I told him about Frank. He remembered meeting Frank.

"I liked him. He was very considerate," he said. But that had brought us back to homicide. He opened a desk drawer and was very quiet all of a sudden. I looked over to see him holding a red candlestick—or rather, the inch or so that remained of a candlestick—in his right palm. Tears were streaming down his face.

"From a special evening?" I asked.

He nodded. "Our first. I asked her to save it. I didn't think she had." He drew in a breath, then covered his eyes with his left hand. I put a hand on his shoulder and he broke down completely. I've seen men cry before, but it wasn't the sight of him crying that was so hard to take. It was a soft sound he tried hard to hide, the kind of sobbing sound a person sometimes makes when he realizes that no matter how long he waits, the one he loved will never again share a knowing smile or call his name from another room or weigh the bed down beside him.

He got up after a while and tucked the candle carefully into his pocket, then went off to wash his face. I finished packing up the last of the books and stuff from the desk drawers while he was gone.

"What kind of car do you have?" I asked when he returned.

"A pickup truck."

"Thank God," I said, looking around at the stacks of boxes. We had managed to fill all of them.

"I feel bad about making you do all of this," he said. "You—"

"I know, I know, I didn't even know her. I know you. Now I even know the name of your elementary school. You'll just have to accept my help. You're saving me from having to buy indulgences."

"I can't picture you being much of a sinner."

I thought of the string of blasphemies I had uttered down in the basement of the *Express* that very morning and laughed. "Don't make me confess," I said.

I was relieved to learn there was an elevator in the building, and we used it to haul the boxes down to his truck. When the last one was loaded in, he turned to me and said, "I won't ever be able to repay you for this. But I won't ever forget it, either. Thank you, Irene." He gave me a quick hug and drove off before I could tell him he didn't owe me a thing.

It wasn't until I got home and had sat around for an hour or two that I realized I had really overdone it. My hand was especially loud in protesting, my shoulder not far behind. I put on some soft music and tried to relax. I changed into one of Frank's pajama tops, which came to just above my knees, and crawled onto the couch to wait for him. I tried not to think about what hurt.

When he hadn't made it by midnight, I put ice on the hand. Still it throbbed. I finally broke down and took a painkiller. It had been a few weeks since I had taken one and I had forgotten how powerful they were. I conked out on the couch.

I don't know how long I had slept when I felt a draft of cold air. It was dark in the living room, and I was still very drowsy. A little later, I felt a pair of strong arms lifting me carefully from the couch and murmured, "You're home." He carried me into the bedroom and tucked me under the covers. I heard him walking back out of the room and fell asleep waiting for him to get into bed.

Later, I finally heard him undressing. "Frank?"

"Sorry, I was trying not to wake you."

"Thanks for tucking me in."

"What?"

Something fell into place then. Some gnawing feeling that something wasn't right. I reached over and turned on the light.

There was a jar of ants sitting on the night stand.

# 11

"DON'T TOUCH IT," FRANK SAID.

Not a problem. I found myself scrambling off the bed and as far away from it as I could, into Frank's arms. I'm not afraid of insects. I do have difficulty with calling cards left by killers.

"What happened?" he asked.

I told him about being carried into bed. "I thought it was you. He was here. He got inside the house. He touched me—"

Frank held on to me, trying to calm me down. I don't know if I was more angry or afraid. When my composure returned, Frank called the department and asked for a forensics team. I stayed close to him as he walked into the living room. He went over to the patio door, and without touching it, pointed out that the sliding-glass door was off its tracks.

"I felt a draft," I said.

"He jimmied it up. We didn't set the bolt," he said with exasperation. The door was equipped with a bolt lock that would have made it much more difficult for Thanatos to enter the house that way. But we only fastened that lock when we were leaving the house, since it would be awkward to unlatch in case of fire. We had talked once or twice about replacing the weak handle lock—the one Thanatos had overcome so easily—with one that would be both strong and easy to open from the inside, but never got around to it.

I could tell that Frank was silently berating himself, and knew it would be useless to protest that it was a case of mutual procrastination. We searched the house together, but as far as we could tell, nothing was missing or disturbed. Unless you count me in the latter category.

Pete came over, and other officers not long after. They tried to ask questions that might elicit some description of Thanatos from me. All I was able to say was that he had been strong enough to lift me; I thought he probably had a build that was similar to Frank's, but I couldn't be sure.

It was frustrating for all concerned. No fingerprints other than Frank's and mine were on the glass door. They didn't find any prints on the jar of ants, but they took it with them. I knew Thanatos' hands weren't gloved when he carried me to the bed, but it came back to me that neither his clothes nor his hands were cold.

How long had he watched me sleep?

By the time everybody left, we were both worn down. We crawled into bed and held on to each other. I thought I would fall asleep quickly, but I didn't. I could tell that Frank was still awake as well.

"You're worrying," I said at last.

"And I'm pissed."

"At me?"

"No, no—why would I be angry with you?"

"Because I missed a chance to see who he is. You could have had a description of him if I had just opened my eyes. And your home has been broken into because of me."

He pulled away to look down at me. "*Our* home. Right at the moment, I don't really give a shit about the house. I'm angry because I left you here alone at night, and he could have harmed you."

"Stop it, Frank. You know how I hate it when you try to take over for God."

He had nothing to say to that.

"I'll be fine," I said.

"Hmmph."

I decided it was time for a change in tactics. I moved up against him in a positively nasty way, running my fingernails over his chest. He groaned and gave me a kiss. One thing led to several others, and eventually we worked off all possible tension. Just before we fell asleep, I scraped his earlobe lightly with my teeth and whispered, "Merry Christmas, Adam."

"Merry Christmas, Eve," he whispered back. I could hear the smile in it.

MORNING CAME WAY TOO EARLY FOR ANYONE'S LIKING, BUT WE managed to crawl out of bed. We made arrangements to meet at home before the Christmas party, and trundled off to work.

I was talking to Lydia about my visit from Thanatos when the phone rang.

"Good morning, Cassandra. Did you sleep well?"

"No thanks to you," I said, trying to hide my nervousness. This time I was able to get Lydia's attention, and she picked up the extension. We both took notes.

"Did you enjoy my Christmas gift?"

"I've already put the little devils to work sorting seeds."

He laughed. Synthesized and changed into an electronic replica of laughter, it was a chilling sound. I fought an urge to hang up on him. I wanted to know where Rosie Thayer was, so I waited. As it turned out, he wasn't going to disappoint me.

"Since I so enjoyed watching you sleep, I've decided to give you another present. If you want to find the other Myrmidons, think of the story of Aeacus, and where he saw his future army."

The line went dead.

"The other what?" I asked Lydia, reaching for a mythology book.

"Mur-mi-dons?"

I thumbed back to the index. "Here it is, Myrmidons—men created from ants by Zeus. Oh, now I remember—they became part of Achilles' army in the Trojan War."

"So we're back to ants."

I nodded as I skimmed through the section on the Myrmidons.

"He said something about the story of a cuss?" Lydia asked.

"Aeacus," I said absently, still reading. "He was a mortal, a son of Zeus. He ruled the island of Aegina. Hera caused the island's streams and rivers to be poisoned. Almost all of the island's inhabitants died. Aeacus prayed near an oak, which was sacred to Zeus. He saw a long line of ants carrying grain up the tree, and begged Zeus to give him as many subjects as there were ants. That night, he dreamed of ants becoming men, and when he awoke, his son Telamon was calling him outside, to see the throng of men approaching their home. Aeacus recognized their faces from his dream."

"So does Thanatos think you're going to dream the answer?"

"I don't know. Maybe he's talking about the oak tree. I can't decipher it yet, but we've got to let John know about the call."

We hurried into his office. After hearing our story, John put in a call to Frank, who wasn't at his desk. "What's the name of that city department that maintains the trees?" he asked me, while waiting for Frank to answer a page.

"The Tree Department," I answered.

"Wise ass," he grumbled.

I shrugged. Would he have felt better if I made up a more obscure name?

"Do you think they know where all the oaks in town are?" he asked impatiently.

"Probably know where to find the ones the city has planted. Private property would be another story."

"At least it's an oak we're looking for, not something scrawny."

Frank came on the line and John put him on the speakerphone. We filled him in; there was a brief pause, then he said, "I know what we'll want to do, John. But if you're asking to involve the paper, I'm going to have to bring my lieutenant in on this."

"We are involved," John answered. "We called you, remember?"

"Hold on, then," Frank replied, seeming unruffled by John's curt tone.

John picked up the receiver, so that the speakerphone was off. Lieutenant Carlson came on the line, and apparently a lot of angry haggling and talk about press rights and police prerogatives ensued. We could only hear John's side of it, but he was unbending. He argued that the call had come into the paper, not into the police, and that his reporters had the right to be on the streets, which were public places, looking at all the public acorn-bearing trees they could find. Eventually Carlson saw that it was useless to protest. The whole conversation probably took about three minutes, but it seemed like forever to me. I wanted to get going.

John stuck his head out his door and started shouting reporters' names. He filled them in, then had two or three of them calling tree surgeons, another pair going down to the Tree Department. "Ask about the biggest oak trees. Something tells me this guy picked out something on a grand scale. After all, it has to be fit for the gods."

"What do you want me to do?" I asked.

"You stay here—who knows what he's up to. Maybe he's just trying to draw you out of the building." At my mutinous look, he added, "Besides, if he calls back, you'd better be here."

"If he stays true to form, he won't call again today. Let me go out on it. I'm the only one reading about the mythology. Maybe I'll see something the others would miss."

"Forget it," he said, and shooed us out of his office.

I drew some quick sympathetic looks from the others as they hurried off. Cassandra.

I went back to my desk and reread the story of Aeacus, more carefully this time. A plague of serpents caused the island of Aegina's water to be poisoned. Additionally, the locals had suffered drought, famine, and a pestilent wind from the south. Aeacus awoke from his ants-to-men dream to discover it was raining, the serpents were gone, and a new populace of hard-working subjects was at his command. Talk about sweet dreams.

I thought of Thanatos' letters, and of what he had said on the phone. Aeacus had seen his future army on an oak. But perhaps, as with many of his other references, Thanatos didn't literally mean that I could find Rosie Thayer near an oak tree. What about the other places in Las Piernas which might be connected to oaks, or to the word "oak"?

I logged on to my computer terminal and asked for a program that serves as a guide to the city; it lists streets, public buildings, developments, parks, schools, and other points of interest in Las Piernas. Given any address, it will also display an area map. I searched under the word "oak." A few seconds later, a list appeared on the screen. A restaurant called The Oak Room. A development called Oakridge Estates. Oak View Apartments. The Oakmont Hotel. Oakwood Elementary School. Oak Knoll Shopping Center. About twenty streets: Oak Park, Old Oak, Oak Point, Oak Meadow, Twin Oaks, Oak Grove, Sleeping Oak.

Sleeping Oak Road. That one caught my attention. Aeacus had seen the army of ants twice: on an oak, and while he was asleep.

I brought the map display up on the screen. Sleeping Oak was a long, residential street that wound its way through the hills. I debated with myself for a while, tried thinking of other ways to look at Thanatos' messages. But the street name was the only possibility that really nagged at me.

I saw that John's door was closed, and gathered up my coat, purse, and keys. I pulled out a copy of the photo of Rosie Thayer and tucked it into a pocket. I had almost made it to the newsroom door when a hand caught my shoulder. I turned to see Lydia.

"Where are you going?" she asked in a low voice.

"Just out to my car for a minute."

"Then where?"

No use trying to fool her. "Listen, Lydia, I can't sit here all day. I've got an idea I want to follow up on."

"If Thanatos doesn't kill you, John will."

"I'll take my chances."

"That's what I thought you'd say. Come over to the desk for a minute." When she saw that I would protest, she said, "Come with me or I'll walk right into John's office before you can make it out of the building."

At the City Desk, she unlocked a cabinet and handed me a cellular phone.

"You know the lecture on how much a call on one of these costs the paper," she said, "so I won't make you listen to it again. But take this with you and use it if you need help. That way, when I'm at your funeral, I'll feel like I did what I could to save an old friend."

"Aren't you the chipper one. Okay, I'll take it."

"Will you tell me where you're going?"

"Sleeping Oak Road. Thanks for the phone—and the concern."

LAS PIERNAS SITS ON A CURVE OF THE CALIFORNIA COASTLINE; MOST OF its beaches face the south. As some custom-home builders have noticed over the past five years, the views from the south side of hillside streets like Sleeping Oak Road were some of the best in the inland part of the city. You could see almost all of Las Piernas below, and the ocean beyond it. The view from the north side of the street was not so picturesque, but some homeowners had overcome this handicap by trying to build taller houses than their neighbors across the street.

Many of the homes were old by Las Piernas standards, modest dwellings built in the 1920s. About every fourth or fifth house had been razed and replaced with a larger, more modern structure. I didn't see an oak tree anywhere.

I started on the south side, and walked from house to house, knocking on doors, asking the few people who were home if they had seen the woman in the photo, or noticed any unusual activities on the street. I asked if any of their neighbors had moved in fairly recently. If they hadn't closed the door in my face by then, I got around to asking about their neighbors' habits. I came across people who had grudges against others on their block, and got the lowdown on who never cut their lawn, whose kids were holy terrors, whose dog barked endlessly, and which couple got drunk and played loud music in the middle of the night.

I listened to it all, knowing that neighborly snoopiness is nothing to ignore. In among all that apparently useless information, someone may have a little gem of observation that will prove to be invaluable. But I didn't come across anyone who had seen Rosie Thayer, or who knew of a neighbor who got home late on the night she disappeared, or who had heard or seen anything that might help me find her.

As I hiked closer to the crest of the hill, I noticed that there were more empty lots near the top, staked signs promising more new construction where the view was best. As I passed each lot, I stopped to look for trampled grass or newly turned earth. Although I was looking for Rosie Thayer and believed she was probably dead, I was quite pleased not to discover anything that looked like a shallow grave.

I had almost run out of houses on that side of the street and still had the north side to check out on the way down. I was discouraged, feeling certain that my street-name hunch was a total waste of time. By now, the police had probably found Rosie Thayer, perhaps under an oak tree in a city park, or on an embankment near a big tree. I considered using the celluar phone to check in with Lydia, but remembered the cost of calls and decided to wait.

The thought of walking back down to my car made me wish I could whistle and get it to come up the hill for me. I had no sooner formed the image than I heard a sharp whistle from somewhere behind me, and turned to see a huge woman whose gray hair was wrapped in pink spongy curlers. She was calling to a white toy poodle as it bounced its way across a pair of empty lots.

"Brutus!" the woman screeched. "Brutus, you get your fluffy white butt right back here!"

Brutus paused, looked at her, then noticed me. That brought on a canine change of program. He made a yapping charge toward me, full of purpose. The purpose looked to be a bite out of my own fluffy white butt. His plans were foiled when the woman moved with amazing speed to scoop him up. She smiled and said, "I hope he didn't scare you. He's not as mean as he looks."

The dog kept yapping, and I realized that he was the one which had been described to me as the neighborhood nominee for most annoying pooch.

"No," I said, "I'm fine." I introduced myself, and showed the photo to her. She stared at it for what seemed like half an hour, dog barking the whole time, then handed it back and shook her head.

"Sorry, I thought I remembered her, then it just came to me that this photo is in this morning's paper."

"I was wondering if I could ask you a few questions about the neighborhood."

"Sure. My name's Molly Kittridge, by the by. Be glad to talk with you," she said, "but let's go inside so I can get Brutus settled down. He's busier than a bagful of bumblebees."

I followed her into her house, one of the smaller homes on the block. She nodded toward a chair at the kitchen table; I took it gratefully, happy to be off my feet for a while. What I could see of the house was neat and clean. The kitchen was warm and filled with the aroma of baking bread. She put Brutus behind one of those indoor gates people use to keep small children out of a room. He stopped yapping, but when I looked toward him, he gave me a growl for good measure.

Molly came back into the kitchen, suddenly touching her hair. "Lordy, I must look a sight," she said, reaching up and pulling the curlers out.

"Don't worry about it. You weren't expecting company."

"Well, that's a fact," she said, and proved it by talking nearly nonstop for over an hour. In that time, she told me the name of every neighbor within a dozen or so houses of her own, their children's names and approximate ages, where they worked, and at least one of their habits, interests or problems. She told me which ones had left to visit relatives for Christmas, what state the relatives lived in, and even gave a weather forecast, saying, "White Christmas" or "No White Christmas there" depending on the family destination. She paused only twice, to take the bread out of the oven and when the phone rang. It took both of us a minute to realize the ringing was coming from the celluar phone. I answered around a mouthful of warm bread.

Lydia was calling, certain I was in mortal danger. I swallowed the bread, reassured her, learned that no one had found Rosie Thayer yet, and went back to Molly Kittridge.

"How is it you know all your neighbors so well?" I asked.

She smiled. "Well, two reasons. First off, I've lived here since God was a baby. My grandaddy on my mother's side built this house as a sort of a retirement place, I guess you'd say. Southern California was a paradise then. My folks ruined his retirement by packing up the family and following him out here from Oklahoma during the dust-bowl days. Lots of Midwesterners settled in Las Piernas. That's why you can find more basements here than most places in Southern California. They're great for tornados, but lousy for earthquakes."

"So your family moved here before any of the others?"

"The only ones that had been here longer was the Nelsons, up at the end of the street. They died and their kids sold it to that young couple that got transferred to North Dakota."

"This is the vacant house, the one three doors up the street?" I asked, remembering her discussion of the couple who had lived there for less than a year, were "asking way too much for that old place in this market," but were too stubborn to lower the price before they were forced to move. After several months without any offers, the couple let their listing expire and were looking for a new real estate agent. I had heard enough about them to write and ask them how they were doing. (No kids; he, a distributor for a shoe company and she, an engineer; both crazy about bass fishing.)

She chuckled. "Not three *doors,* exactly. There's no doors, windows, or anything else on half of these places up here on the crest. The old Nelson place is at 1647. There's two vacant lots between us now."

"You said there are two reasons you know your neighbors. What's the second?"

"Brutus."

He started yapping in response.

"Hush!" she commanded. He gave one more bark and settled down again. "He's a wild little fellow. Wilder than a fox raised by wolves. I have to chase him all over the neighborhood. Now all of a sudden he's crazy about the old Nelson place. I think he knows I don't like hauling my old buns up to the top of the hill. And all the grass in these lots gets my hay fever a-going. But most times Brutus will come back when I whistle."

"He does seem to be well-known around here."

She cackled at that. "I'll just bet everyone you talked to griped about him. He's a barker, I admit it. He's very protective of me. He's usually good about being quiet at night, but for the past week or so he's been a little bothersome."

"The past week?" I asked, suddenly feeling a chill in that warm kitchen.

"Oh, about that long, I guess. Something just got into him. Middle of the night, two, three in the morning, he starts barking. 'Bout to drive me crazy."

The hair on the back of my neck was rising. "Do you remember which night he first started barking?"

She thought for a moment. "Wednesday, maybe?"

Wednesday night. The night Rosie Thayer had disappeared.

"No idea what he's barking at?"

"The top of the hill, for all I can tell. I get up, I turn the lights on, ask him what's the matter, let him out in the backyard, show him there's not a living soul to be found. He stops barking, follows me back into the house, hops back up on the bed, and looks at me like I'm crazy to be up at that time of night. And he's probably right."

She was disappointed when I said I'd have to be going. I gave her one of my cards and thanked her for her help. I started to leave, and felt myself losing my nerve.

"Molly, I have an unusual favor to ask."

She looked up from studying my card. "Sure, honey, what is it?"

"I need to look around the Nelson place. Would you watch me

from your window for a few minutes? I mean, just in case anyone else happens to be there . . ."

Her eyes widened. "Holy smokes, I just got it! You think she might be in there. You're the one he's been writing to . . ."

"Yes. The house is probably empty, he's probably miles away, but just in case —"

"I'll get Brutus on the leash and come with you."

She refused to hear my objections.

I had expected Brutus to be nipping at my heels, but the leash seemed to change his personality. As we neared the house at the crest of the hill, he pulled like a huskie in his traces. Molly sneezed once, twice, three times. "What'd I tell you?" she said, reaching for a handkerchief.

From a distance, 1647 Sleeping Oak appeared to be a modest, white wood-frame house. Grass grew up around the ankles of a "For Sale" sign in the big front yard. The lawn was due for a mowing and the windows were dirty, but otherwise it looked as if it had been a place someone cared about not so long ago.

Molly kept sneezing, her eyes red and watery now. When I suggested that she just wait for me back at her house, she gave me a congested version of "not on your life." I walked up the steps and knocked on the front door, not expecting an answer. Brutus suddenly started going berserk, making me wonder if someone was waiting inside. He would alternately bark and wheeze as he strained against his rhinestone collar. I walked over to one of the larger windows at the front of the house and looked in. I saw a sun-faded beige carpet in a bare room. Dark marks and nail holes outlined the places where pictures had been taken down. The stigmata of an abandoned home.

"I don't think anyone's here," I said over the dog's barking, hoping to God I was right. "But would you mind letting Brutus off his leash? Maybe he can show us what's got him so worked up."

"I guess I can catch him again," she said, unsnapping the leash as he twisted in impatience. He bolted around the corner of the house, stopping at a wooden gate. He looked back at us, yapped, then suddenly disappeared. We could hear him in the backyard.

"Brutus!" Molly cried, but he just yapped louder.

As we came closer, we could see that Brutus had wriggled through a hole in the ground beneath the gate; apparently a project he'd worked on during his previous visits. The gate had a latch with pull string on it. I tugged on the string and cautiously stood aside as the gate swung open. I peered into the backyard. No one there but Brutus.

Still, there were signs of another presence having preceded me—something much larger than Brutus. The grass was taller in the backyard, almost to my knees. Molly and I cautiously followed the pathway of flattened grass toward the sound of Brutus's toenails, scratching furiously.

He seemed determined to burrow through what once had been the entrance to a basement. The weathered doors had been nailed shut long ago; rusting metal bands bolted across their width further secured them.

"Brutus, get back from there!" Molly said, picking him up and suffering another sneezing fit. He squirmed in her arms for a moment, then resorted to whining.

"Is there another entrance to the basement?"

"Oh sure," Molly said, talking rapidly, nervously. "The Nelsons boarded this one up long ago. Most of us did that—to make the houses more secure, I guess." She stopped to blow her nose. "We all built staircases and an entrance from inside the house. Some people had a door going off the kitchen, like mine. Others had trap doors in the floors. The Nelsons had one of those. Put in a laundry chute, too. I thought that was overdoing it." She sneezed. "Kids throw clothes down the chute, they land all over the place. I always made my kids carry their clothes down the stairs. It was good for them."

I wasn't listening very carefully. I was watching the crevice near the edge of one of the doors. Ants were streaming in and out of the basement. An army of them. And there was a faint but distinct odor in the air, one that made my hopes plummet.

"Maybe you should take Brutus home now, Molly."

She looked at me in surprise, then looked down at the doors. "Oh, my Lord! Oh, my Lordy-Lord-Lord-Lord. She's in there! Call her name, maybe she can answer you."

I tried it once, but my voice caught. "Molly, go home, please. I'll come over in a while. There's . . . there's a smell."

"I don't smell anything."

I looked over at her, but didn't say anything.

"Even with all that sneezing, I'd smell a dead body! Besides, if there is a smell, you don't know that it's a-comin' from her! Could be a cat, or a possum or something else dead."

She was right, of course. I couldn't see into the basement.

She was waiting for me, silent and afraid, but her eyes pleaded with me to do *something*. Brutus yapped once, then stared at me in much the same way.

I looked at the trail blazed by our unknown predecessor and sighed in resignation. "Try not to step on the flattened grass," I said, knowing she would follow me. I made my way alongside the trampled path, which led around the corner of the house to a set of concrete steps. At the top of the steps was the back door. It wasn't wide open, but it hadn't been closed hard enough to latch.

Sometimes the last thing on earth you want to do is the very next thing you need to do. My curiosity demanded I go into the house, see for myself what was in there. My fear, or perhaps my common sense, said to let someone else take care of it.

"She might still be alive," Molly said.

Curiosity had an optimist on its side. It always does.

I climbed the steps and used the toe of my shoe to budge the door. It creaked open, and I stood staring into an empty kitchen, yellow linoleum peeling and stained where a stove and refrigerator had once hidden its faults. The counters were bare, the sink empty. I waited. Silence.

Brutus's sharp yap behind me came close to scaring me right out of my skin. Just as I had decided to listen to the pessimist within me, the dog wriggled free and scurried through the open door, into the house, and out of sight.

"Brutus!" Molly wailed.

"Stay here," I told her, blocking her attempt to follow the dog. "If I'm not back out in five minutes, or if you have any inkling that something's happened to me, get the hell out of here. Go home and call the police. Don't come in looking for me or the dog."

She didn't say anything, just peered inside the house. It was silent again.

"Promise," I said firmly.

"I promise," she said.

The kitchen had two interior doorways. One led out into the dining area of the living room I had seen from the front window. A quick glance showed this area to be empty of man and beast. The doorway at the other side of the kitchen was darkened.

With every step I took across that kitchen floor, I was sure I wasn't alone in that house, that I had walked into a trap. REPORTER KILLED IN POODLE RESCUE ATTEMPT. What a headline that would make. Undoubtedly, the subhead would read, "Poodle Found Unharmed." I kept listening, hearing the soles of my shoes moving across the linoleum, the rustle of my clothing seemingly amplified to shout my presence. I noticed a trail of ants moving along one corner of the kitchen floor— toward the darkened doorway. I swallowed and tiptoed to it.

The smell was stronger here.

I peered cautiously around the corner. A long hallway, as near as I could tell. I held still, hearing a noise to my left. I waited. Nothing.

I glanced behind me, saw Molly watching from the door to the backyard, and tried once again to screw up my courage.

There was only enough light coming from the kitchen windows to allow me to determine that the hallway ran in two directions. I hung back in the kitchen, poised for flight as I groped for a light switch on the hallway wall. I found one. Outside of making a loud snapping noise, it did nothing. The electricity was off.

I reached into my purse for my keychain flashlight. Felt the comforting weight of the cellular phone. If I couldn't call for help, maybe I could use it to bean an attacker. I switched on the little flashlight, held it to the left, where I had heard the noise, and even its small circle of light revealed enough to make me feel weak in the knees.

An opening gaped in the floor. If I had stepped into the hallway without the light, I might have fallen through the trap door and down the basement stairs.

"Bruuu . . . tus," I crooned.

I could swear I heard the little bugger panting, but in the distance. Down in the basement.

I pointed the beam in the other direction, passed it from one closed doorway after another. Three altogether. Thought of opening those doors first, just to try to get more light in the hallway. Didn't know if I had the nerve to find out what was behind them.

I crept up to one and shoved it open, then ran back into the kitchen, purse raised.

"Irene?" I heard Molly call.

"I'm okay, I'm okay," I said. *Liar, liar, pants on fire.*

I took a breath and looked into the hall. A little more light. No bogeymen. Not yet, anyway. Two more rounds of hit-and-run with the doors brought the same result. The house had two bedrooms, one bath. I had the shakes.

Brutus barked. He was down in the basement.

"That's him!" Molly called. "Do you see him?"

"Not yet," I said. I was not pleased with the dog.

I thought of giving in and calling Frank right then and there. Let him explore the damned basement.

But what if I called Frank away from a homicide investigation only to find there was nothing more down there than a toy poodle and something like, oh, maybe a smelly old dead gopher? The woman who cried wolf. Over a poodle.

I walked over to the edge of the trap door opening. My flashlight beam showed nothing more than wooden stairs. I stepped down on one, then another, and another, until my head was just above the opening in the hallway floor. I made myself duck a little, and held the flashlight out in front of me. Cobwebs. I could hear Brutus. I lowered the beam a few degrees and saw a concrete wall. I caught a movement and gave a little yelp. But it was Brutus, sniffing along the wall, apparently unconcerned by my presence. For a few seconds, I felt a slight easing of the tension that had my stomach in knots. Brutus wouldn't act so nonchalant if there were anyone else in the basement. Would he?

I moved the light a little to the left, and I could make out a card table, with what looked to be a bowl of fruit and a pitcher of water. Tantalus.

My mouth went dry.

I knew what would be behind me. I forced myself to take two more steps down the stairs, clinging to the handrail.

I heard a noise above me and cringed. "Molly?" I called.

I waited. Nothing.

Brutus came closer to me, his nails clicking along the cement floor.

Slowly, I turned around.

I saw the wide piece of tape first. It covered her mouth. She was bound to a large pipe against the back wall. Even in the faint light, I knew she was dead.

The trap door slammed shut above me.

# 12

I WAS STILL SCREAMING MY HEAD off when it opened again, not more than a few seconds later. Molly, red-faced, was leaning over the opening, saying, "I'm sorry, I'm sorry." Brutus, unhappy with both of us, shot up past me and out of the basement. I gained a modicum of control over myself and did the same.

"I thought I heard you call to me," she said, only slightly less upset than I was. "It's so darned dark in this hallway, I accidentally knocked the door shut. I'm so sorry, honey, I know I scared the bejesus out of you. Are you all right?"

"Yes, I'm fine," I said. "Let's get out of here."

As soon as we were out of the house, she said, "So there wasn't anybody down there after all?"

The optimist.

"I wish I could say there wasn't."

She stared at me a moment, the color draining from her face. "She's dead?"

I nodded, then put an arm around her big shoulders and walked out to the front yard with her, leaving the gate open. I stayed there; she kept walking, her eyes on Brutus, who waited in her own front yard.

I used the cellular phone to call Frank's pager and left a message on his voice mail, asking him to meet me at the address on Sleeping Oak. I dialed the City Desk next. Let John bitch about the order of the calls, I thought. Lydia answered on the fourth ring. I stood in the ankle-deep grass, watching Molly walk back to her house, looking twice as old as she had just moments before. I told Lydia to call the police, but to mention to them that I had already called Frank's pager. I told her I would be waiting in front of the house. I heard John yelling, "Is that Kelly?" in the background, told Lydia I didn't want to run up the bill, and hung up.

The phone rang almost immediately. I thought it might be John, but it was Frank.

"I'm on my way," he said. "I'm not too far from you."

"Hurry," I said, looking through the gate, suddenly noticing that there were long leafy stems growing out of a place at the far corner of the yard. The stump of an oak tree.

"You think she might still be alive?" he asked.

At my feet, another trail of ants.

"No. But hurry."

By the time I finished writing my contribution to the story on Rosie Thayer, I was fighting off a serious case of the megrims. The story itself made me feel down, but that wasn't all that was getting to me. The general atmosphere at the paper was tense. I learned that Lt. Carlson had argued with Wrigley and others over a new issue: whether or not the police should be allowed to put a wiretap on my phone line. So far, Carlson was being forced to live with the paper's refusal.

I felt restless and decided to get some fresh air. Let the chronicling of cruelty be left to others for a while. I put on my coat and stepped outside.

Holiday decorations lined the street, as they had since Thanksgiving. I walked aimlessly, listening to the sounds of the downtown streets—the rumble of passing traffic, snippets of pedestrians' conversations, horns echoing off tall buildings, the sharp staccato of a jackhammer at work in the shell of an old building. I heard a street musician playing "Fever" on a flute. The same guy played this same song every day, so that by now "Fever" seemed to be the anthem of this block on Broadway. He was getting better at it. Some days I noticed the improvement, heard the notes one by one; some days the flute's song was nothing more to me than all the other sounds of the street. As I walked that afternoon, whenever I thought of Rosie Thayer, I tried to listen for the flute again. It worked for a little while. I turned up the collar of my coat against the chilly air and kept moving.

I walked east a couple of short blocks to Las Piernas Boulevard, and then south a couple more, past the old post office and bank buildings and found myself standing in front of Austin Woods & Grandson Books, a used bookstore not far from the paper. I know a remedy when I see one, so I pushed the front door open and stepped inside.

The bookstore occupies a huge brick building that has withstood both earthquakes and city redevelopment plans over the last century. I've been told that it was once home to a market, then a car dealership, and later a machinery warehouse, but I've only known it in its present incarnation.

Once inside, I stood still for a moment, letting the store's warmth and cathedral quiet welcome me. Skylights in the high, arching ceilings overhead brought softened sunlight into the cavernous rooms. Around me, wooden crates were nailed together to form walls of bookcases. Ten feet high or higher they stretched, holding row upon towering row of musty tomes. Each cover and spine seemed to long to be held again, the way a widower might long for his late wife's embrace.

I took a deep breath, inhaling the distinctive old-book fragrance of yellowed paper and aged binding glue. Images of dark basements and bloodstained offices faded. I walked down the aisles, reading titles, and eventually began smiling to myself. You can find just about any book in this store, provided you aren't really looking for it.

The shelving system was designed by Austin Woods, who has a mind that apparently views the universe of printed matter in a unique way. Books should not be subjected to silly things like alphabetical order or genres; even a division between fiction and nonfiction was unnecessary, since the latter might have less to do with the truth than the former. This whimsical approach was not to his only son's liking; Louis Woods refused to work in the store and went on to start one of Las Piernas's oldest accounting firms.

In one of those twists of fate that have long caused parents to go gray and balding, Louis' own son, Bill, rebelled against the accountant's orderliness. Bill spent most of his childhood helping his grandfather; Austin rewarded this loyalty by giving him half-ownership and adding the "& Grandson" to the name of the store.

O'Connor had introduced me to the place, and taught me that the best strategy was to relax and browse and let something intrigue you on its own; if you really wanted a specific title, just ask one of the Woods and they'd miraculously make a beeline for it. O'Connor sometimes asked for a certain title just to watch Austin or Bill do this; he figured the entertainment value was worth the price of a book.

Austin is a dried apple of a man, with a face that can hardly be found among his wrinkles. At ninety-six, he spends most of his time sleeping at an old desk in a cluttered back office, glasses atop his head and buried in wisps of thin white hair, some favorite tome opened and serving as a pillow beneath him. Bill, his wife Linda, and his daughter Katy carry on the business, which has attracted a faithful clientele over the years.

I browsed for a while, then made my way over to the counter, where the fourth generation was at work. Katy Woods looked up from a beautifully bound volume of *The Master of Ballantrae.* She's about nineteen, very pretty, but shy. "Hi, Irene," she greeted me. "I didn't think I'd see you until Christmas Eve. Are you doing some early Christmas shopping?"

I laughed. "I suppose I should, Katy. In fact, you've just given me an inspiration. I'd like to purchase one of Stevenson's other works to give to my former brother-in-law."

"*The Strange Case of Dr. Jekyll and Mr. Hyde*?"

"You know me too well."

She called to her mother, who took over at the register while Katy unerringly steered me directly to the book, which was next to a 1948 high school science textbook. All the other works on the shelf appeared to be science fiction or relatives of science fiction.

"I give up," I said. "Why's the textbook here?"

"This science book has a few pages in it that espouse some pretty silly ideas about radiation. Austin says this shelf is where we should have works about what happens when scientists don't fully understand the impact of their discoveries."

With Katy's help, I found an old edition of Jane Austen's *Emma,* and decided to buy it for Barbara, quite sure that she would never get the hint it might offer about sticking one's nose in where it doesn't belong.

Katy found a few books on mythology for me as well. Hermes, or Mercury, was pictured on the cover of one of them. It sparked a memory, and I reached into my coat pocket and pulled out the message slip I had taken from E.J. Blaylock's office. Hobson Devoe.

"Could I use your phone for a local call, Katy?"

She nodded, and I followed her back to the front counter. The phone was made of black metal and had a rotary dial. "I'll bet it really rings, too," I said.

She smiled. "Yes. I like it better than an electronic chirping."

I called the number on the message slip. I got a recording. A woman's silky voice, saying, "Thank you for calling the Mercury Aerospace Museum. The museum will be closed for the holidays from Monday, December 17 through Tuesday, January 1. The museum will reopen on Wednesday, January 2. Museum hours are ten A.M. to three P.M. on weekdays; other hours by appointment. To make an appointment, please press the pound sign, located below the number nine on your Touch-Tone phone. If you are calling from a rotary dial telephone, or wish to speak to an operator, please stay on the line."

I waited. And waited. I feared my call was a captive in that strange electronic dimension where transferred calls wander without direction until the end of time. I finally heard a voice say, "Mercury Aircraft. How may I direct your call?"

"I'm trying to reach Hobson Devoe—" I began.

"One moment," she interrupted, and transferred me right back to the recording about the museum.

I hung up, muttering to myself, but softly enough to hear Katy clear her throat.

"I couldn't help overhearing," she said. "You want to talk to Hobson Devoe?"

"Yes. Do you know him?"

"I'm assuming there aren't too many Hobson Devoes in Las Piernas. But if he's the one who works at Mercury, he's one of my great-grandfather's friends."

"Austin knows Hobson Devoe?"

She nodded. "Austin's taking a nap now, but when he wakes up, I could tell him you need to talk to Mr. Devoe. I'm sure he'd be happy to pass a message along."

I took out a card and wrote my home number on it. "Please ask him to tell Mr. Devoe that it's urgent that I speak to him. I'd consider it a great favor."

She waved a hand in dismissal. "Remember that column you and Mr. O'Connor wrote about the store? Back when the city wanted to tear down this building?"

"It made more sense for the city planners to put the convention center where it is now, anyway," I said. "They probably wouldn't have stayed with the plan to close the store down."

"Well, that's not how we see it. You kept us from being closed down while they made up their minds. Austin will be happy to do a favor for you. Mr. Devoe is in here quite often. Austin talks to him about Las Piernas in the good old days. I like to listen to them—I love history. I'm thinking of majoring in it."

"Are you dating anybody special these days, Katy?" I asked, thinking of Steven Kincaid. She blushed, then, as she rang up my purchases on the antique cash register, proceeded to describe her boyfriend. I had to admit that he sounded like a perfect match for her. She paused and looked at me over the top of the register. "He knows how to find the books," she said, pushing down the keys that made the bell ring, the cash drawer open, and the total-with-tax appear behind dusty glass.

Well, that settled that.

I went along to other downtown shops and picked up gifts for almost everyone else on my list. I bought a couple of pairs of sweatpants for Frank from Nobody Out, a sporting goods store. Helen, my favorite salesperson there, was working that afternoon, and I briefly considered introducing her to Steven. She's a college student, very bright, and gorgeous. Closer to Steven's age than Katy. She's not stuck on herself, and I can't understand why.

Then I thought about the book I had just bought for Barbara and decided to stay out of the matchmaking business. I wished her happy holidays and left without mentioning available males.

I lugged all of my purchases back to the *Express* and piled them into the Karmann Ghia. I drove home, then walked next door to talk to Jack. I needed his help with my plans for a gift I had in mind for Frank, and he was willing to lend a hand. As we drove off together toward the animal shelter, he asked me if I was sure Frank wanted a dog, given all the work Frank did on the yard.

"Oh, sure. We had a long talk about dogs the other night. I know he wants one, or I wouldn't do this."

"Don't you think it would be better to let him pick out the one he wants?"

"Well, I did wonder about that, but I think I've got a pretty good idea of what kinds of dogs he likes best."

"Hope you're right."

"If he doesn't like the dog I pick out, I'll just tell him it's my dog."

For some reason, Jack found this funny.

There were lots of people touring the pound that day, the last day the city animal shelter was open before Christmas. After Jack and I went through all of the kennels, and he had finally convinced me that owning eighty-seven dogs would not be practical, we found a huskie-shepherd mix that won my heart. I paid the fees and bought a leash. Fortunately, the dog was already neutered, so we didn't have to wait three days to take him. He was not quite done with being a puppy; the shelter said he was about a year old. He had a long, creamy coat, a dark muzzle, and big feet. He was very affectionate.

"I'll tell you what, Irene," Jack said as we tried to get the dog to crawl in behind the seats, "If Frank won't let you keep him, bring him over and I'll adopt him."

That made me feel much more at ease, and I thanked Jack. I was mortified when the dog showed his gratitude by getting carsick on Jack's right shoulder on the way home, but Jack graciously took it in stride.

"What are you going to name him?" Jack asked when we finally pulled up in front of the house.

"Frank gets to name him. His family has a knack for naming pets."

If Jack thought that was an odd compliment to give to the Harrimans, he didn't say so. I gave the pooch a good-bye scratch on the ears and let Jack take him home. Knowing Frank's schedule, I figured the ever-observant detective could be kept from discovering the new dog in Jack's backyard for a day or two at the most. And not wanting to abuse Jack's generous offer to temporarily stable the mutt, I wasn't willing to leave the dog at his house much longer than that. So we arranged that Jack would keep an eye on the dog until late the next night, when Frank and I got home from the party. Jack's a night owl, so he was likely to be awake no matter when we got home.

I made a quick trip to the local market and bought dog food, bowls for food and water, and a rawhide chewbone. Jack had changed shirts and was playing with the dog by the time I brought all of this by his place.

"By the way, Jack, did Frank ask you if you had seen anyone around our place late last night?"

"Yes, he did. But no, I'm sorry, Irene. You sister called me and we went out to grab something to eat at Bernie's last night. I guess it was right around the time the jerk broke into your house. I feel bad about it."

"Forget it. It's not as if you're supposed to be our guard service."

With effort, I held back any comment on the dinner with Barbara. The only time I ever wished Barbara would marry Kenny again was when I wanted Jack to be safe from her. She had met Jack on one of her visits to our house, and I knew she was attracted to him. Jack didn't seem to be able to figure out that she had the red hots for him, and never seemed to treat her as anything more than a friend. Still, these late-night dinners . . .

"Well, I'm glad you're getting a dog," he was saying. "I know it doesn't make you perfectly safe, but it can't hurt. And I think this fellow will be good company."

I thanked Jack again for dog-sitting and went home. Cody sniffed curiously at my clothes, but was easily distracted when I fed him.

FRANK CAME HOME ABOUT AN HOUR LATER, AND WE HAD A QUIET DINNER together. We share silences fairly easily, but I noticed that this one had an edge to it. He wasn't eating much, but he was looking at his plate more than he was looking at me. I wondered if he had reconsidered our truce.

"Did you learn anything more about Thanatos?" I asked.

He shrugged, then said, "Is this for publication?"

"Does it really matter?"

He sat back and pushed his plate away. "Yeah, I guess it does. Carlson is hot under the collar. John Walters really ticked him off today, so if I tell you something and it ends up in the paper, I'm in trouble. He threatened to take me off the case at least once an hour this afternoon."

"He's mad at John and he's taking it out on you?"

"Right now, anything or anyone that reminds him of the *Express* can send him into a fit. Needless to say, I remind him of the *Express*. And it's not just John. It's Wrigley as well—the lieutenant is convinced that a wiretap would lead us to Thanatos."

"I wasn't involved in that discussion, but I understand why the paper said no."

"Other papers have said yes under similar circumstances."

"Not without a lot of soul-searching. In the only case I know of, the reporter's life was being threatened."

"Oh, I see. And in this case, it's just a few unfortunate members of the public that are in danger. The paper would protect you, but not E.J. Blaylock or Rosie Thayer—or whoever is next."

"That's not the problem and you know it. I get calls from sources on that phone, people who would clam up on me for good if they ever thought the police could trace or record their calls. And I don't like the idea of the cops listening in on my calls all day long."

"You could set up an outgoing, separate phone line—a secure line without a tap—and tell your callers you'll call them right back."

"Because the call they've just made is being recorded and traced? I'm sure they'd be in a real hurry to thank me for that. I don't find myself on Wrigley's side very often, but this time I agree with him. A police wiretap would have a chilling effect on our sources, and in turn, on our ability to report the news."

He sighed, looked like he would say more, then stood up and started clearing the table.

"Frank—talk to me."

He hesitated, then sat down again. After a moment, he said, "I had to listen to arguments about this all damned afternoon, and I guess I'm just tired of hearing about it. The funny thing is, I'm arguing with you, and taking a position directly opposite the one I took with Carlson."

"What do you mean?"

"I wasn't as hot as he was on the idea of a tap—although for different reasons than yours. From what you've told me, Thanatos doesn't stay on the line long enough to trap it. And from what we've seen of the guy's methods, I can't believe he'd be careless enough to call from his home or office. He's a man who makes plans. He's probably calling from pay phones or using an electronic device to hide the origin of the call. Even if he's not, I knew what the paper would say when Carlson started talking about a tap, and hassling the *Express* won't help us with this case. I figured the request for that kind of surveillance would only create a greater strain in the department's relations with the paper."

"You were right. I heard a rumor that the lieutenant is going for a warrant."

"He's already tried it. Judge wouldn't give it to him. That didn't improve his humor any."

"I'm sorry you're having to take flak off him on my account. Is there anything you can do to avoid his temper?"

"Just ride this out. And try not to give him grounds for any complaints. I know I can trust you not to report our private conversations, but Carlson doesn't know you as well as I do. So he's going to assume that anything that's in the paper came straight from me to you. I'll talk to you, but you've got to keep it out of the paper for now."

"That's not going to solve your problem. What if Mark Baker or one of the other reporters hears something from another cop?"

"Look, that could happen whether I say anything to you or not. I just want to have a clear conscience."

Assured that I'd keep quiet for the time being, he told me what he had spent his day on whenever Carlson wasn't bitching at him. Frank and Pete had talked to neighbors, to the realtors who were selling the house, and made phone calls to the people who owned the house. There was no sign of forcible entry at the house. They were tracking down anyone who might have had a key. They were talking to anyone who might have had any excuse to go near the house.

Just as Molly had said, the real estate listing on the house had expired three weeks ago, and the owners were considering finding a new agent. The realty company that had listed the property was trying to talk them out of switching. Frustrated, the owners had decided to leave the house off the market until after Christmas; they were planning to fly out in January to talk to other realtors. All of the people who had been contacted by the police claimed they hadn't been in the house during the last three weeks. The Las Piernas Board of Realtor's lockbox was still on the house, the key to the house still in it.

"Any of these people know Rosie Thayer?"

"No, at least they say they don't. Hernandez is still working on cause of death."

That surprised me. "Is there really any doubt?"

"Yes, there is. Hernandez doesn't think she starved or died from dehydration. She's been dead for a while, but with the ants—well, I won't go into that at the table."

"Thanks." When it comes to the coroner's work, there's still a big gap between what Frank can stomach watching close at hand and what I can stand to hear him refer to in more than a vague sort of way.

As we finished clearing off the table and started to wash the dishes, something he said stayed with me. I frowned down into the sinkful of suds and scrubbed a plate. "How long is 'a while'? More than two days?"

He reached over and stilled my hands, making me realize that I had done a fairly good imitation of Lady Macbeth as a scullery maid. His voice was gentle when he said, "She was dead before you got the letter."

"You're sure?" Not too steady. Sort of squeaked it.

"Definitely." He pulled me into his arms, and even though I was getting lemon dishwashing soapsuds on his white shirt, held me there. "He never really gave anyone a chance to save her—not by sending you the letter, anyway."

"Why is he involving me in this?"

"I don't know. Publicity, for one thing. He does things to frighten you, it comes across in your stories, and other people feel afraid. Maybe it makes him feel more powerful to have the whole city running around in a panic because of him."

I leaned back. "You think I'm helping him? That we shouldn't publish the letters?"

He hesitated, then said, "It's a useless question. It's not up to me."

I knew that meant he thought we shouldn't, but figured he'd had all he needed of arguments about the police and the press for one day. I let it drop.

• • •

I WENT TO WORK THE NEXT MORNING, EVEN THOUGH IT WAS SATURDAY. Like other people at the *Express* who were scheduled to have time off on Monday and Tuesday, which were Christmas Eve and Christmas Day, I was trading my weekend for the holidays. The weekend before Christmas is, however, a nearly impossible time to reach anyone by telephone. I wanted to contact officials at Mercury Aircraft, to try to persuade someone to help me look for a link between Rosie Thayer and E.J. Blaylock's mothers. A couple of phone calls confirmed that I would have to wait until Mercury's offices reopened on Wednesday—if I made any progress that soon. Corporations that do work for the government are not hasty to let reporters snoop around their plants, let alone ferret through confidential—and legally protected—personnel files. Big companies are often sensitive about their public image, but the fact that two murder victims were children of women who once worked for Mercury Aircraft wouldn't give me much to push with. Mercury had long been one of the largest employers in town, and my finding out that a couple of local residents had links to it would not scare anyone into giving me an interview.

In the meantime, my imagination was going wild: I wondered if the two mothers had worked on some secret military project together. But why would Thanatos attack their daughters and not the workers themselves? Why wait until years after the workers had died? And even if Mercury Aircraft turned out to be the link between the victims, how was I linked to them? I was still confounded by the fact that Thanatos had singled me out for his contact with the paper.

I kept hoping Hobson Devoe would call.

I also wondered if Thanatos would call to gloat over all the attention he was getting with the second murder.

I had plenty to keep me busy in the meantime. Fortunately, the political beat had slowed a little as the holidays approached, or I would have been hopelessly behind in my work on City Hall stories. I did some catching up.

After a couple of hours in the office, I noticed that some of my coworkers were avoiding me. Stuart Angert seemed to notice it, too.

"It's not your breath, in case you wondered," he said, sitting on a corner of my desk.

"I wondered. Glad you stopped by. So what is it?"

"It's the letters. Same thing happened with me over Zucchini Man. Only this is much worse."

"Zucchini Man?"

"Let me tell you the story. We had a couple of slow news days one summer, and Wrigley gets a brainstorm. Decides we should have a contest among local amateur gardeners, see who can grow the biggest zucchini. You ever plant zucchini?"

"Frank has the green thumb, Stuart. If he's smart, he won't ask me to do more than look at the garden. If the army had known about me, they could have saved a lot of misery by using me instead of Agent Orange."

"Me, too. I am the bane of the botanical world. Nevertheless, Wrigley decided this contest should be run from my column. I didn't like it, but what the hell, he's the boss."

"Ever stop to think of how much trouble that phrase causes around here?"

"Plenty. And boy, did I get plenty of trouble. Zucchini, I thought, were these skinny little Italian squash I bought in the grocery store. Six, seven inches long, max. 'Mail in your entry,' I foolishly said. We were inundated with them.

"As you probably know—I didn't, but learned very quickly—left to grow on the vine, zucchini can best be described with words like humongous and gargantuan. People couldn't afford to mail them; some of them weighed as much as a watermelon. So they'd bring them into the paper, hand-carrying them to the security desk. Geoff was calling me from the lobby every few minutes, asking me to come down and get these three-foot, twenty-pound vegetables."

"So you became known as Zucchini Man?"

"No, Zucchini Man came on the scene a little later. As you can imagine, I quickly tired of lugging the things around, so I was happy when the contest deadline arrived. I declared a winner as quickly as possible, gave out the check for one hundred dollars in prize money, and prayed I'd never see another squash of any kind. I had become the butt of a lot of newsroom jokes.

"However, this one participant was very unhappy with the outcome. He was certain that he should have won. He kept bringing in zucchinis. They would be accompanied by long, rambling notes that didn't make much sense. He signed them 'Zucchini Man.' Geoff warned me that the guy who dropped them off was wearing a tinfoil hat."

Stuart did not need to explain the tinfoil hat. They are worn by a small segment of our downtown population, and can be seen in many other cities. To the people who wear them, the hats are not a fashion accessory, but a device whereby they attempt to deflect the radio waves that are interfering with their thoughts.

"And people in the newsroom started avoiding you because of that?"

"No, it was when he managed to get past Geoff one day and into the newsroom itself. He knew me from the picture on my column; headed straight for me. This guy has a huge zucchini with him, probably one of the twenty-pounders. He was carrying the zucchini on his shoulder like a baseball bat. Geoff had already called up to warn me, and he had called the police, but it took them a little while to get here.

"Zucchini Man calmly asked me where his million dollars was, his prize for the biggest zucchini. I kept my cool, told him that we were getting the editor's signature on it at that very moment, and if he would just have a seat and wait, it would soon be here. Everything was going fine until Wildman Winters decided to play John Wayne."

Wildman Billy Winters, a former staffer, was a walking Bad Hemingway Contest. He had none of Papa's talent for writing, but that didn't stop him trying to emulate the lifestyle. His successes were generally limited to accolades like "person who made the ugliest scene at the party." I winced thinking of what he would have added to the situation Stuart was describing. "Not the best defender you could have asked for."

"Right," Stuart said. "He tried to grab Zucchini Man from behind, but he didn't make it. Zucchini Man ducked, then came up swinging. Walloped Winters but good with this great green gourd. Knocked him out cold; Winters ended up in the hospital for a few days. The Zucchini Man was going berserk then, whomping one surface after another with this zucchini. He didn't try for anyone else, just objects, but it scared everybody and made a huge mess. Pulp all over the place.

"The cops got there about then. The LPPD was smart, sent a couple of guys who knew Zucchini Man. They greeted him like he was an old friend. When he saw them, he calmly set the remainder of the zucchini down and walked out with them. He paused near the door and asked me to send his check to him in the mail."

"Not to speak ill of the dead, but I'm not so sure that Winters wasn't a bigger menace to society."

"I agree. You ask me, a guy like Winters was scarier than a guy who's proud of his vegetables. But what I was trying to explain to you was that for a few weeks after this event, some of the people in the newsroom avoided me. They sort of blamed me for the guy being here, and for Winters getting hurt. It was as if they thought I might attract other people like this Zucchini Man—standing next to me was like standing next to a bull's-eye."

"I see what you mean. If Thanatos is coming by my house, he might visit the newsroom."

"Right. You've already brought him too close. He calls you here. He sends things to you. Apparently watches you now and then."

"And he's more dangerous than someone with a large squash."

"Don't get too discouraged."

"Thanks, Stuart."

He started to walk away.

"Stuart?"

"Yeah?"

"What happened to Zucchini Man?"

He smiled. "He was lucky. Too many people said Winters went after him first, and Winters didn't have too great a reputation with the cops, so Zucchini Man wasn't charged with anything. We ran his picture in the paper; turned out his family had been looking for him. They got him on some meds that worked for him, and they make sure he stays on them. He's still around—he helps out with a community garden program over on the west side of town."

I DIDN'T GET A CALL FROM HOBSON DEVOE OR FROM THANATOS. When I got home that evening, I took a nice, hot bubble bath. It was relaxing, but my thoughts kept returning to Stuart's story about Zucchini Man and Billy Winters. Stuart didn't need to tell me what had happened to Billy Winters. Everyone on the staff knew about the night when Winters got himself good and lit, drove off in a drunken rage, and died in a head-on collision. The Wildman himself might have thought of it as going out in style, if he hadn't also killed a family of five in the other car.

I'd rather ride home with someone wearing a tinfoil hat.

# 13

As I got ready for Frank's office party, I thought that it might be good to take his mind off his troubles at work, and chose an outfit that would have made a mnemonics expert forget what he was about to say. It was a sleek little blue number that accented the color of my eyes—if anyone bothered to look that high. I was feeling devilish, and set a personal challenge for myself: to get Frank to leave the party an hour after we arrived.

He came home and gave me one of those looks that make you want to shout *Vive la difference*, and I had to convince him that we should go to the party in the first place. He got back at me to some extent by looking pretty spiffy himself, and I started to wonder if maybe we should stay home after all. But by now we were both enjoying the sparks that were flying, and we put on our coats and left.

The party, I soon learned, was at Bredloe's house, which added an obstacle. Bredloe is captain of the Robbery-Homicide Division. Boss to the second power—Frank's boss's boss. I glanced at my watch: 7:30, and the damn party was at the captain's house. This was going to be tough, I thought with a grin. But not too tough.

I had a drink in my hand and all the male attention I could want by 7:32. Frank stuck to me like a Siamese twin, and I started to wonder if I was going to be able to be as effective at such close range. Pete arrived, and I was happy to see that Rachel was back in town and with him that evening. She's a real stunner, a tall Italian beauty. She ran over and gave me a big hug, and pulled me aside. Pete started yammering away at Frank, who watched us walk away with an anxious look. I loved it.

"What a terrific dress!" Rachel said, then added more softly, "Frank's looking at us like we might disappear. I get the idea he'd like to go home and take that dress off you. Why are you looking at your watch? Am I boring you already?"

Noting that it was already 8:14, I told her my plan. We started laughing, and I saw both Pete and Frank look up in dismay. I noticed a couple of women had moved over toward them, trying to start conversations. Our boys were acting distracted but tried to be courteous.

"Well," Rachel said, "I won't have time to talk to you tonight, then. But Lydia tells me you'll join us tomorrow?"

"Yes, looking forward to it. We decided to put off going up to the mountains, and we'll see his family on the day after Christmas."

"*Bene.* We'll see you tomorrow. Now, quit wasting time."

"Don't worry, this hasn't been a waste of time. This works better than standing next to him." A glance at my watch told me it was time to go in for the kill: 8:24. Rachel crooked a finger at Pete, and he made his way over as I made my way back. Frank put a possessive arm around me, but continued to give polite attention to a redhead who was still doing her best to converse with him. I leaned over and spoke softly into his ear. "Frank," I said in my huskiest whisper, "I'm not wearing any underwear."

We thanked Bredloe and were on our way home by 8:27.

PETE CALLED AT 10:30. I COULDN'T MAKE MUCH OF FRANK'S END OF the conversation, but the result was that he got out of bed and put on jeans and a sweater; not the type of clothes he wears when he's going out on a case. "What's up?" I asked.

"I've got to go over to Pete's for a minute. I'll be right back."

"Is something wrong?"

"No, no, he's fine. Rachel's fine. Everyone's fine." He was acting fidgety.

"Well, fine. I'm so glad everyone is fine. Want me to go with you?"

"No, no. I'll be right back," he said, scurrying out the front door.

I decided this was a perfect opportunity. The minute I heard Frank drive away, I called Jack and warned him I was coming over for the dog. I put on jeans and a sweatshirt, then closed the bedroom door on Cody. He doesn't like being locked in rooms, but once he figured out there was a dog in the house, he'd appreciate the sanctuary.

Before Jack would part with the mutt, I had to tell him that the dog would be right next door and that he was free to come over and see it any time. The dog was easygoing about it all, walking along on the leash with the kind of manners that said someone must have taken some time to work with him. I brought him into the living room and brushed his coat. He was calm and well-behaved. He even put up with the indignity of having a ribbon tied around his collar. After all, he was a Christmas present.

I was amused to see his ears perk up when Frank's car pulled up in the driveway. I heard Frank opening the door, and suddenly the dog bolted and went bounding down the hallway. I ran after him, heard Frank swearing, and came outside to see my intended lying flat on his ass in the front yard.

"Quick! They ran toward the beach!" he shouted as he scrambled to his feet. I wasn't sure who "they" were, but I closed the front door and caught up with Frank as he made his way down the steps to the shore. In the moonlight I could see two large dogs cavorting and chasing each other along the beach.

"Where'd that other dog come from?" I panted.

"I don't know, I could swear it came out of the house —" He suddenly stopped running. "Irene?"

I stopped too. "Oh, no. You got a dog for me for Christmas."

"Yes, that's why I went over to Pete's. I was going to wait until tomorrow, but she was tearing up Pete's yard."

"Oh, yeah? Well, guess what I got you for Christmas?"

"Does it have four legs and a mean tackle?"

"He seemed well-mannered until you opened the door. Jack was keeping him until I could come over and get him tonight. Jack helped me pick him out."

"Jack? But Jack knew I was getting a dog for you."

Suddenly I remembered Jack's amusement at my saying that if Frank didn't like the dog, I would just keep the dog for myself.

"I think Jack figures he'll take your dog if you don't want him."

"No way."

We watched them run part way into the cold water and come tearing out again. Great. Two wet, sandy dogs. Remembering that Frank's dog—that is, the one I was giving him—had such good leash behavior, I whistled as loud as I could. Sure enough, the pair came galloping toward us, tails wagging, and getting us as wet and sandy as they were when they reached us. We each grabbed a collar, and I got my first close look at my Christmas present.

She had long black fur, and seemed to be some kind of Labrador retriever mix. She had a white patch on her chest; floppy ears, and big soulful eyes. She was about the same size as Frank's dog. She gave me a friendly nuzzle and reached out a paw for a shake. "Happy to meet you. What did you say your name was?"

"She doesn't have one yet. I'm not familiar with the names of all of Tennessee Williams's characters."

"Well, he doesn't have one yet either, since I'm not willing to call him all those things you said when you first met him."

"Too bad. But I guess the neighbors wouldn't enjoy hearing you shout that from the front porch every time you called for him."

We made it back to the house and carried the dogs into the bathroom. They weren't light, but we didn't want them tracking sandy paw prints all over the house. We cleaned them up in the tub, rinsed it out, then made them sit outside of it while we got into the shower. While I lathered up his back, I thanked Frank for the present.

"Think you'll want to keep her?"

"Yes. What about you?"

"Yeah, having two big dogs and Cody will be a handful, but let's try it, okay?"

They started barking. In the confined space of the bathroom, it sounded like we had them on a boom box in an echo chamber.

We got out, dried off, and put on clean jeans and sweatshirts while pandemonium reigned. Telling them to be quiet was useless. We let them out, and they both went charging for the front door, barking. "Oh no, you don't," Frank said, going after them. "You two are going out to the backyard for a while." But when he reached the front door, he stood stock still for a moment, then yanked open the door for them. They went charging out again, still barking, while Frank grabbed his gun.

"Frank, what the hell are you doing?"

"Stay inside and lock the doors!" he shouted over his shoulder, following the dogs. "Call 911 and tell them to roll a unit!" I heard the dogs quieting down and hurried toward the open door, but stopped cold about three feet away from it.

On the floor, just inside the doorway, was a bright red envelope with a computer label on it.

# 14

*Dear Cassandra,*

*You must tell them that I have no quarrel with Alcyone. It is Ceyx who was to be punished. Poor Alcyone, still unaware. But it is done. Poseidon will bring him to you. Soon my work will be complete. Then we can be together, my beloved.*

*You see that I always know where you are, and who you are with. This does not concern me now. You will set these others aside in favor of me when you realize how powerful I truly am.*

*Your beloved,*
*Thanatos*

Frank had carefully opened the letter, trying not to disturb any fingerprints that might be on the envelope. In addition to the letter, the envelope contained a small, shiny, odd-shaped key. A number was stamped into it.

"Lockbox key," Frank said. "Probably show up on the Board of Realtors 'lost and stolen' list. I guess he wanted to let you know how he got into the house on Sleeping Oak."

A helicopter passed overhead, searching for signs of the person who had hand-delivered this latest message. The dogs must have heard him skulking around the front door before he pushed the envelope though the mail slot. Frank never saw him; he was gone by the time Frank let the dogs out.

Jack came over, having heard the commotion. He sat down in the living room and read the letter without touching it. Frank and I were sitting on the couch, both feeling dejected. The dogs mirrored our mood, lying side by side with their heads on their paws. I distracted myself by lighting a fire in the fireplace, and checking on Cody, who had heard the barking and retreated to a closet shelf. I couldn't seem to get warm. Frank put an arm around me, but still I was shivering.

"I'm sure you've figured out that he's telling you he's already killed his third victim," Jack said.

I nodded. Frank said, "I know Poseidon is the god of the sea. Tell me about Alcyone and Ceyx."

"He's probably basing the letter on Ovid's version of their story," Jack began. "Ceyx was a king. He and his wife, Alcyone, were very devoted to one another. Ceyx planned a long sea voyage to visit an oracle."

"His wife didn't want him to go," I said, remembering the story. "Alcyone had a sense of foreboding about it, and begged him to stay home, or to take her with him. He was reluctant to be separated from her, but didn't want to endanger her. He promised to return as quickly as possible and began his voyage."

"He should have listened to her," Jack said. "The very first night, the ship was caught in a heavy storm. All hands were lost. Ceyx was grateful that his wife would not share his fate, and died saying Alcyone's name over and over.

"But Alcyone, not knowing what had happened, passed her days weaving a new robe for him, and thinking of how happy she would be when they were reunited. She prayed to the gods for his safety, and they took pity on her."

"She prayed to Hera, the goddess of marriage, right?" I asked.

"Yes, but Ovid, being Roman, called her Juno. Juno was moved to intervene. She called on Morpheus to help her."

"The god of dreams?" Frank asked.

"Yes," I replied. "Morpheus could assume any form or shape. He changed himself into the shape of Ceyx—Ceyx as he appeared drowned. Weeping, he stood by Alcyone's bed, and told her—in Ceyx's voice—that he was her husband's ghost, and asked her to mourn for him."

"Alcyone cried out to him in her sleep," Jack said, "and suddenly awakened, feeling certain that Ceyx was dead. She went to the shore at dawn, and as she watched in agony, saw Ceyx's body floating toward her. She ran into the water, and suddenly, instead of sinking, she was flying over the sea. The gods changed Alcyone and Ceyx into birds—kingfishers—and they're always seen flying or riding the waves together."

"The term 'halcyon days' comes from their story," I said. "According to the legend, for seven days in winter, the days when the kingfishers nest, the gods forbid storms to break, and the sea is peaceful."

Frank reread the letter. "Nothing peaceful here."

"He's drowned someone," I said. "A man, this time."

"I'm afraid that's what it looks like," Jack agreed.

Frank got up and made some phone calls. When he was done, I called the *Express*; they contacted John Walters, who had just gone home for the night. One of the nightside reporters called me back and told me John expected me to come in the next morning, and took a story from me over the phone. Another story on the Thayer murder was already planned for the front page. The staffers in Design were unhappy about seeing their day's work on the A section completely rearranged, but John didn't want to delay the story of the third letter.

WE TOOK THE DOGS OUT AND WATCHED THE ACTIVITY ON THE BEACH from the top of the stairway at end of our street. We could see searchlights from boat patrols out on the water; more lights as jeeps and foot patrols searched the beach, pier, and marina. I wondered, with a chill, if Thanatos was watching it all with glee. I moved closer to Frank.

We went home after an hour or so, both of us feeling worn down. I tried to get Cody to come out of the closet and got clawed for my efforts. The dogs gave up scratching at the bedroom door. I tried not to make too much of the fact that Frank checked his gun before we crawled into bed. I don't know what time it was when we finally managed to fall asleep.

The phone rang at dawn. An unidentified man's body had washed ashore.

We dragged ourselves out of bed. Frank tried to talk me into staying home, knowing something about what bodies look like when the ocean has had a little time with them. I reminded him that even though I didn't always like to talk about corpses, I'd seen my share of gruesome sights in my years of reporting. That probably didn't sway him as much as my admission that I didn't want to be left alone in the house.

We walked in silence to the end of the street and took the stairs down to the sand. A police department jeep met us there, and drove us to an area on the beach which had already been cordoned off and shielded from the stares of curious early morning joggers.

The trick in these situations is to not identify the object on the sand as another human being. The trick, I told myself, is to distance yourself, observe, and not think about this waterlogged casing as a person, and certainly not anything at all like yourself. If you start to think about who it might have been or about your own vulnerability to death, you'll probably pass out or get sick or both.

So I used the trick. I noted the fancy yachting shoes and the Rolex and the neatly trimmed hair. Absolutely refused to let my glance settle for more than a brief moment on what was once the face. The thing on the beach wasn't in as awful a condition as "floaters" usually are, leading the county coroner, Dr. Carlos Hernandez, to say the body probably hadn't been in the water more than a few hours.

THAT SUNDAY'S EDITION OF THE PAPER WAS PRINTED BEFORE THE BODY was found, but a story on the third letter and an interpretation of its meaning ran on the front page. The *Express* got phone calls all morning from women who were frantic about their missing husbands, but it wasn't until about nine o'clock that I picked up the one that I knew was Alcyone.

Her voice was shaky, and she started by saying, "My name is Rita Havens. I've been reading your articles, Miss Kelly. I think—" She took a deep breath and started over. "My husband, Alexander Havens, went sailing to Catalina Island yesterday. He's fifty-four years old." That made the hair stand up on the back of my neck. But it was as she whispered her next statement that I became convinced that she should get in touch with the police.

"His mother used to work at Mercury Aircraft. Have they found Ceyx?"

# 15

RITA HAVENS' CALL TO THE *EXPRESS* had resulted in negotiations that came just short of requiring a U.N. Resolution. When I went into John's office and told him about her call, he got in touch with Frank, but didn't give out any names or addresses. Frank handed it over to Lieutenant Carlson, saying he couldn't do otherwise.

Carlson, in turn, went bananas. When he started making threats, John hung up the phone, then called Carlson's boss, Captain Bredloe. Bredloe, fortunately, saw the wisdom of seeking the help rather than the ire of the paper. He promised to get back to John within the hour.

Meanwhile, my own situation at the *Express* wasn't exactly comfortable. Rita Havens insisted I was the only reporter she would talk to, but the *Express* was wary of putting me on a story involving the cops. John only gave in when it looked as if he wouldn't get an interview with her any other way.

Bredloe called back as promised. In the interest of finding the killer as soon as possible, he was encouraging a more cooperative spirit. He told us he had "worked with Lieutenant Carlson" on "better defining a team for this set of cases." Frank and Pete were to act as liaisons with the paper, and he asked that we forward any leads we received to them. Mark Baker was free to talk to any of the detectives assigned to the case, but Bredloe made it clear that the detectives would continue to use discretion regarding what information they released to the paper. No detective would release information which might jeopardize the apprehension or prosecution the murderer. I could tell that John wasn't happy about the possibility of Frank working with me, but he could hardly complain, since Bredloe was basically giving him what he wanted, and getting Carlson off his back at the same time.

I CALLED RITA HAVENS TO TALK ABOUT FRANK AND PETE JOINING ME when I came to see her.

There was a long silence, then she said, "So you are quite sure it's Alex."

"I'm no more certain than you are, Mrs. Havens. But if it is, then the police will need to be informed."

"I suppose I'm only delaying the inevitable." There was a little catch in her voice, but after a moment she said, "Bring them, of course."

• • •

## DEAR IRENE,

We pulled up in the sweeping drive of the Havens' mansion, a great monument of a place. The door was answered by an honest-to-God butler, and I caught myself developing a bad attitude as we stood in the entryway. I find I have to fight a prejudice I have about the wealthy when I encounter them. However, while I've certainly met my share of the obnoxious well-to-do, I'd be lying if I said that I haven't found the same types among the other economic strata.

But if Rita Havens was a *nouveau riche* snob, then she fooled me. In any other setting, I think she still would have been as genuine and as warm. She was a petite salt-and-pepper brunette with dark brown eyes. There was something about her manner that made me feel instantly comfortable with her. Although it was easy to see that she had been crying, she greeted us as if we were there to visit as friends, rather than to discuss the possibility of her husband's death. She invited us to join her for a cup of coffee in a cozy sitting room, and asked us to call her by her first name.

We chatted about the weather, about the newspaper, about a new building that was going up where the Buffum's department store used to be. Frank didn't rush her, and neither did I. She took a sip of coffee, looked outside for a moment, and then, as if realizing that small talk would not change what had happened, started talking about her husband.

Alexander Havens was a prosperous manufacturer of special fasteners used on airplanes—airplanes made by none other than Mercury Aircraft. Alex, as she called him, had gone to work at Mercury while his mother was still working there. He had seen an opportunity in Mercury's need for reliable fasteners, left on good terms, and started his own business. It had been a highly successful venture for all concerned. He had branched out into supplying other aerospace companies with a variety of parts, but Mercury had always been his mainstay.

I asked her about his business, his hobbies, his interests. As she worked her way toward the question at hand, her devotion to him was apparent.

"Alex loves to sail. He's very good at it. I get seasick just looking at the boat, so usually he finds someone else to go with him. This close to Christmas, and with the weather so chilly, he couldn't find anyone who wanted to brave the choppy seas between here and the island. I tried to get him to forget about it . . ." She couldn't finish. She didn't start crying again, just bit her lower lip and looked away from us.

"Forgive me," she murmured.

I'm not sure she meant it for us.

"So he went sailing alone?" Frank asked.

She nodded.

Pete, usually an animated chatterbox, was quiet and still. I remembered that he once told me that contacting victims' families was always hard on him, no matter how often he had done it. I wondered if he usually left this part of the job to Frank.

Frank continued asking questions, his tone gentle. "Your husband left yesterday—the twenty-second?"

"Yes."

"From the Las Piernas Marina?"

"Yes."

"Could you describe the boat?"

"It's a small sailboat, at least, Alex says it's small. A thirty-foot Catalina—I think that's right. It's white—I guess most of them are."

"And the name of the boat?"

She waited a moment before whispering, "*Lovely Rita.*"

Frank gave her some time to recover, then asked a few more questions. She thought there were at least six or seven other people who knew he was sailing; she named them. He had left early yesterday morning.

She looked over to me. "He was going to sail back today. He was supposed to call before he left. I became worried, and then I read your article. I had this—well, call it a feeling, a very strong feeling—that Alex was Ceyx.

"Alex and I had talked about this serial killer whenever there was a story in the newspaper. One of your stories mentioned that Dr. Blaylock and Miss Thayer were daughters of women who worked at Mercury Aircraft. Alex was upset when he read that. He thought he might have known the two women who were killed—when they were children. Thought they might have gone to school together. But he said he couldn't be sure, because it had been so long ago."

"Any recent contact with them?"

"Oh no. As I said, he wasn't even sure he had known them in school. But since they were all the same age and their mothers all worked for Mercury, maybe he did know them."

"Did he mention any ideas or theories he may have had about the murders?"

"No, I can't say that he did. At least, none that he discussed with me. Just that the killer sounded like a very sick individual."

Frank asked her a series of questions that brought her around to describing what Alex Havens was wearing when he left the house to go sailing, as well any other articles of clothing he might have taken with him. She watched Frank's face as she described them. If he gave something away, she was the only one who saw it.

"You need for me to come with you, don't you?" she said suddenly. "You've found him, haven't you?"

"We may have. Is there someone you would like to call to be with you?"

"No, no, I—we have friends, but—no, I'd rather not call anyone else."

"Why don't you ride with us?" Pete said, speaking for the first time since they were introduced. "I'll make sure someone takes you home again."

She nodded, unable to stop the tears as she rose from her chair. I stood beside her and she reached for my arm, suddenly seeming very unsteady on her feet. I put my hand over hers, and Frank asked the butler to please get her purse and coat. Frank helped her put the coat on, and we slowly walked out with her between us. I sat in the back-seat with her as we drove down to the morgue.

I hadn't intended to go in with them, figuring this to be a private moment, but she never let go of my hand. I didn't have time to do any mental bracing. This time, the view of Alex Havens' body was more disturbing. This time, I knew who he was. This time, someone who cared about him was holding my hand as if it was the only thing keeping her from collapsing.

No tricks would work against that.

LATER, BACK AT THE PAPER, I ENCOUNTERED A RARE MOMENT OF writer's block. I found myself staring at the flashing cursor on the computer terminal, willing it to help me get going. Every opening line sounded corny or trite when considered next to what I had actually seen and heard. I had given up on the screen and was staring blankly at my fingers—lifting them up one at a time from the *a-s-d-f-j-k-l* and ; keys—when the phone rang, startling me into pressing them all down at once. The terminal beeped in annoyance as I answered the phone. It was Steven Kincaid.

"Irene? I thought you might be working today. I saw the article. Are you all right?"

"I am, but it's been a hard day. They found Ceyx. A man named Alexander Havens."

"Oh God."

"E.J. ever mention him to you?"

"No, I'm sorry. I'll look back through her papers for his name, though. I just can't believe Thanatos is getting away with this. Every time, it's . . ." His voice trailed off.

"Steven?"

"Every time this happens—I keep wondering what it was like for her. I worry that she suffered, like Rosie Thayer."

"If it's any comfort at all, the coroner has said that E.J. and Alex Havens died quickly. He's fairly certain the first blow killed E.J., and he suspects Havens was strangled before he was put in the water."

Silence, then a quiet, "Thanks."

"Frank and I will come by for you at about a quarter to six tomorrow, okay?"

"I'm not sure I'm up for this."

"It doesn't matter. I insist. No more sitting around by yourself. Can you hang in there until Christmas Eve?"

"Sure. I'll see you tomorrow."

The receiver wasn't back in the cradle more than five seconds when the phone rang again.

"Kelly."

"Irene Kelly? Oh, drat! Now I owe Austin five dollars. I told him you wouldn't be in on a Sunday. Shouldn't gamble on the Lord's day, I suppose."

"Mr. Devoe?" I ventured.

"Yes, Hobson Devoe. Mr. Woods tracked me down and urged me to call you."

"Thanks for getting in touch. I'd like to ask you some questions about Mercury Aircraft—you work there?"

"Oh, well, in a manner of speaking. I'm officially retired, but they pay me a little something to act as the museum curator. I started working for Mercury back in 1938. I was in charge of what is now called Human Resources—personnel. But Mercury has a public relations department that I'm sure would—"

"—I'd rather talk to you first, Mr. Devoe."

"Just exactly what is this about, Miss Kelly?"

"You knew Dr. Blaylock?"

"Oh my, yes, poor Edna," he said, and was quiet for a moment. "I spoke with her a few times about her research, but I didn't know her very well. I knew her mother—a longtime employee of Mercury. You are the reporter who received the letter from the killer, are you not?"

"Yes. Three letters, now."

"Three! This has happened more than once? Oh, my!"

"I take it you don't read the *Express* . . ."

"But I do! I read it religiously. Oh! I've failed to tell you, haven't I? I'm not calling from Las Piernas. I'm visiting my daughter in Florida. Austin has been leaving messages on her answering machine, but we were in Orlando, taking my granddaughter to Disney World. Just got in today."

"I'm sorry, Mr. Devoe, I didn't realize this was a toll call for you. Let me call you back."

"No, no. Austin is the one who'll need help with his telephone bill. He left . . . I'll just say *numerous* and lengthy messages exhorting me to call you. Tell me about these other letters."

Briefly, I described the letters and the murders which followed them.

"Oh. I understand the urgency. Oh, my goodness, yes."

"You said you knew Edna Blaylock's mother. Did you know Bertha Thayer, or . . ." I flipped through the notes I had taken at Rita Havens' house. ". . . or Gertrude Havens?"

"Gertrude, yes, of course. And Bertha as well. Amazing, really, that I should. I've met tens of thousands of workers over my years at Mercury. But Gertrude and Bertha were some of the very first women to work in manufacturing. War workers, as you've noticed. I was responsible for programs for them at both of our Southern California plants."

"What sort of programs?"

"Oh, I tried to help those first women workers feel welcomed and at ease. And to help workers cope with the transition, both for the women and the men. It was considered quite the new frontier in those days. Viewed as something of an experiment at first."

"Experiment?"

"Goodness, yes. Something temporary. Most of the women lost their jobs not long after the war. There was even some gearing down after V-E Day. It was simply expected that the women would all be laid off—well, the corporation expected it, but I can tell you that not all of the women expected it. Not that they begrudged veterans a job; no, they had simply become dependent on the income. And I, in turn, hated to lose some of those women workers. I managed to persuade . . . oh my. Oh my."

"Mr. Devoe? Is something wrong?"

"Wrong? No, no. Oh, my goodness. Why, Miss Kelly! I just realized that the workers you named had something very unusual in common."

# 16

MY PEN FROZE ABOVE THE NOTES I had been writing. "What did they have in common?"

"Those three workers weren't laid off at the end of the war."

"Was that really so rare?"

"Oh yes. Oh yes indeed."

"Do you remember why were they allowed to keep their jobs?"

"Of course I do. There was only one hardship plea that J.D. would listen to."

"J.D.?"

"J.D. Anderson, founder and president of Mercury Aircraft. Deceased now, of course. But back then, I begged J.D. to let the war widows stay. That wasn't good enough for him. War widows with good work records, I asked. Still not enough. But then I practically got down on bended knee and begged him to allow war widows with young children to support to stay on. He finally agreed to that, provided they had good work records."

"Wait a minute. You're saying that all three of these women were widows?"

"Not only widows, war widows. And war widows who had not remarried by the end of the war. I lost my own father in World War I, when I was eleven. So I knew something of what these children would know, growing up without a father. My goodness, yes, I think that's why I fought for them. I had watched my own mother struggle to find work that would pay a decent wage. She eventually went into business for herself, and managed quite well, but at first it was simply horrible."

"How many of these women were kept on, would you say?"

"Oh, at a guess, well, perhaps no more than a hundred."

One hundred. Manageable research, even if it turned out to be a dead end. "Would Mercury still have records on these women? The ones who were allowed to stay?"

There was a long silence. "Yes," he said at last.

No "oh my" or "goodness." Shaky ground.

"Mr. Devoe, before you answer my next question, please think about what happened to the children of three women you helped—and what might happen to the children of other women war workers if we don't learn more about why Thanatos is targeting them." I drew a deep breath. "If I never published or revealed how I learned . . ."

"I understand," he interrupted in a firm voice. Another long silence. "The personnel offices will be empty on Wednesday," he said at last. "The employees who work there won't be back until the day after New Year's. Perhaps Wednesday would be a good day for you to come to see my museum. I'll call you again after I've arranged a flight back to Las Piernas."

"I can't tell you how much—"

"No need to. Merry Christmas, Miss Kelly."

"Merry Christmas, Mr. Devoe. And thank you."

I CLEARED THE COMPUTER SCREEN OF THE JUMBLED LETTERS. HOBSON Devoe had given me a thread of hope. I found I was able to start writing the story of Rita and Alexander Havens.

As I finished and signed off for the day, I looked at the blank screen, seeing my reflection in its darkened glass. Images of Rita Havens staring at her dead husband came unbidden. I stood up and left quickly.

CHRISTMAS EVE DINNER WAS EVEN BETTER THAN I HAD IMAGINED IT would be, which is saying a lot. We ate, laughed and chatted happily over cioppino and linguini con vongole and a variety of other meatless pasta dishes.

Apparently, most women suffer a standard reaction of near catatonia when they first look at Steven, because even Mrs. Pastorini—Lydia's mom—spent some time . . . well, *appreciating* him. But once that wore off and Rachel and Mrs. Pastorini found their speech restored, Steven fit right in with the gathering.

At midnight, the non-Catholics humored the rest of us and we all went down to St. Patrick's for Mass. Even though I'm basically a lapsed Catholic, I seldom miss this tradition.

Afterwards, we thanked the chefs, and with a last "Merry Christmas!" headed for home.

"Did you have an okay time?" I asked Steven as we dropped him off.

"I had a great time. You have terrific friends."

I acknowledged it was true. As much as I look forward to those rare times when Frank and I can spend a day alone, this time, I was glad we hadn't run off to cocoon with one another in the mountains. Our close friends, in many ways, comprised a family.

The dogs had completely torn up the backyard by the time we got back home. Cody had shredded part of the couch. None of it mattered. Our problems were small ones and we knew it. We climbed into bed and held each other. I was grateful just to be able to hear his heart beat. It was Christmas.

AS IT TURNED OUT, FRANK AND I BOTH HAD TO WORK ON CHRISTMAS Day. John called and said that since my story on the Havens was causing the phones to ring off the hooks, I should get my ass down there, and Merry Christmas. The *Express* was inundated with calls from children of Mercury Aircraft wartime workers; from people who were sure they knew who Thanatos was; from readers who had been angry to find murder on the front page on Christmas Day; from readers who thought we were aiding and abetting a murderer by running the letters at all.

I left the Thanatos identifications and the editorial complaints to the handful of other people who were working that day; I concentrated on the children of war workers.

I took names and numbers and whatever useful information I could, including the caller's age, marital status, and parents' names. I asked if the caller's parents were still living—and if not, when they died. I asked about any current connection the caller might have to Mercury Aircraft or to the three victims. Finally, I sought opinions about Thanatos' identity. I had to assure each and every one of them that there weren't any new letters from Thanatos. I made a list of the callers; there were over sixty by late that afternoon.

Fewer calls were coming in by then, so I found time to make a second list, eliminating those who weren't fifty-four years old, praying to God that wasn't just a coincidence. From the third list, the smallest, I excluded the ones whose fathers had survived the war. The third list had twelve names on it.

I remembered Hobson Devoe's guess that about one hundred women had stayed on after the war; I worried that I had somehow eliminated too many of the callers.

John and I had one of our conferences to review what I had learned and decide what could be discussed with the police. He gave me his consent to tell Frank about my discussion with Hobson Devoe. I noticed that John was backing off from his previous hard-line attitude about my working on the story. I suppose he had come to trust Frank a little more as well. "For a cop, he's done all right by us," he confided. Merry Christmas again.

I called Frank. For the past two days, he had been trying to talk to people who saw Alex Havens set sail. The police had located only two or three people who had noticed Havens, and they didn't see anything unusual. The *Lovely Rita* had been found smashed to pieces on a rocky jetty several miles south of Las Piernas. The police were working with the Coast Guard to figure out if it could have drifted there by itself, or if it was deliberately wrecked there, just as Havens' body must have been deliberately left where it would most likely come ashore at high tide.

Friends and coworkers of Alex Havens spoke repeatedly of the couple's devotion to one another. As it turned out, over a dozen people knew of his plans to go sailing, and he had mentioned the trip to Catalina in places where he could have been easily overheard.

The police had also received numerous calls from children of Mercury Aircraft workers, with about the same percentage of promising names. Frank had already used much of the same criteria to narrow his list of callers. I told him about Hobson Devoe's call.

"Hmm. That does add another factor. I guess I'll have someone call the people on my last list and ask them if their mothers were war widows," he said. "Then we can combine our final lists before we talk to Devoe."

"*We?*"

"Do you mind if I tag along?"

I thought about it. "If Hobson Devoe doesn't mind, it's fine with me. But if he has any qualms—"

"Just run it by him and see what he says."

We talked about our schedules for the evening. It looked like we'd each get off work in time for round two of the Christmas festivities. Frank would be home first, so he agreed to take care of the animals. "One other thing, Frank. It doesn't look like I'll be able to take tomorrow off. Will you still be going out to see your mom in Bakersfield?"

"I've already called her," he said. "I'm not going to be able to leave, either. Don't worry about it. She was married to a cop for a lot of years—she knows all about cancelled plans."

"She's probably disappointed all the same."

"Probably. But I told her we'd get out there to see her as soon as we can."

MOST OF THE DAYSIDERS WERE GONE FROM THE NEWSROOM WHEN I signed off the computer. I was clearing off my desk when the phone rang.

"Kelly."

Nothing.

I hung up. I was putting on my coat when the phone rang again. I hesitated, then picked it up again.

"Kelly."

"Questioning the scared little rabbits about their fathers, Cassandra? My, you've been a very clever girl. Too clever, perhaps. But oddly, it pleases me."

"Whoopity-damn-do."

"Don't make the mistake of ridiculing me!" Even synthesized, the growling voice betrayed his anger. But his next words were spoken calmly, quietly, and distinctly. "Keep in mind that I always know where you are, what you're doing, and with whom you're doing it. Remember that, Cassandra. As I've remembered you with a little gift. Merry Christmas."

He hung up.

When I told John and Frank about the call, I had to listen to warning after warning from both of them about not tempting Thanatos to turn his anger toward me.

I WAS CAUTIOUS WHEN I WALKED OUT TO MY CAR THAT EVENING; I asked Danny Coburn to escort me. I dreaded any thought of what Thanatos might consider a "gift."

But when we got to the car, everything seemed to be just as I had left it. No parking lights on or strange men watching me from nearby shadows. Danny, who was just ending a long shift in the press room, waited patiently in the chilly night air while I walked around the outside of the car, looked underneath the hood and below the car. Nothing. I opened the door and glanced around the interior. No jar of ants on the front seat. I climbed in and started the motor. No windshield wipers flapping or horns blaring or any of the other problems I half expected. I wished Danny a Merry Christmas and drove off.

I looked in the rearview mirror. No one following me. Maybe he had given up on the car, having grown bold enough to enter our house, to leave letters on our doorstep. What might be awaiting me at home? I shivered. I turned on the heater to take the chill out of the car. It warmed up quickly, but I was still shivering.

A present for Cassandra. Having done some reading on the subject, I decided I didn't enjoy being called Cassandra. Her family thought she was nuts, men mistreated her, and she met a bad end.

I had just stopped at a red light when something cold and sinewy moved across my right ankle.

# 17

I DON'T REMEMBER OPENING THE car door or jumping out of the car. I might have yelled or screamed—I think I must have. But I only remember finding myself standing next to the car, shaking. Another driver got out of his car. For a moment, I wanted to run from him.

"Lady, are you all right?"

He took a step closer, and I stumbled toward the front of the Karmann Ghia. I must have looked about as calm as a horse being led from a burning barn. But as my initial panic subsided, I realized that he was a teenager. I pictured Thanatos being much older. The boy had long, straight brown hair and big brown eyes.

"What's wrong?" he asked, staying where he was.

I found my voice and said, "Snake. In the car. There's a snake in my car."

"Really?" He walked toward me, slowly this time, holding his hands out at each side, as if to show me he meant no harm. I glanced around and realized traffic was backing up. It had all but come to a complete standstill as other people started getting out of their cars and walking toward us. I calmed down a little.

The boy came closer. "I'm Enrique."

"I'm Irene."

"You're not scared of me, are you?"

I took a deep breath. "No, I'm not. I'm not even afraid of snakes. I just wasn't expecting to find one in my car."

"Little cold out for snakes," he said as he came closer. He looked inside the car, then said, "Damn, whatcha know? There *is* a snake in there!" He started to reach into the car.

"Don't!" I warned. "It could be poisonous."

"Him? Naw," he said, not taking his eyes off the reptile. "He's a little ol' gopher snake."

Before I could stop him, Enrique had moved like lightning to grab the snake behind the head. He pulled it from the car and held it out, away from his body. The "little ol' gopher snake" was over two feet long and mad, if all that hissing meant what I thought it did.

"Can I keep him?" Enrique asked.

"I wish I could give you a simple 'yes,' " I said, watching a traffic cop on a motorcycle make his way toward us. "But the snake is probably going to jail for a while."

"Lousy thing to do on Christmas," he said. "Even to a snake."

WE WERE A LITTLE LATE PICKING STEVEN UP FOR DINNER, GIVEN ALL the hullabaloo which followed my close encounter of the serpentine kind. Frank asked me if I wanted to just stay home, but by then I had gone from scared to angry, and I was determined not to let Thanatos spoil my Christmas the way he had spoiled the snake's.

At first, the snake was the talk of the dinner gathering. Steven theorized that the warmth from the car heater might have made the reptile restless.

Jack recalled the story of Cassandra—that she and her brother were left in a temple one night, and when her parents looked in on them the next morning, the children were entwined with snakes, which flicked their tongues into the children's ears. "That's what enabled Cassandra and her brother to tell the future."

"A lot of good it did Cassandra," I said.

"Disgusting!" Mrs. Pastorini made a face, and then waved a hand as if to ward off a bad odor. "Snakes licking children's ears! It's not good to talk of such things on Christmas."

"You're right," Guy said. "No more talk of sadness and danger and worry." Guy nodded slightly toward Steven, who was looking a little pale. Steven didn't notice the subtle gesture, but the rest of us caught the hint. Throughout the rest of the evening, a concerted effort was made to distract Steven from his grief.

You wouldn't think that we could stuff ourselves two nights in a row, but we did. It was after ten o'clock when we finally got home. Frank lit a fire and asked me to stay up with him for a while. We sat on the floor, on the big rug in front of the fireplace. I reached behind the couch and pulled out the package with his sweatpants in them; he opened it and thanked me. He moved over closer to me. He put his arms around me, gently pulling me between his thighs, my back against his chest, then handed me a neatly wrapped, small box. I started crying.

"What's wrong? Aren't you going to open it?"

"I give you sweatpants, and you give me this?"

"It's not as big a package, I admit, but . . ."

"Very funny. You know what I mean."

"Open it. I don't believe in gift-giving as a competitive sport."

I didn't say or do anything.

"Open it." He said this gently, kissing my neck. Frank has learned that kissing my neck gives him a big advantage in the persuasion department.

I tried to open the package with shaking fingers, fumbling with the wrapping until I gave up and ripped the damned paper to pieces.

Frank laughed and said, "Well, I guess that won't get pressed into the family Bible."

I opened the small velvet case. Two sapphires and a diamond twinkled back at me. I shut the case and started crying again.

He put his hands around mine and opened it again, took the ring out of the box, and put it on my left ring finger.

"Have I asked you lately if you'd marry me?"

"We'll check our files. What was the name again?"

I got a bite on the earlobe for that one.

"Yes, I will marry you. Will you marry me?"

"I thought you'd never ask."

We fell asleep on the rug in front of the fire, moving to the bed after waking up in a cold room with cricks in our backs and necks, but this is a small price to pay for true romance, which is generally harder to come by than square eggs.

# 18

Hobson Devoe called me at work early Wednesday morning. "My conscience troubled me after we spoke, Miss Kelly."

Uh oh, I thought. He's got cold feet. "Troubled you how?"

"I've worked for Mercury for many years. Oh my, I've worked for Mercury for more years than you've been alive, I'd wager. I decided I wasn't willing to go sneaking around behind Quincy's back."

"Quincy?"

"Quincy Anderson. J.D. Anderson's son. He's been the president of the company since J.D. retired. Quincy is my boss."

His habits of speech must have been contagious, because the sound of my hopes sinking was reduced to a simple "Oh."

"So I called Quincy and I explained what I wanted to do. He was a little perturbed with me at first. But eventually I persuaded him that it is in the company's best interest to allow you to investigate this particular group of records. Can you meet me in the museum at nine o'clock?"

"Yes, I can. Mr. Devoe—I have to admit, you had me worried for a moment."

"Oh, I'm sorry!"

"Which entrance should I use to get to the museum?"

"Well, first I should explain one other matter. Quincy did ask that you meet a few of his conditions."

My worry button was back in the "on" position. "What kind of conditions?"

"Just three rather simple ones. First, he wants us to cooperate with the police. Quincy doesn't want to deny the police access to information that might help them catch a serial killer. Will this be a problem?"

"In this case, no. I'll even bring a homicide detective with me today." So far, Quincy Anderson had saved me some trouble. "What are the other two?"

"Second, he doesn't want the names of the workers released to the public, by you or the police."

"I can't speak for the police, of course. As for the paper, we already know some of the women's names, both from our own research and from calls we've received from children of war workers. So I can't promise their names won't be printed. But my purpose in going through Mercury's files is not to present confidential information about individual workers to the public. I'm just trying to find out why Thanatos is chosing certain people to be his victims."

"Oh, my. I should have remembered that you already knew three women's names when I first spoke with you. Well, I'll talk to Quincy about that."

"What's the third condition?"

"Ahem, that you, ah—mention that Mercury was cooperative."

"If Mercury is cooperative, I don't have a problem saying so. Whether that kind of statement stays in the published version of my story is up to my editor."

"Oh, of course. Well, let me talk to Quincy. I'll call you back in a moment, Miss Kelly."

ABOUT AN HOUR LATER, I WAS MEETING FRANK OUTSIDE THE MUSEUM doors. It had only taken Hobson Devoe about fifteen minutes to call me back to say we had the go-ahead from Quincy.

Devoe was a skinny twig of a man who looked like a strong breeze would snap him in half. But his eyes had an intelligence in them strong enough to overcome any frailties of his body.

"This museum means a lot to me," he said, gesturing with a bony hand toward the models of planes and historical photographs along the walls. "It's important to know where you've come from if you ever want to know where you're going." He paused and smiled. "Forgive me. You're not here to see the museum. We have more pressing matters to attend to—and I don't want you to think I'm ungrateful to be included. I am looking forward to helping you. I haven't had anything this challenging to work on in years!"

We followed him out of the museum, trying to walk as slowly as he did.

If I had seen a big piece of cheese in one corner of the offices which housed Mercury Aircraft's Human Resources Department, I wouldn't have been surprised. The place was a maze. Hobson Devoe took a slow but sure path through the cubicles, dividers, and desks, using a key card to open one locked door after another. I suppose it's easier to find your way around a place after you've spent more than half a century there.

We ended up crowding ourselves into a small office with a computer terminal in it. Devoe put on a pair of glasses that magnified his eyes so much I could count his lashes. How the hell had he seen well enough to walk us back here, I wondered? He sat down at the keyboard, then slowly but steadily entered a series of keystrokes. He grinned up at us.

"Oh, ho! Bet you didn't think I'd know how to use one of these contraptions, did you?"

"Mercury has records from the 1940s on the computer system?" Frank asked.

"Oh, yes. Unusual, isn't it? Most places don't even save those records on paper. But every employee record we've ever had is on our system. J.D. Anderson was quite fond of doing statistical studies on personnel."

That statement raised an eyebrow or two, but he looked between us and said, "Oh, oh, all quite legitimate, I assure you."

He slowly hunted and pecked a few more keys. Good grief, I thought, Thanatos is going to kill off half of Las Piernas while this old geezer learns to type. "There," he said with satisfaction. "Now, where would you like to start?"

Frank and I had already discussed this. After some further work on the list of people who called the LPPD, our combined list now had fifteen women war workers' names on it. But there was a much smaller group of war workers who were unmistakably linked to this case. "With the mothers of the three victims," I said. "Could we look at Josephine Blaylock's records?"

Devoe tapped in her name, then moved closer to the screen, its light reflecting off his lenses.

"Born January 11, 1922," he read, as Frank and I took notes. "Hired October 5, 1942. Widowed. There's a star here, which indicates that she lost her husband in the war. One child—we could ask about that in those days . . . oh goodness, don't let me get started on that subject."

"What else does it say about her?" I asked.

"Let's see. She started out at our Los Angeles plant. We had the two large plants then, one here and one in L.A. We had about seven smaller satellite plants as well, in other parts of Southern California."

"When did she come to Las Piernas?" I asked.

He moved a little closer to the screen. "Transferred to the Las Piernas plant on November 6, 1944. Worked in plating."

We outlined Josephine Blaylock's work history, then asked him to look up Bertha Thayer.

"Born June 3, 1924. Hired August 17, 1942." She was a little younger than Josephine, but as he read on we learned she was, as Hobson had remembered, a war widow. Thelma was her only child. "Started in the L.A. plant," he went on, "transferred to the Las Piernas plant on November 6, 1944. Worked in several areas, mainly in de-icer assembly, though."

"Hold it," Frank said, looking up from his notes. "She transferred on the same day as Josephine Blaylock?"

"Why, yes," Hobson said.

"Let's take a look at Gertrude Havens' records," I said.

Devoe was working up some speed now, and it took less time to pull up her file.

"Transferred November 6, 1944. Worked in wiring." His snow white brows drew together. "I don't know what to make of that November 6 business. Sometimes we would transfer groups of workers as projects ended in one plant and new ones began in the other. Let me take a closer look at their records."

He typed a command and, indeed, peered closer at the screen. "Mr. Devoe," I warned, "that's probably not safe." He was close enough to leave smudges on the monitor. That close to the screen, even if radiation wasn't a problem, he'd get static electricity in his nose hairs.

"O-L-Y," he said to me, then leaned back. "O-L-Y . . ."

"Beg pardon?"

"O-L-Y. That's what's listed as the reason for the transfer."

"What does it mean?"

"I have no idea," he said unhappily, clearly outraged that a personnel record could contain something he didn't understand. "On Leave of . . . no, I can't imagine what the Y stands for."

"Could you tell us the names of any other workers who transferred on that same day?" Frank asked.

He scratched his head, and then tapped in another set of commands. It took the computer just a little longer to come up with matching records.

Thirty-eight names. A short list, but longer than our fifteen.

"Oh my," he said, frowning, "I forgot to specify females. There are some men on this list. Here's one from our San Diego plant. I'll redo that search."

"Could you also narrow it to those who came from the L.A. plant and who have 'O-L-Y' as the reason for leaving?"

He began typing in the search specifications, saying each aloud as he entered them. "And Oly," he said as he put in the last, then pressed the command to start the search.

Oly. He said it as a word that time, reminding me of other words in my treasure trove of mythological terms.

"Olympic? Olympiad? Olympus?"

Devoe looked at me as if I had conjured a ghost. "Olympus!" he whispered. "By God, it's Olympus."

He stared silently at the screen for a moment, as Frank and I exchanged glances.

"Mount Olympus, home of the gods. Was that the name of a special project?" I asked.

"Perhaps it was," he said absently, his thoughts obviously drifting for a time. He looked up at me. "Olympus was the name of our child care center."

The computer beeped and he looked back to the screen. "A list of twenty-five names," he said, printing them out.

"Why would the child care center be listed as the reason for a transfer?" Frank asked.

He sighed. "That, I'm afraid, is a very sad tale. I had quite forgotten it until Miss Kelly mentioned its name." He looked between us. "You're both too young, I suppose. Born in the 1950s?"

We nodded.

"Yes, well, many people your age don't realize it, but in the years just before and during the war, there were a great many federally funded child care centers."

"*Federally funded child care?*" I thought about the defeat of such proposals in the 1970s and since. "They built them for war workers?"

"Yes, but we had some even before that, as a part of the WPA. After the U.S. entered the war, of course, the number of them grew by leaps and bounds, especially in places like Las Piernas and Los Angeles, where there were so many war-related industries."

"So this Olympus was one of the federally funded centers?"

"No, it was our own."

"Mercury's?"

"Yes. The government funded centers usually closed early in the evenings. We were working three shifts, twenty-four-hours a day, seven days a week. We needed child care centers to match. We couldn't wait for the federal government to decide it could sponsor such centers, so we sponsored our own."

"In Los Angeles?" Frank asked.

"The Olympus Child Care Center was in Los Angeles. The one in Las Piernas was simply called the Mercury Child Care Center. They were both closed before the end of the war."

"Why?"

He shifted uncomfortably in his chair. "Old J.D. would spin in his grave if he knew I was dredging all of this up again. But I'm an old coot now, and past scaring.

"Life in Southern California was very different in those days. It was different everywhere. But you cannot imagine how much this area has changed. Los Angeles! Oh, my." He closed his eyes, as if picturing L.A. and Las Piernas as they were then. "Aircraft companies and the people who ran them were very powerful. Everyone saw their importance to winning the war. No one wanted to stand in the way." He sighed and opened his eyes. "It was wartime. People your age have never seen anything like it. The World War II homefront was something beyond what your generation can imagine. Everyone had a brother or a husband, a father or a son, in the military. People weren't just patriotic. The war effort was a personal matter. And this plant and the one in Los Angeles were vital to that effort. Whatever we asked for, we got. It's impossible for you to understand . . ." He paused. "Oh, forgive me. I'm rambling. You want to know about Olympus."

He hesitated again, then began speaking in a low, confiding voice, as if he were dishing the dirt on the bride at a wedding reception. "There was a very strange and sad incident at that day care center. A little boy died. I don't remember all of the details, but as I recall, one of the workers at the center was blamed for the boy's death. The center was closed."

"You don't remember anything about the person who was blamed?" Frank asked. "Was it a man? A woman?"

"A woman, I believe. Yes. There was a big trial." His brows drew together again. "I'm sorry, it's so long ago. I was so busy after they closed that center, I didn't follow all of that very closely, I'm afraid."

"What happened to all the children who were being cared for at the Olympus Center?"

"Now, that part I remember. I handled most of that. The company offered to transfer a few of the mothers and their children down here, and to help them get settled in Las Piernas. As I recall, J.D. offered that only to the war widows, not every woman who had a child there. Most of the other women were forced to make other arrangements. But he had a soft spot for the widows. The first women he hired were Pearl Harbor widows. He got great press out of that—but I wouldn't want to disparage his motives."

"So these twenty-five came down here, to Las Piernas?"

"Yes. I was in charge of helping them to find housing down here, which wasn't easy, I can tell you."

"How *did* you manage that?" I asked. "I've always heard that housing was scarce around here then."

"Oh, it was. Very much so. But as I said, Mercury Aircraft had a tremendous amount of power in Southern California in those days, and we got it all worked out. J.D. wasn't above pressuring officials for favors when he needed them. And as I said, he also knew how to milk the publicity value of a good deed, and he made the most of what we were doing for these women."

We started comparing his list to ours. We had six exact matches to the names of mothers on our list, including the mothers of the three victims:

*Josephine Blaylock*
*Bertha Thayer*
*Gertrude Havens*
*Peggy Davis*
*Amanda Edgerton*
*Louisa Parker*

Most of the others didn't match in one of two ways. If a woman was on Devoe's list, and not ours, her child's (or children's) current age would not be fifty-four. If she was on ours, but not Devoe's, a check of the Mercury records revealed that she was not transferred with the Olympus group.

There was one exception. A woman named Maggie Robinson had transferred with the Olympus group. Her only child, Robert Robinson, would be fifty-four, but hadn't called the police or the newspaper.

"Maybe he didn't scare as easily as the others," I said.

"Maybe." Frank was concentrating on writing down social security numbers; although it would take a little time, with that information, he could probably find any of the women who were still alive. "This information is almost fifty years old. Robinson could have moved out of the area. He could have died when he was forty. There are lots of possibilities."

I looked over his shoulder and noticed that even if they didn't match the list, Frank noted the women's social security numbers. "We don't want to be too cocky about this connection through the Olympus Child Care Center," he said. "Things could change. Maybe his next victim will be someone younger or older than fifty-four."

WE THANKED HOBSON DEVOE AND LET HIM GUIDE US OUT OF THE building.

"You'll have to come back and visit the museum sometime," he said as we were leaving.

"I'd like that," I told him. "And someday I'd like to sit down with you and Austin Woods and eavesdrop while you reminisce about Las Piernas."

He laughed. "You'd fall asleep faster than Austin does at that old desk of his."

"One other thing," Frank said, "if you don't mind my asking, is there a story behind your name?"

"Devoe?" The old man smiled mischievously. "Oh, you must mean Hobson. Well, yes. I am my parents' youngest child. They had six girls before me. When my mother went into labor with me, my father told her he wanted a boy this time. She said he could have Hobson's choice."

I LOOKED OVER MY NOTES AS WE WALKED TO THE CAR, READING OFF the names of the seven women who were on both lists.

"You still have some time this morning?" I asked.

Frank looked at his watch. "Not much. I want to get something set up for keeping an eye on anyone he might be after. And I've got an appointment with the Coast Guard about Havens' boat. They thought they might have more information for me today."

I flipped back to the names of people who had called into the paper or the police. "Don Edgerton, Howard Parker and Justin Davis. Those match up with the Mercury records for children's names. Plus this Robert Robinson."

"I'll see what I can do to track him down."

"I'll go to the morgue when I get back to the paper, Frank. I want to see if I can dig up some stories about this incident at the child care center."

"Good. I need to talk to the other three soon, though. I think we're going to need to divide the paper's interests from the department's on this one. What if Pete and I talk to them, and you interview them on your own, provided they're willing to talk to the paper?"

I considered objecting, but some intuition told me that it was more important to find out what had happened at the Olympus Child Care Center. I went along with his suggestion because I had a strong feeling that the key to understanding Thanatos was probably waiting for me back at the paper.

Unfortunately, that wasn't all that was waiting for me.

# 19

*Dear Cassandra,*

*Did you enjoy the Christmas present? Truly, I am sorry that I cannot continue to demonstrate my power, but there is a purpose to which I must remain faithful. You have tempted me, and I have allowed myself to be distracted—but no more! Only when Nemesis is satisfied will I pursue my own heart's desire.*

*Time has softened the heads of my tormentors. There are so few left for me. They drink from the River Lethe, but justice is due all the same.*

*Do you feel it, Cassandra? Yes, I know you do. Our time together draws near, and you are a little afraid.*

*Your feeble attempts to protect yourself amuse me. Cerberus will be no obstacle. One cannot escape one's destiny. I am yours.*

*Icarus will be the next to die.*

*Your beloved,*
*Thanatos*

"Postmarked from the airport," I said absently to John. I was trying to force myself to calm down by studying notes he had scrawled on the dryboard near his desk. I had been standing there for several minutes, but to this day, I can't tell you what any of them said about plans for the next edition of the *Express*. John cleared his throat as he finished reading the letter, and I turned to face him.

"The airport, huh?" he said. "I guess that makes sense for Icarus. Better call your sweetums and tell him to advise the folks on your list not to get on any airplanes."

I ignored the gibe and told him I'd call Frank.

"The River Lethe," he said, frowning. "Something to do with the dead, right?"

"Yes. The river of forgetfulness. The shades drink from it before passing into the kingdom of the dead."

"Hades?"

"Or Tartarus, depending on who's telling the tale. Drinking from Lethe brought a kind of oblivion, made those who drank from it forget all that they were before they died."

"So Thanatos is telling us that even if the victims have forgotten something—or forgotten him?—they are going to be punished all the same."

I nodded. "Nemesis is the goddess who represented divine vengeance."

"That leaves Cerberus," he said. "The three-headed dog who guards the gates of Hades."

"I think Thanatos is telling me that our dogs aren't going to stop him from getting to me."

He was silent. He seemed to be at a loss for words. It's fairly remarkable to find John Walters in that state.

"I'll call Frank," I said, and left his office.

TALKING TO "MY SWEETUMS" CALMED ME DOWN. FRANK APPRECIATED the information, but didn't have time to come by for the letter. He told me the department would send another detective to pick it up. He also said they would post someone at the airport and warn airport officials not to let anyone on our list get on a plane without talking to the LPPD first.

I WENT DOWN TO THE MORGUE, WHICH WRIGLEY HAS BEEN TRYING (in vain) to get us to call the "library," and asked for the reel for November 10, 1944. Since Devoe claimed that J.D. Anderson was a publicity hound, I hoped there would be a story about the transfer. With luck, there might also be some mention of the earlier childcare center story.

It took some searching, but sure enough, there was a small story about Mercury Aircraft transferring twenty-five war widows from the Los Angeles plant. Arrangements included housing and child care. "Each of these women was married to a man who made the greatest of sacrifices for this country. These women deserve our utmost care and concern," J.D. was quoted as saying. No photos, no childrens' names. The article closed by saying that Mercury was trying to help these women because they had faced special difficulties following the closure of the Olympus Child Care Center the previous spring.

The previous spring. At least my search was narrowed down from "the war years."

I went back and asked the guy at the counter for March, April, May, and June of 1944. But no matter how much I grumbled or scowled, the assistant (I couldn't bring myself to call him the librarian, but of course mortician isn't the proper term, either) wouldn't let me take more than seven reels at a time.

I tried to keep my eyes from crossing as I scanned each page, afraid that the item was bound to be buried on a back page. After my fourth trip to the counter, some twenty issues into March, I suddenly came across something that made me shout "Eureka!"—startling the hell out of the assistant.

WOMAN CHARGED WITH MURDER
IN CHILD CARE CENTER TRAGEDY

*Pauline Grant, the child care worker who allegedly struck and killed an eight-year-old boy last week, has been taken into custody and will be charged with second-degree murder, a spokesman for the Los Angeles District Attorney said yesterday.*

*Grant, who was supervising children playing at the Olympus Child Care Center, reportedly became infuriated when young Robert Robinson engaged in fisticuffs with her own child, who also attended the center. Grant is said to have given the Robinson child a blow which knocked him into a wall. The boy struck his head and lost consciousness. He was taken to Mercy Hospital, where he died shortly thereafter.*

*The District Attorney notes that although the only witnesses to the event were other children, their accounts are consistent and are believed to be reliable.*

*Olympus Child Care Center is owned and operated by Mercury Aircraft, and serves its workers. The center remains closed following the incident.*

Now I knew why we hadn't heard from Robert Robinson: he had been dead for about fifty years. I couldn't figure out why Maggie Robinson's name was included among the transfers, though. Maybe she had another child. Or maybe J.D. Anderson felt sorry for her. I decided to ask Hobson Devoe about it; he might recall something more about her if I showed him the article.

The article also said all of the witnesses had been children. I did some quick subtraction. At the time of Robert Robinson's death, Alex Havens, Edna Blaylock, and Rosie Thayer would have been his same age—eight years old. Were they the witnesses?

I briefly considered the possibility that Pauline Grant was Thanatos. But if her child was at the Olympus Center in 1944, by now she would probably be at least seventy years old. No woman—let alone a woman of seventy—had carried me from the couch to the bedroom that night.

I wondered if her child was a boy. "Engaged in fisticuffs." Well, I did my share of fist-fighting in elementary school, but I had a professional attitude about being a tomboy.

I had to look through a hell of a lot of microfilm, but I eventually found other articles. I learned that Pauline Grant had pleaded not guilty, and repeatedly denied that she had intended to kill the Robinson boy. Only Alex Havens and Edna Blaylock had taken the stand, but apparently they made calm and unflustered witnesses.

As for Pauline Grant, she was sentenced to ten years in prison for manslaughter.

I made copies of all the articles that tied in. Much to the relief of Mr. Seven-Reels-at-a-Time, I left the morgue.

I had a terrific headache from looking at bright screens in a dark room by the time I walked back to my desk, but it didn't last long. I had a feeling that ran right down to the marrow of my bones: I was getting closer to discovering Thanatos' identity.

I called Hobson Devoe and asked him about Maggie Robinson.

"I don't really remember her," he said. "As I told you, I didn't meet all of the women. I tend to remember only the ones who stayed with Mercury for a while. Maggie Robinson. Maggie Robinson." He repeated the name a few times, as if chanting it would bring some image of her back to mind. "Her boy was the one who died, you say? A pity I can't recall the details. But I'll take another look at the records."

I thanked him and hung up. The phone wasn't in the cradle two minutes when Frank called.

"Good news," he said. "I think we've finally frustrated Thanatos. Turns out Justin Davis has a small plane and was planning to go flying today. We stopped him and had someone look the plane over. Someone had tampered with it. I haven't got all the details yet, but apparently it was rigged so that he would have crashed soon after becoming airborne."

"Thank God Mr. Davis didn't fly his plane before I read my mail."

"Yeah. Thanatos' luck may be changing. I can't tell you how good it feels to be beating this bastard at his own game." He didn't have to tell me; I could hear it in his voice.

"By the way, I've got good news, too." I told him about Pauline Grant and what I had learned. "Let's compare notes again tonight. For now, I'll have to transfer you to Mark Baker so you can tell him about what happened at the airport—they'll have my head on a platter if I try to cover the story myself."

I transferred the call and then made appointments to talk to Justin Davis, Don Edgerton, and Howard Parker. It was going to take up most of the rest of the day, but I didn't want to delay seeing them. I'd be meeting with each of them later in the afternoon.

I had a sense of drawing closer to my quarry. I remembered my old beagle, Blanche, and how she'd bay when she caught a scent. If I hadn't been certain that my coworkers would peg me as an up-and-coming Zucchini Man, I probably would have bayed right there in the newsroom.

I had a couple of hours before my first interview, so I used the time to write a piece on the possible connection between Thanatos' activities and the Olympus Child Care Center case. I read it through a couple of times and filed it long before deadline.

I looked at my copy of Thanatos' last letter and smiled.

"Your fate is linked to mine, all right, Thanatos. But you won't believe what old Cassandra here envisions for your destiny."

Aah-whoooooooo.

# 20

At John's insistence, Mark Baker came with me for the interviews. I wasn't unhappy about it; I enjoy Mark's company. Mark had a lot of work to do, but figured that talking to these three men fit in with most of it. Mark is tall and broad-shouldered, so to avoid resting his chin on his knees in my Karmann Ghia, he offered to drive.

As we made our way across town to our first stop, Howard Parker's house, I filled Mark in on what I had learned from the microfilm.

"Did I ever tell you that my mother worked in one of those aircraft plants?"

"No, you didn't. For Mercury?"

"No. She worked for Lockheed. She worked there for years, just retired not too long ago. She started out on wing assembly. Being able to work in a factory was a big change for her; she had cleaned houses before that. She always said that if that war work hadn't come along, she'd just be one more black woman working in a rich white gal's kitchen. War plants paid a lot more than maid's work, needless to say. Made a big difference to our family."

"Did your dad work there, too?"

"No, he was in the military during the war years. After that, he went to work for the *California Eagle*. The *Eagle* and the *Sentinel* were L.A.'s African-American newspapers in those days. So now you know why I ended up studying journalism."

AS WE DROVE DOWN HOWARD PARKER'S STREET, MARK NODDED toward a car parked near a jacaranda tree, about two doors down from Parker's house. "Gee, two guys in suits sitting in a Plymouth on a weekday afternoon. Don't suppose they could be the law, do you?"

"You know those guys as well as I do. Reed Collins and Vince Adams. They go drinking with you at Banyon's on Friday nights."

He laughed.

When we pulled up in front of the house, Detective Collins got out of the car and walked up to greet us. "Hello, Irene. This guy have any ID?"

"You'd like to forget who I am, Reed," Mark said. "Like you want to forget that Kings game. So much for honest cops."

"Baker, you wound me." Reed reached into his back pocket and pulled out his wallet, then handed Mark a ten-dollar bill.

"Mr. Baker," I said in mock-horror, "are you going to accept a gambling payoff from an officer of the law right here on a public sidewalk?"

"Absolutely."

"To hell with that," Reed said, walking away. "Ask him why he bet against the Kings."

At my narrowed gaze, Mark shrugged and said, "Edmonton had Grant Fuhr in goal. I can never bring myself to bet against him."

I have to admit that Mark's bet was not too iffy. Fuhr's goaltending often made the opposing team wonder why they bothered to put on their skates.

HOWARD PARKER WAS A TALL, THIN MAN; HE WAS SO SKINNY, YOU HAD to wonder what the hell his belt was resting on. But his big brown eyes and easy smile gave him a pleasant face, and his handshake was firm.

A grandfather's clock chimed three o'clock as he ushered us into his living room. The furnishings were highly polished and old-fashioned. Lots of dark wood and soft fabric. Family photographs—Parker with a smiling, robust-looking woman; high school graduation pictures of two boys who appeared to be twins—covered a mantelpiece over a brick fireplace which had been painted white. But the house was quiet, as if none of these other people were home. There was a combination of neatness and stillness that gave it a museum-like quality, amplifying the ticking of the clock and the sounds of cupboards being opened as Parker busied himself in the kitchen.

He came back out bearing a large silver tray ladened with a plate of store-bought cookies and three delicate china cups filled with coffee. He was nervous, and the cups rattled a little as he handed them to us. "Since my wife passed on, I'm afraid I don't get to play the host very often," he said, finally taking a seat. The overstuffed chair he sat in seemed to be in direct contrast with his own body shape.

A widower's house. Relatively recent and beloved, I thought. Mark was already gently asking the question.

"About eight months ago," Parker said. "Heart trouble." He was a little misty-eyed for a moment.

We expressed our condolences, and took turns getting him to talk a little about himself. He told us that he was a retired math teacher. "I've lived in Las Piernas since the day my mother transferred down here. I graduated from high school here, went to college here, met my wife here—worked here almost all my life. My twin boys were born and raised here. They decided to go away to college, though. I think they were half afraid they'd never leave Las Piernas if they didn't do it to go to school. But they stayed together—they're both at Cal, up in Berkeley."

"Mr. Parker, do you recall an incident at the Olympus Child Care Center, when a child about your age was injured?" I asked.

"Injured! He died. Of course I remember it. I was eight years old. Wait a minute—do you think all of this killing has something to do with that?"

"Can you think of any reason that it might?"

"I don't know. I don't know. It's just that the child care center had something to do with Mercury Aircraft. And when the kid who was hurt died, we all got sent down here."

"Did you see it happen?"

"No, no. I was on the other side of the playground. But some of the other kids were right there—started screaming. That brought the rest of us running. Ambulance came and took him away. Robbie. That was his name. He died later."

"You knew Robbie?"

He made a face. "Yes. I suppose you shouldn't speak ill of the dead, but I don't have any fond memories of Robbie. He was a bully. A little bigger than the rest of us and mean. I was just as skinny then as I am now, and Robbie used to pick on us all the time."

"Us?" Mark asked.

"Oh, any of us that he could intimidate. Jimmy, me, other kids. I don't remember their names. Only Jimmy. What happened to Jimmy scared me so much, I had nightmares about it for years as a kid."

"What happened to Jimmy?" I asked. "I thought Robbie was the one who was killed."

He made a gesture of impatience. "Yes, Robbie was the one who was killed. But at the time, we all just thought he had a nasty crack on his head. He went into a coma and died, but that was later. It was the first time I had ever heard of anyone going into a coma, so I guess that part did scare me. I just saw him lying on the ground, all pale and quiet before the ambulance came, but he was still alive then."

"So who is Jimmy?" Mark asked.

"Jimmy Grant. We were friends. His mother was the one they arrested. That's what scared me. It was just an accident, and all of a sudden, they took Mrs. Grant away and then they took Jimmy. As a kid, I remember being worried that someone would take my mother away, too. I was scared to death of it. I never saw Mrs. Grant or Jimmy after that. Next thing I know, the child care center is closed, and we moved."

I tried to imagine the impact those events would have had on Howard Parker as a young boy—a young boy who had already lost his father. To a child his age, the thought of losing his mother would be terrifying. Perhaps it would be terrifying to any child—I remember being inconsolable after seeing *Bambi*, years before my own mother died.

"Did you know Jimmy's mother, Pauline Grant?" I asked.

He shrugged. "Vaguely. I don't really remember her as much as Jimmy."

"Did you ever hear from Jimmy after you moved here?" Mark asked.

"No, I have no idea what became of him. I don't even know who took him in. His relatives, I suppose."

"Did he have any brothers or sisters?"

"No, none that I remember."

"Is your mother still living?" I asked.

Parker smiled. "Yes, she's still here in Las Piernas. She'll probably be able to tell you more than I can." He gave us her name and number.

We talked with him a while about the three victims, none of whom he remembered clearly. We asked about other ideas he might have on Thanatos' motives, but he had no suggestions. We gave him our cards and thanked him. After waving good-bye to Reed and Vince, we made our way to Justin Davis's house.

"If he's telling the truth," Mark said, "Parker doesn't seem to have been a witness to Pauline Grant hurting Robbie Robinson."

"No. But at least we learned the name of Pauline's son."

"Oh, we learned a lot. But I was just thinking that Howard Parker may not be a target, since he couldn't have been one of the ones that testified."

"Only two of them testified, Edna Blaylock and Alex Havens. But even though Rosie Thayer didn't take the witness stand, she was killed. And he tried to kill the guy we're on our way to see. So who knows what Thanatos is using for his criteria," I said.

"Yeah, you're right. And besides, Thanatos said they drank from Lethe, so maybe Parker just doesn't remember what role he might have played in it himself."

"Let's hope that Justin Davis has a little clearer memory of it all."

# 21

JUSTIN DAVIS LIVED IN MASON Terrace, a gated community on the cliffs above the beach. The development was built in the early 1980s, a subdivision of what had once been a single parcel owned by one of Las Piernas's older families. There were only fifteen houses in the entire development, but they were so huge that they still ended up being somewhat crowded together. The gatehouse had lost its human gatekeeper long ago, replaced by a fancy electronic security system. We entered a code that Davis had given us when we set up the appointment; he had told us it could only be used once. We were buzzed through a double set of gates. The gates were apparently designed to prevent a second car from riding through on another car's tail without clearance.

He had one of the choice lots, a little larger than most, on the staggered row that lined the cliff. The stark, white stucco house was built on lines drawn by an architect who apparently forgot to carry anything more than a T square that day. There was a patrol car out in front of it, which I'm sure must have thrilled the neighbors. The officers on duty seemed to be expecting us, and merely waved to us as we walked up the front steps.

The front door was white and unadorned except for a fancy electronic lock—one that had both a keycard slot and number pad on it. We were searching for the doorbell when Justin Davis himself opened the door.

"Hidden video camera?" I asked.

"Yes, and a pressure-sensitive doormat," he said. "Please come in." He was a tall man, broad-shouldered and narrow-waisted. He had that kind of lean, muscular sleekness that comes only to those who work at it, and that kind of grace in motion that belongs only to those who are born with it. He was dressed in a gray sweater and jeans, but made them look as if they would be acceptable attire at a coronation.

Except for a small scar on his cheek, his face was not remarkable, but neither was he plain or unattractive. He had pale gray eyes and thick, straight black hair, which was cut in a conservative style. He either hadn't acquired any gray hair yet or his hairdresser knew some neat tricks to make a dye job look natural.

He took our coats and hung them on a metal object that I assumed to be an advanced form of hall tree, but it could have been artwork pressed into doing double duty.

High ceilings, skylights, and tall windows gave the house an open and airy feeling. The inside was as white and bare as the outside. A painting here, a vase there, were all that would break up the starkness of white walls, ceilings and carpet. As a result, my eyes were immediately drawn to these few objects. I found myself anticipating the paintings as soon as I saw the edge of a frame, ready to savor any kind of respite from the blankness that governed the rest of the house.

But soon we rounded (not literally, since it seemed nothing was round in that house) a corner and came into a room that made me feel a certain appreciation for the spare decoration that had gone before. A wall of windows facing the Pacific gave Justin Davis an incomparable ocean view. The sun was just finishing its business day, and the rich sunset colors displayed beyond Davis's windows and balcony were stunning. The Pacific and sky combined to make a natural mural.

We declined his offer of a drink. He seated us on a low white couch at one end of the room, near a fireplace. A fire was burning behind a glass screen, somehow as removed from us as the ocean, but warm and fragrant.

Davis poured himself a scotch on the rocks and took a seat across from us, in a chair that matched the couch. His voice, when he spoke, was soft and low. "I can't tell you how grateful I am to you, Miss Kelly. If you hadn't contacted the police about that letter today, I wouldn't be here to welcome you."

"I'm just glad you didn't have a chance to fly that plane before the police found you," I said.

"Perhaps you could give us some details about what happened this afternoon," Mark suggested.

The corner of his mouth quirked up for about a nanosecond. "Wouldn't the police tell you?"

"Yes, but it would be good to hear from you, as well."

"Certainly. I understand that Miss Kelly and—Lieutenant Harriman, is it?"

"Detective Harriman," Mark said easily. "I'll let him know you wanted to give him a promotion, though."

"Thanks. Perhaps I'll contact his superiors. I really would like to see that the man's efforts are appreciated."

"I'm sure Miss Kelly will see that he's rewarded," Mark replied. "He's definitely been more than cooperative with certain members of the press." Mark managed not to laugh as he said this. Barely. He was avoiding eye contact with me at all cost.

"So what did happen at the airport today?" I asked.

"Detective Harriman said the police were already looking for me when you received the letter. He said that you had helped him prepare a list of people who might be ..." His voice trailed off, and he took a swig of scotch, then got to his feet. He walked over to the windows, looking out at the darkened sea. "I wasn't in my office today, so they hadn't located me yet." His voice caught, and he paused again. He looked back to us, embarrassed. "Sorry. I think all of this is just now hitting me."

"Take your time," Mark said.

He came back to the chair and then looked over at me, giving me another quick smile. Two or three nanoseconds this time. He didn't strike me as someone who found it easy to smile, not even for that long. "Where was I?" he asked.

"You were saying that you weren't in your office when the police looked for you," I said. "What kind of work do you do?"

"I own a security systems company. Everything from industrial to home security."

"And your office didn't know how to locate you this morning?" Mark asked.

"I took the day off. My business has reached a point where I don't have to spend every single day in the office. It's a nice switch after years of never being home, always being in the office. In those first years, I was often there all day and night—except for a couple of hours at the gym. I'm a big believer in exercise—and even then I knew that if I wanted to be a good manager, I needed the stress-relief a workout brought me. Later, I'd catch a quick nap on my office sofa and be ready to roll.

"But now I have a team in there that I can trust, and I have time to pursue my real interests—especially flying and skydiving. I own my own plane. A Cessna 182."

He stood up, and again he offered us a drink. When we declined, he refilled his own and took a sip before continuing.

"Today, I didn't even get close to my plane. Airport Security met me at my car and walked me into their office. A Detective Baird was there, and he asked me to wait for a moment. Then Detective Harriman came in, and explained that he had asked my mechanic, Joey Allen, to check my plane while Airport Security looked on. Poor Joey. It's his first day back from a two-week vacation in Hawaii, and he gets hit with investigations and questioning—I probably caused his whole schedule to go to hell."

"It took a long time to find the problem?" Mark asked.

"No. Joey saw it within minutes. Someone had put the wrong fuel in my plane."

"How could he tell?"

"Color. To explain it in simple terms, each type of fuel is color-coded; it's a method of preventing mix-ups in fueling, a mistake which can be deadly. So by looking at the color, Joey knew that the wrong fuel had been mixed in with the one I would usually use. I probably would have been able to start the plane, even take off, but I would have had engine trouble in no time."

"Is Joey the one who would normally fuel the aircraft?"

He shook his head. "I take care of that sort of thing myself. I know my own plane, and I pack my own chute. I use Joey's help mainly for safety's sake—to check my work and to take care of problems that are beyond my skill level."

"When did you last fly the plane?" I asked.

"About a week ago."

Well, I thought, that lets Joey off the hook. "And no one saw anyone near your plane since then?"

"No. But over the course of a week, any number of people could have been near it and not attracted any special attention. The airport is busy and there are a lot of Cessnas out there."

We asked him a few more questions, none of which got us much of anywhere on the matter of the airport, but Mark did get some great quotes for his story. We started asking about the Olympus Child Care Center.

"Oh, yes, I remember it. Probably as much from hearing my mother talk about it as being there, to tell the truth. There were a lot of changes in our lives as a result. We moved to Las Piernas, for one thing. But as for the incident itself, I can't tell you much. I remember a group of kids yelling at Mrs. Grant, remember the ambulance coming for the kid who got hurt—Robbie, I think it was. Not much else."

He said he didn't remember any of Thanatos' victims. "No, I haven't had contact with any of them. It's been a long time. I don't think I would have recognized any of them if I saw them on street. We were all just kids."

"What about Jimmy Grant?" I asked.

He was quiet for a moment, swirling his drink. "What kind of monster wouldn't pity Jimmy Grant? He was sort of an outcast to begin with. Didn't have many friends—he was the one I thought about when my mother used to tell the story. Funny.

"Maybe it was because I didn't understand enough about death to feel sorry for Robbie. I thought, well, he's gone. But Jimmy—I remember people talking about how Jimmy would never see his mother again. She killed kids, they said, so they wouldn't ever let her near Jimmy again. I don't think anyone ever heard what happened to him." He sighed. "As I said, who couldn't understand what that must have been like for an eight-year-old boy?"

"Is your mother still living?" Mark asked.

He was quiet again. When he spoke, his voice was flat. "Is my mother still living. Good question."

"You don't know?" I asked, surprised.

He gave me another one of those faint smiles.

"Sorry, that's a philosophical question at this point. Peggy Davis, the body, is alive. Peggy Davis, the mind, is dead. She suffers from a severe memory-loss disorder. She's in Fielding's Nursing Home—a very good one, but still a nursing home.

"Putting her there was difficult decision to make. I guess in her own way, she made it for me in October. Mother was being taken care of by a private nurse in her own home. This was about the tenth nurse I had hired within the past year. I paid top dollar, but unfortunately, my mother's condition is one that causes her to be violent and verbally abusive at times.

"Her memory loss has become much, much worse this past year as well, so she's harder to care for. Anyway, she wandered out of the house when the nurse got a phone call. Managed to catch a bus. I didn't find her for another five hours—downtown, in Sheffield Park. She had a scrape on her head, never knew how or where she got it. She didn't know me. She didn't even know who *she* was. That was about all I could take."

We talked a little longer, as much to take his mind off his problems with his mother as to gather any information. When we were leaving, he thanked me again, bestowing one last, rare smile on me.

It didn't endure any longer than the other smiles. When I looked from the car to his doorway, where he stood watching us, I thought he looked sad. For a moment, I was certain that sad look meant that he had more to tell us, but dismissed this as the product of an imagination still suffering from lack of visual stimuli.

"WHAT'S ON YOUR MIND, IRENE?" MARK ASKED.

I realized that I had been brooding as we made the long drive from Justin Davis's house toward Don Edgerton's place.

"Not very good company, am I, Mark? Sorry. I was just thinking about Peggy Davis."

• • •

## JAN BURKE

THE ANCIENT GREEKS BELIEVED THAT THE DEAD DRANK FROM THE River Lethe and were transformed from beings with remembered lives into shades, existing in a state of oblivion.

Now, it seems, some of us come to that river long before we die.

# 22

THE TWO DOBERMANS BEHIND the chain-link fence were barking at us as if it were something personal—loud and unrelenting, their lips curled and bodies bristling with focused tension. It was clear that they wanted to release that tension by ripping our throats open.

Show no fear, the old wisdom says.

You have to have a lot of faith in fence-builders to trust the old wisdom.

Across the street, three young men leaned against a car parked on a lawn, huddling in their jackets and smoking cigarettes. We were the best show on the block. They weren't the only ones with front row tickets. Two detectives sitting in an unmarked car were clearly amused by this spectacle of the intimidation of the press. Mark recognized them, but didn't know them by name.

"Shit," Mark said. "I hate this."

I could tell it was more than an expression of irritation or embarrassment. No one else could hear what we said to each other over the racket the Dobermans were making, so I ventured to ask him if he was afraid of dogs.

He gave me a tense shrug. "I was attacked by one when I was ten. I'm a married man, or I'd moon those two jerks in the car so you could see my scars."

A porch light came on, and a man opened the front door. The dogs became even more determined, jumping against the fence and causing the metal to sing. "Are you from the *Express*?" the man yelled out to us.

"Yes!" we shouted in unison.

He whistled once and the dogs immediately stopped barking.

"Are you Mr. Edgerton?" Mark asked.

The man nodded. He said something to the dogs in a low voice, some words I couldn't make out, and they ran over to his side. "You can come on in now," he called to us.

I glanced at Mark. "Mr. Edgerton," I called, "I wonder if you could pen the dogs for me."

"They're very well-trained," he answered. "They won't hurt you."

"It's okay, Irene," Mark said, but I wasn't convinced.

"Mr. Edgerton, I'm sure those dogs are very well-trained, but I've got a real fear of dogs. If you can't pen the dogs, maybe we could meet you somewhere else."

There was snickering from the trio behind us.

Edgerton looked thoroughly disgusted with me. "If you're going to be a baby about it, I guess I'll put them out back." He walked into the house, dogs in tow.

"You didn't have to do that," Mark said. "We're off to a bad start with him now."

I put my fists on my hips. "He knew we'd be here about this time, we called him a few minutes ago from a pay phone to let him know that we're nearby, and he lets us sit out here for ten full minutes while his Doberman pinschers bark their asses off. We were off to a bad start before we got here."

Mark started laughing.

"What's so funny?"

"Remind me never to piss you off, Kelly."

DON EDGERTON WAS ABOUT 6'2", LANKY AND LEAN. HE WAS AS FIT AS Justin Davis had been, but his face had a kind of rugged handsomeness. A cowboy without hat or horse or rope. Or cows. His skin was leathery, as if he worked in the sun, or had done so before we all got the bad news on tanning. He wore running shoes and faded jeans and a long-sleeved T-shirt. There was gray in his light brown hair, and a kind of tired but wary look in his blue eyes. James Dean, all grown up?

No, James Dean would have slouched a little by now. Don Edgerton's nearly perfect posture made me wonder if he had been in the military.

The house was small, one of the wood-frame bungalows that populated this part of town. The only part of it we saw much of was the first room we walked into. A table and four chairs sat at the far end of the room, a worn sofa and a television at the other. A cheap stereo and a record collection sat on a set of shelves made from four cinderblock bricks and two unpainted pieces of particle board. Don Edgerton was apparently unworried about the advent of compact-disc players.

Except for a cheap battery-operated clock and one framed black and white photograph, the walls were bare, but in this house, the effect was not the same as in Justin Davis's. It was as if Don Edgerton hadn't really decided that he wanted to stay here.

The framed photo was of a baseball team. From where we sat at the table, I couldn't make out the team insignia, but it was obviously one of those posed team photos. Not exactly gorgeous, but at least it gave me the idea that he might have interests beyond training his dogs.

Edgerton picked up the beer that had been sitting half-empty on the table and drank from it, not saying anything. I was tired and didn't like ending an otherwise productive day with this apparently hostile source.

Mark didn't let Edgerton faze him. He began by gently reminding Edgerton that we were there in part because *he* had contacted *us*. He went on to make it sound like Edgerton had done a major public service to Las Piernas, that receiving Edgerton's call had been this terrific turning point in the investigation. Edgerton started looking a little less sullen, more interested. Mark commended him for his courage and said that the *Express* shared many of his concerns about Thanatos.

"The *Express* is especially concerned," Mark said, "not only because of the way this affects our community, but also because this individual who calls himself Thanatos has focused on Miss Kelly here. We don't know why, and we don't know what he has in mind. But he has done his best to make her fearful of him. He has discovered where she lives and on one occasion, broke into her home."

"He broke into your *home*?" Edgerton asked, looking directly at me for the first time since we walked in.

"Yes," I said, and told him the story of being carried into the bedroom.

"Jeee-zus." The sullenness was gone. He shook his head. "Too bad you're afraid of dogs," he said to me. "I feel a lot safer with the Marx Brothers around."

"The Marx Brothers?"

"Harpo and Zeppo. My dogs. My ex-wife kept Groucho and Chico."

"Irene's not the one who's afraid of dogs," Mark said. "I am. She was just trying to keep me from being embarrassed in front of those two detectives out there."

"You covered for him?" he asked me.

I shrugged. "He would have done the same for me."

He shook his head again.

I asked him about the Olympus Child Care Center, going over the same ground we had covered with Justin Davis and Howard Parker.

"No, I really don't remember much about it," Edgerton said. "Some kid got taken off in an ambulance. I remember that."

"Do you remember moving to Las Piernas?"

"Yeah, sure. During the war. I liked the kids here better than the ones at my school in L.A. And before my mom met her second husband, there was a nice old couple that took care of me in the afternoons. Mr. and Mrs. York. He taught me how to play baseball."

"So you didn't go back into child care after that?"

He laughed, but not as if he were amused. "No, not unless you call running from the end of some drunk's belt child care."

"The Yorks abused you?" Mark asked.

"No. My stepfather was a drunken asshole." He turned to me. "Pardon me, Miss Kelly, but it's the truth. I used to run away all the time. I'd go over to the Yorks' place. He'd fetch me back. One day, about three years after they were married, he was driving over to the Yorks' to come get me. I remember seeing the car come down the street—in one lane, then the other. He was looped, as usual. Then all of a sudden, a dog ran out in front of the car. He swerved to avoid hitting the dog, and ran the car up over the curb and hit a tree instead. Killed him. I've loved dogs ever since."

We sat staring at him for a fraction of a moment, then Mark said, "So your mom wouldn't have met your stepfather if the child care center hadn't closed?"

He shrugged. "I guess not. But I wouldn't have met the Yorks either, or lived in a better house. To tell the truth, I'd forgotten about that day-care thing having anything to do with moving to Las Piernas."

We asked about his memories of the Olympus Child Care Center. Although he vaguely remembered the routine of being taken there after school each day, he didn't remember Pauline or Jimmy Grant, and had no real recollection of Robbie Robinson.

"Is your mother still living?" Mark asked.

"No, my mom died in 1977." He paused, then asked, "How come all you ask me about is this child care center?"

I explained that the victims had all come to Las Piernas at the same time, following the closure of the center.

He frowned. He kept his eyes on the beer bottle when he asked, "Does this mean I haven't helped you out after all?"

"You've helped," I said.

Mark surprised me by changing the subject. "Mind if I look at that photo over there?"

Edgerton shifted a little in his chair, and suddenly became fascinated with peeling the label off the bottle. But he said, "No, go ahead."

Mark stood up and walked to the other end of the room.

"Sorry if I was a little abrupt with you when you first got here," Edgerton said, still concentrating his gaze on the label. "I've been on edge since I read about the Mercury Aircraft thing, and having the cops around here all the time—well, I feel like I'm the one who's done something wrong. I feel hemmed in. I was supposed to go hunting tomorrow, now they tell me I probably shouldn't be off alone anywhere. Guess I blamed the paper for the cops camping out here."

I was about to reply when Mark shouted, "The Dodgers! Good Lord, look at this, Irene!"

Edgerton glanced up at me, then shrugged. I went over to where Mark stood.

"Duke Snider, Gil Hodges, Jim Gilliam, Carl Furillo, Johnny

Roseboro," Mark was saying. "And check out the pitching! Hell, there's Koufax, Podres, Drysdale—what year was this taken?"

"1958," Edgerton said.

"1958? The first year they played in L.A.?"

"Yeah. Otherwise not a banner year for L.A. We were 71–83 at the end of the season."

"We?" I asked, but Mark had already picked him out.

"Look, he's right here!"

Sure enough, a younger Don Edgerton stared back at us from the photo, his posture just as good in those days. He was right in among those people whose baseball cards I used to carry in my back pocket like a family photo album. My collection didn't start until the 1960s, but I was a devoted Dodgers fan. While Barbara screamed her way through ten or eleven screenings of A *Hard Day's Night*, I was wondering if Sandy Koufax would marry me.

"You played with the Dodgers?" I was still amazed.

"Just about long enough for them to take that photo," Edgerton said. "They called me up for a cup of coffee. I was back in the minors after three games that year."

"Still, you made it to the big show," Mark said. "And it was tougher then. Fewer teams, smaller rosters."

"Oh, I got called back a few times. I was a utility infielder with a decent glove, but I couldn't consistently hit a curveball, so I'd always end up back in the minors again."

"How long did you play in the minors?"

"Oh, about eight years. Coached for a while in the minors. Then I came back here and worked for Las Piernas College. Coach baseball, teach fencing and archery."

"Fencing and archery?" I asked. The guy was full of surprises.

"Yeah, outdated skills, some might say. But I'm a believer in them. I have this theory. Men aren't men anymore. We're all getting too soft. Fencing requires grace and agility and quick reflexes. I'd like to see some of these kids that are so hot with video games try it. As for archery, well, that's how I do my hunting—strictly bow and arrow. Guns aren't sporting, if you ask me."

Before I could make a response, he turned to Mark and said, "You did pretty good on that photo. Most people your age can't name half those guys. Are you a player or a fan?"

Mark smiled. "Both, I guess. I played center field for a semester in college before I ruined a knee."

The next thing I knew, a serious—and I mean serious—baseball discussion ensued. "Let me show you some other photos," Edgerton said. He took us down a hallway to a small back bedroom that had been converted into an office.

There was an old olive green filing cabinet and a big wooden desk. A computer sat on the desk, a bulky plastic cover tossed to one side of it. There were framed photos covering almost every inch of wall space. Most were of the Dodgers, many much more recent than the one in the living room.

"These are terrific," Mark said. "Are you friends with the team photographer?"

"No," he said, turning red. "I took them. Hobby of mine." He saw me walk over to the desk—I admit I was hoping to snoop a little—and quickly ushered us out of the room again. "Look, if there's nothing more I can do for you . . ."

"Nothing more at the moment," I said. "Thanks for your help. And for the opportunity to see your photos."

We said pleasant, if somewhat rushed, good-byes and left.

"OKAY, OUT WITH IT," MARK SAID, STARTING UP THE CAR.

"He's a strange one. And he's nervous about something—I noticed that even before he gave us the bum's rush."

"I have the same feeling. And I don't think it's the threat of Thanatos coming after him. I just can't figure out what it is."

We saw Edgerton's front door open again. The Marx Brothers ran across the porch to the fence and started barking wildly at us. The audience across the street was long gone, but the detectives were laughing like they had been treated to a double feature of the original Marx Brothers.

"Shit," Mark said, and drove off.

# 23

FRANK AND CODY WERE WAITING up for me when I came in at midnight that night. I had called and left a message on our machine saying I would be late, but the look of relief Frank gave me served as a reminder that he was still easily worried about me.

"I was just getting ready to call the paper," he said.

"I'm safe and sound. Any messages?"

"You got a call from a woman named Louisa Parker. She said you talked to her son today—Howard Parker?"

"Yes. It seems he's the only one whose mother is still living and mentally competent."

"She said she wanted to talk to you, asked me to have you call her tomorrow. Mind if I go along with you?"

"I'll have to clear it with John, but I don't mind."

"I talked to Carlos Hernandez today. He's fairly certain Rosie Thayer died of a coronary, and that the coronary was induced by a lethal injection of some type. Toxicology reports will take a while yet."

"He found an injection mark on her?"

"Yes. That took some time because of the ant bites, but they found it."

"So then everything else was just staged? The death by starvation or dehydration never happened?"

"No, she died quickly."

"Strange, isn't it? As if he felt he had to kill her, but that he couldn't bring himself to go through with the cruelty of starving her."

"Maybe," he said. "But I suspect that's wishful thinking on your part. From his point of view, it's much more practical to kill the victim quickly. He's careful, and a careful man wouldn't want to risk a victim's escape. If she's dead, she doesn't make noise. Less risk of interference or discovery by others."

Given Thanatos' desire for control, I decided Frank's interpretation of the lethal injection was probably right.

I went out to pet the dogs, who looked up at me quizzically when I told them they would not be named after film comedians.

AS IT TURNED OUT, I ALMOST CHANGED MY MIND ABOUT HAVING FRANK go with me to talk to Louisa Parker. We started the morning off with an argument, another round in our ongoing fight about what he calls my carelessness and I call his overprotectiveness. I had awakened before he did, and gone for a run on the beach with the dogs. He was furious with me for going out alone.

"I had the dogs with me," I protested.

This did not appease him in the least. We argued while he drove me to work. We argued in the parking lot. The argument wasn't really settled before I got out of his car. Throughout the morning, I wondered if it would ever be settled.

JOHN WAS PLEASED WITH THE STORIES MARK AND I HAD TURNED IN THE night before, though as usual, we didn't learn that directly from him. He works very hard at keeping his staff from thinking too highly of themselves.

Mark got a break on another story he had been working on, and wasn't free to see Mrs. Parker. John asked me if I wanted to take Frank with me. He could see that I was surprised at the suggestion. "Just consider this a little belated Christmas gift from me to you, Kelly."

"A gift from *you*?"

"Look, no use having you take any chances." He smiled at my scowl and added, "If Thanatos kills you, Wrigley will probably freeze your position, and I'll be out a reporter."

"Now, that's more like the old Ebenezer Walters we've all come to know and love."

I figured this was a sign from on high and called Frank.

"Harriman," he answered. He sounded unhappy. I hadn't thought our argument affected him that much.

"Hi, Harriman. Still want to talk to Louisa Parker?"

"Irene? Yeah, I do. More than ever."

"What do you mean, 'more than ever'?"

"I guess Hobson Devoe hasn't called you yet."

"No, why?"

"Hope we don't need to look up anything else in those personnel records we went through."

"Mercury had a change of heart?"

"I wish it was something that simple. The records have been wiped out."

"Wiped out? How?"

"Apparently it's the work of a hacker. Wiped out all kinds of records, not just the war years."

"A hacker? At an aircraft company? Don't they have security systems on their computers?"

"I asked the same thing. They have very sophisticated protection on the computers that store accounting, design, production, and other records. A small percentage of employee records, mainly those of people with very high-level government security clearances or people connected with sensitive projects, are well-protected records. But most of the personnel records, especially the older ones, aren't as difficult to gain access to—the ones we looked at were just used for J.D. Anderson's studies. And Devoe said the hacker really knew what he or she was doing."

"When did this happen?"

"About three o'clock this morning, but they're not exactly sure that's significant. Could have been a destructive program someone planted before then. It may not be connected to Thanatos; Devoe said the other records included a group of pending workers' compensation cases. In some ways, that's more likely, because the cases include those of two people who worked on computers in Human Resources. They're out with carpal tunnel syndrome complaints."

"Do you believe that's who did this? Workers' compensation complainants?"

There was a long pause before he answered, "I don't know. To be honest, I'm just too close to this. Carlson has someone else checking that out, which is fine with me."

Neither of us said anything for a minute.

"Irene? You want to have lunch with me?"

"Sure. How about meeting me at the Galley?"

"Great. I could go for a pastrami sandwich. And I may have something for you on Pauline Grant by then."

He told me his afternoon plans were all things that could be shuffled around or handled by Pete, so I was free to set up the appointment with Louisa Parker for whatever time worked out best.

When I called her, she was quite excited about talking to me, and had no objections to having Detective Harriman join us. She was taking an art class and wouldn't be free until the late afternoon. We made an appointment for three o'clock.

FRANK WAS A LITTLE LATE FOR LUNCH, BUT HE MADE UP FOR IT BY handing over some startling news.

"I tried to look up Pauline Grant's probation records," he said. "I figured she would have been paroled a long time ago, but that maybe I could track her down."

"And?"

"And she's dead."

"Well, I guess that's not too much of a shock. She probably would have been about seventy-something by now, right?"

He shook his head. "No, I mean, she never made it out of prison."

"What? I thought she was only up for manslaughter."

"She was. And to be honest, I'm surprised they made that stick."

"So what happened to her?"

"She was killed in prison. Not long after she was sentenced, in fact. I don't have all the details yet, but from what I could learn, she was stabbed to death by a group of inmates."

"Good Lord." I thought about the interviews Mark and I had conducted the night before, how Justin Davis and Howard Parker had talked of Jimmy Grant. Bad enough to have been separated from his mother for a few years; worse yet, he had been orphaned. "Any idea what became of her son?"

"Not yet. The usual procedure would be to place him with family members. If no family members could be located, he would have been placed in foster care, maybe adopted, although he would have been hard to place at that age. The records are in L.A. County and too old to be readily accessible. Besides, for this kind of information, I'd need a warrant. That will take some time."

"If the Department of Social Services is reluctant to open his records, what else can you do?"

"Oh, we'll still have some options. Track down his mother's Social Security records, see if anybody is collecting her payments. Look for school records, things like that."

"A lot of work."

"Yes, and a lot of time. No telling if he's the one we want. He could be dead by now, or living in some other part of the country, maybe not even aware all of this is going on. But the victims sure as hell point back to *somebody* connected with what happened that day."

"I can't think of anyone who would have a stronger motive for revenge than Jimmy Grant. Alex Havens and Edna Blaylock testified against his mother. He was separated from her, and later she was killed."

"But why did he wait so long? He has to be about fifty-four years old himself. Why didn't he do this when he was in his teens or his twenties? And why involve you—choose you as his Cassandra?"

"I don't know." I doodled on my napkin as I thought about it, then noticed I was drawing figures shaped like fawns. I was the only person on earth who could discern them as such, of course. Film animators have nothing to fear from me.

"The people we've talked to so far were all children at the time," I said. "Maybe Louisa Parker will be able to tell us more."

He smiled. "I'm kind of surprised you asked me to come along with you to talk to her."

"It wasn't my idea."

There went the smile. "Still pissed off at me?"

"No, but I'm thinking of seeing a doctor. Something's really wrong with me—I can't hold a grudge like I used to."

At least the smile was back, and he did have the good sense to withhold any arrogant remarks on his ability to charm me out of a bad mood. He skated dangerously close to the edge, though, when he started whistling as we walked out to the car.

LOUISA PARKER LIVED IN AN AREA CALLED KELSO PARK, AN OLDER PART of town. It was an oddball neighborhood; little wood-frame houses built in the 1930s were sandwiched between large buildings of fifty or more condos each.

Developers would buy a couple of the old houses, which were on large lots, tear them down, and replace them with four-story buildings. At most, the builders provided one parking space per condo in underground, gated lots. Street parking was a bitch.

If, like Louisa Parker, you were one of the people who owned a house, you were suddenly living in a canyon. And with three walls of condo balconies surrounding you, you didn't have much privacy. Not exactly conducive to things like nude sunbathing in your own yard. Not that I imagined Louisa Parker was into baring all.

"I wonder what the air quality is like when all those condo folks get out on their balconies and barbecue," I said to Frank as we walked down the sidewalk toward her house. He just gave me one of those looks that said he would never understand how my mind works.

I like it that way.

He knocked on the front door, and it fairly flew open before his knuckles left the wood. He had his ID in hand, but she didn't so much as glance at it. "Irene Kelly!" she said. "I can't believe I'm going to have Irene Kelly right in my own home! Come in, come in!"

My photo will run next to one of my occasional commentary columns, so once in a while I'm recognized on the street. Although

I'll get mail or phone calls from readers, I rarely encounter people who are what you might call fans. Louisa Parker was a true fan. I would be a first-class liar if I said this wasn't pleasing, but I'm never quite ready for it when it happens.

She was a bundle of energy. She was grinning from ear to ear as she shook my hand with a firm grip and ushered us inside. As she led us into the living room, I could see why Howard Parker thought she might outlive him. She was tall, like her son, but not as thin. She wore her gray hair like a crown of glory, and had a few wrinkles, but you wouldn't find it easy to guess her age without missing by a couple of decades. She looked great.

The house wouldn't tell her age, either. The furnishings were sleek and contemporary. Her son had far more old-fashioned furniture in his home.

"This whole Thanatos business stinks to high heaven," she said with conviction. She had seated us on her black leather sofa and given us each a cup of coffee in about three minutes flat. "I don't like it at all. Not at all." She turned to Frank, giving him the look mothers reserve for children caught sticking their fingers in the frosting. "When do you suppose you police fellows are going to catch the bastard?"

"We're doing our best, Mrs. Parker," Frank said, managing somehow to maintain a serious expression.

"Well, you damn well better catch him soon." She turned to me and smiled. "What can I tell you?"

"Do you remember much about the Olympus Child Care Center case?"

"Of course I do. I don't mean to be a shameless braggart, but I have an excellent memory. At my age, that's something to crow about. If you're as gray-headed as I am and you so much as misplace your keys, people think you've got Alzheimer's."

As she continued on, I noticed that she hardly spared Frank a glance. "Yes, I most certainly do remember it. And I think it was one of the saddest things ever to happen to someone I knew personally. Pauline Grant was a lovely young woman, and she truly did love children. I took the time to get to know her a little, since I wanted to know the person who would be caring for my child while I was at work."

"That's always wise," Frank said, but she ignored him, and I could tell he was a little irked about it.

"The children who were Howie's age went over to the Olympus Center right after school, at about two o'clock," she said. "They stayed there until about five-thirty, when we picked them up after work. I guess they call it extended day care.

"Well, Pauline was a woman trying to raise a child all by herself, just as I was. She doted on her son. I suppose that was her downfall. Try to understand. We were patriotic, but that side of the war, losing a loved one, was as painful for us as it ever has been for anybody. For those of us who had lost our husbands—well, that protectiveness of our children was hard to avoid. We were all our children had left, and quite often, the reverse was true as well. Pauline had no other family to turn to. She was all alone. So it was easy for her to become overprotective of her little boy."

"So you knew both Pauline and Jimmy?" I asked.

"Oh, yes. Jimmy, her son, was a sensitive child to begin with, and Pauline's attitude just made him something of a whiner. Clung to her apron strings. I'm afraid the other children didn't give him a very easy time of it. Maggie Robinson's boy was a nasty little booger, if I may speak so ill of the dead. He had a temper on him. A born hell-raiser. And if you want my opinion, in another ten years he would have been one of the people Detective Harriman goes hunting for."

"Maybe so," I said, "but he was only a child, just eight years old. He wasn't much of a physical match for a grown woman, was he?"

"No," she said quietly, "I suppose you're right. But I tell you, that child was the kind of kid that could tempt Mother Theresa to knock the crap out of him."

"Do you know what became of Jimmy Grant?" Frank asked.

She looked between us with wide eyes. "You mean you don't know?"

"We've only known of his existence since yesterday, Mrs. Parker." He caught himself, and quickly added, "We would appreciate any information you could give us." He glanced over at me, then back at her.

She smiled, knowing she had nettled him. Suddenly she looked between us slyly. "Is something going on between you two?"

"Engagement," I answered, noting Frank was slightly taken aback by my directness.

She brightened. "Well, congratulations! I've been married twice myself, and recommend it highly." Now she was eyeing him from head to toe. "Well, well, well. Well, well, well!"

With each "well," Frank apparently received a higher approval rating. He was embarrassed by the appraisal process, which in turn forced me into a hopeless struggle to keep a straight face.

"Jimmy Grant?" he asked, as if in pain.

"Oh, yes," she sobered. "We were talking about poor little Jimmy. Well, I suppose that is exactly what makes the whole thing so sad. Sad and *bizarre*, if you ask me."

"Bizarre?"

"Yes, Detective Harriman. Bizarre. A sign of the kind of corruption we had around here in those days. Pauline, as you know, was jailed almost immediately after the Robinson boy died. The mothers of the children at the Olympus Center were divided into two camps, you might say. Those that lined up behind Maggie Robinson were crying for blood. The rest of us that felt that the whole thing had been an accident. Her lack of self-control meant Pauline should lose her job, but not her child. And certainly not her freedom."

"Did Pauline have many supporters?" I asked.

"Oh no. By supporting Pauline, I was in the minority camp. None of us had the kind of money it would take to get her a good lawyer or to help her get out on bail. So she was in custody from the day of the incident on."

"And Jimmy?"

"As I said, there were no relatives available, so Jimmy was placed into foster care. He was—oh, I hate to say it, but he was a difficult child. He didn't accept what had happened at all. Blamed himself, in the way children will. When Pauline was sent to prison, he became totally uncontrollable, and there was doubt as to whether he could ever be placed anywhere for long. That's when Maggie Robinson stepped in."

"Maggie Robinson?"

"Yes. She somehow finagled it so that she became Jimmy's foster mother."

"What?" We asked it in chorus.

"Yes. She had some twisted notion that this was a just solution. I thought it stank. When Pauline was killed, Maggie adopted Jimmy."

We sat in stunned silence for a moment.

"How was that possible?" I asked.

"J.D. Anderson," she said.

"The president of Mercury Aircraft?" Frank asked. "What did he have to do with it?"

"Rumors were, Maggie was J.D.'s mistress. For all her other faults—and believe me, you don't want to sit here while I name them—Maggie was stunningly beautiful."

I shook my head. "I still don't understand how that could allow her—"

"To adopt Jimmy? Irene Kelly, you surprise me. At that time, J.D. was one of the most powerful individuals in the Los Angeles area. And while you may believe there is corruption now, back then, things were absolutely rotten. Didn't Mr. O'Connor ever tell you about what it was like then?"

"Well, yes, but a child —"

"*Especially* a child. Surely you can see that even now, children have little say over what becomes of them. They're at the mercy of adults. Adoption has changed now, not so much because of the law, but because of supply and demand, if you will. Abortion rights changed the supply. Back then—remember the recent revelations about the judge who made a small fortune from adoption? She ordered babies removed from their parents' custody and then accepted payment to place the children with wealthy clients."

"Wasn't there anyone who spoke up for him?"

She wrung her hands together. "I'm ashamed to admit it, but no, I didn't. Maggie wasn't working at Mercury by then, but we all knew she was J.D.'s kept woman. The rumor I heard was that he had pulled all the strings himself, had even fixed it so that if anybody went looking for Jimmy's records, they wouldn't find a thing. As if the kid didn't exist before he was adopted."

She paused, then continued in a much lower voice. "The war was over, and lots of women had lost their jobs. At the time, I was the sole source of support for my son. I had never worked before the war. Not as a teacher or a nurse, not even as a waitress. If I lost my job at Mercury, I didn't have a thing to fall back on. If it had just been me, well, maybe I would have spoken up. But I had Howie to think of, and I stayed silent."

"I appreciate your telling us now," Frank said. "You've saved me a lot of effort. I'll have a better idea of how to look for him now. Did you ever see Maggie Robinson after the war?"

"Yes, once I saw her here in town, at a store during a Christmas sale. Must have been two or three years after the war. She seemed quite nervous about the encounter. She tried to avoid me, truth be told. I sort of pushed my way over to her and asked about Jimmy. She looked furious, but she said she didn't know any Jimmy, and I must have mistaken her for someone else. Then she managed to disappear into the crowd. I never did like that woman."

"Do you know Hobson Devoe?" I asked.

"Yes, the former head of personnel. I understand he runs the museum out there now."

"Would he have known about Maggie?"

She frowned. "I'm not certain, of course, but I'd tend to doubt it. Mr. Devoe has always been very active in his church. The other men used to call him 'The Boy Scout.' Treated him as something of an innocent—or perhaps I should say, they treated him as if he were prudish. They didn't tell dirty jokes around him, or use foul language, so I'm sure they didn't discuss J.D.'s mistresses—according to rumor, J.D. had several. Maggie was certainly not the only one who let J.D. sample her wares, although she was apparently a favorite over many years. I just don't know. Hobson was a straight arrow, but he wasn't naive or unable to get what he wanted in the corporation."

We talked for a few more minutes, then thanked her and said our good-byes. As we went down the sidewalk, she shouted out to Frank from her front porch. "You be good to her, Detective Harriman, or you'll answer to me."

We waved and drove off.

On the way home, I told Detective Harriman that he had indeed been good to me, and started to list off some possible rewards. He was looking forward to them, but it wasn't to be. When we pulled up in his driveway, we noticed a car parked out in front of the house. A woman was sitting in it.

Frank's mother had decided to surprise us with a visit.

# 24

FORTUNATELY, BEA HARRIMAN hadn't been waiting long. Unfortunately, Frank and I had spent that morning arguing, not housekeeping. The place wasn't a wreck, but it wasn't what I wanted it to look like when my future mother-in-law stopped by for her first inspection tour. Although she had been inside Frank's house several other times, this was her first visit since the dawn of our cohabitation.

I was nervous when we opened the front door, but my fears about her reaction to the house were unfounded, it seemed. She was full of leftover Christmas goodwill and quite pleased with herself for surprising us. As we made our way down the hall, she happily commented on the fact that this was the first time she had seen me out of my casts. She even turned a blind eye to the pile of dishes in the sink.

She was startled to see two big, barking dogs in the backyard. Cody, not to be outdone, bit Frank on the ankle and then ran around like Beelzebub was after him, knocking books and papers to the floor in his wake. The pandemonium was raised to a new pitch by the ringing of the telephone.

Home sweet home.

Frank took over the task of carrying his mom's packages, taking her coat and getting her settled in the guest room. I tried to get the dogs to be quiet. "Shush!" I shouted to them as I picked up the phone.

"What?" the voice on the other end said.

"Oh, not you, Steven. The dogs. They're raising Cain. Hang on just a minute."

I opened the door a crack, intending to get them to settle down. They bowled me over and ran over to Frank's mother, who was still remarkably calm about the whole situation. She petted the dogs, who were giving her a sniffing over and an enthusiastic greeting all at once.

"What are their names?" she asked.

"They don't have names yet. I think we're narrowing it down between Frick and Frack or Yes and No. If it's Yes and No, we might rent them out to spiritualist parties." She looked at me as if I might be serious.

"Who's on the phone?" Frank called from our small spare bedroom.

"Steven," I answered, going back to the receiver.

"I vote for Yes and No," Steven said. "Otherwise, you'll have Frick, Frack, and Frank, and that could get confusing."

"So would saying,'No, Yes,' if Yes misbehaved. Frank thought we should give them mixed-up Western names. Since Cody is a cross between Wild Bill Hickok and Buffalo Bill Cody, maybe we could have Buffalo Hickok and Calamity Annie Oakley."

"You lost me. Besides, too hard to say. Although Calamity isn't a bad name, from what you've told me about your dogs."

"Hang on again, Steven. Now the doorbell's ringing."

The dogs were barking again and got to the front door before I did. "What's wrong with you mutts?" I heard a voice call from the other side of the door. They immediately settled down into anxious whines. Not to be fooled by this, I grabbed on to their collars.

"Come on in, Jack," I shouted.

He opened the door and stepped in. The dogs sat prettily and were quite well-behaved for him. "If I had known you could have this effect on them, I would have made sure you were here when we walked in tonight. They've been candidates for the banana ranch."

Frank stepped out into the hallway and invited Jack back to meet his mom. I could tell that it took everything in her power to control her initial reaction to him, taking in his scarred face and shaved head, his earring and tattoos. But Jack has an ability to make almost anybody like him, so Frank and I no longer worry over people's first reactions to his appearance. I headed back to the phone.

Steven Kincaid was apparently just feeling lonesome, and had no particular reason to call. I chatted with him for a moment, then covered the receiver and motioned to Frank. After a brief discussion, we ended up inviting Jack and Steven to join us for dinner. While we waited for Steven to make his way over, we fed the dogs and Cody. Jack had already won Bea over by the time Steven arrived. Bea wasn't too old to appreciate Steven's good looks, either, so we were happy campers when we headed out to Bernie's All-Night Cafe.

It was just as we were finishing dinner that the trouble started. "Irene," Bea said to me with a smile, "I have the loveliest place picked out for the wedding."

Frank and I exchanged a look.

"Mom, Irene's sister is already working on that."

I tried not to laugh out loud as I added, "We'll probably be picking something out ourselves when the time comes."

The check arrived and we haggled over who would pay, Frank

and I finally convincing everyone that we'd cover it this time. We piled back into the Volvo; I sat between Steven and Jack in the backseat.

Bea took up where she left off. "I'm sure your sister will adore this place. But you two need to set a date and set it now. I think June would be nice. Traditional, I suppose, but still—Irene, have you picked out your dress yet? We need to get going on invitations as well. And set up a florist, and a photographer, a caterer and—oh, of course, a minister."

"Irene's Catholic," Frank said, the moment she stopped to draw a breath.

"What? Catholic? Really?"

"Really."

"Oh, Frank." The disappointment level would have better matched an announcement like "Irene's an ax murderer and cannibal, as well as a polygamist, but by golly I love her anyway." "Well," she said, bucking up admirably, "we're Episcopalian, Irene, and I don't think you'll find it too much of a change."

We had just pulled up in the driveway. Jack took my hand and gave it a squeeze of silent support, or I don't think I could have kept my mouth shut. Steven was looking extremely uncomfortable. I suppose it was Frank's tone of voice that made everyone in the car suddenly snap to attention. It was quiet, but chilled.

"Irene, why don't you and Jack and Steven take the dogs for a walk on the beach?"

I nodded, and we got out of the car. Jack and Steven let the dogs out of the backyard. Frank opened the front door for his mom, who hadn't said another word, then he came over to where I stood. He put his arms around me and bent to my ear and whispered, "Be careful, you unrepentant papist, and don't let yourself wander out of sight of Jack and Steven, okay?" He kissed my forehead and went inside.

The dogs were overjoyed at the prospect of a walk, leaping in circles around us as if they were on springs, bouncing their front and back ends. Their enthusiasm somehow buoyed my own spirits.

We walked along the shore, watching the dogs chase each other. It was a cloudy night, threatening rain. There wasn't much wind, but the air was cold. The moon was up; its bright face broke through the clouds now and again, but the night was dark enough to make me heed Frank's warning—I stuck close to Jack and Steven. Jack was on my left, Steven on my right, as we approached the pier. Each put an arm through one of mine, and we huddled together, listening to Jack tell a story about a job he once had picking pears.

Suddenly there was hollow "thump" to my right, and I turned to see blood pouring down Steven Kincaid's face. He stared at me with a dazed look, reached toward his forehead, and collapsed onto the sand. I cried out, and Jack and I quickly knelt down next to him. He was breathing, but out cold. Blood flowed from a deep gash in his forehead, just above his right eye. The dogs started barking ferociously and charging toward the pier, where I saw a tall man running away.

I looked back to Steven, who was pale and motionless.

"Get Frank, Jack. Hurry. Tell him about the man on the pier." As I spoke I took Steven's head in my lap. I reached beneath my jacket and tore off a wide strip of my cotton blouse and used it to try—gently—to stop the bleeding on his head. Jack whistled for the dogs, who turned and came back. "I'm not leaving you here without them," he said. The man who had been on the pier was nowhere in sight.

Jack saw Frank's dog sniffing at something, and he bent over and gingerly picked it up. He pocketed it, commanding the dogs to stay, then he ran back to the house.

I sat shivering on the sand, holding the cloth to Steven's head, listening to the dogs making small whimpers of concern. Frank's dog licked my face, and I became aware of the fact that tears were coursing down my cheeks.

Now and then the moon would clear the clouds, and I would see

Steven's pale, blood-covered face. The bleeding wouldn't stop. The cloth was soaked and still he bled.

I held back, or thought I held back, a sound of fear and sadness, but I may have made the sound after all, because I heard the dogs echo it. I begged my papist God not to let Steven Kincaid die.

I DON'T KNOW HOW MUCH TIME HAD PASSED BEFORE I SAW THE DOGS prick their ears forward. I looked up to see Frank and Jack running towards us. Probably only a few minutes had gone by, though it felt like hours. Frank knelt down next to me and felt for Steven's pulse. "He's still alive," I managed to say, "but he hasn't moved or made a sound. There's a lot of blood."

"Foreheads bleed easily," Frank said softly, and reached over to lift my hand from the wound. The strip of blouse was soaked red, and as it pulled away, the awful gash below it looked worse to me than it had before. Frank had a first-aid kit with him. He moved Steven's head from my lap onto a sort of pillow. I heard a sound above us, and saw Jack unfurling a blanket. He put it over Steven while Frank made a pressure bandage for the wound.

Before long, we heard sirens approaching. A beach patrol vehicle pulled up next to us, its floodlamp bathing us in bright light. The light only made me feel greater dismay as I looked into Steven's pale, bloodstained face. I felt Frank taking me by the shoulders, gently moving me aside. The beach patrol had a stretcher; they took Steven away on it. I stood watching as they made their way to the pier, then met an ambulance; they transferred the stretcher to that vehicle and it drove off quickly, sirens wailing.

The police arrived on the scene as well, and we talked to them for a few minutes. We had little to tell them. I hadn't been able to see the face of the man on the pier; Jack hadn't seen the man at all.

Frank carefully held out something to a member of a forensic sciences team, saying Jack had found it on the sand.

"Actually, your dog found it," Jack said. Frank reached down and scratched his dog's ears while the forensics man looked it over. It was a bloody rock, about four inches in diameter. Printed on one side, in small, cramped letters, were the words "Hyacinthus Must Fall."

"It's another one of the myths," Jack said. "Hyacinthus was a handsome young man who was greatly loved by the god Apollo. One day, at a competition, Apollo threw a disk that accidentally struck Hyacinthus on the forehead."

He acted like he didn't want to say more.

"What happened to him?" Frank asked.

"He died," I said quietly, taking up the story. "Apollo grieved for him. As Apollo wept, a flower bloomed in the place where the blood of Hyacinthus had soaked the ground."

I stared down at the sand, red from Steven's blood. Frank put an arm around my shoulders, and we turned and started back to the house. I couldn't talk. I heard Jack whistling to the dogs, following us.

When he opened the front door, Frank said, "Change clothes and we'll go down to the hospital. I'll help Jack with the dogs."

I just stared up at him. Had he said something?

"Irene?"

"Okay," I said, and walked in the house.

Frank's mother took one look at me and rushed over to my side. She put an arm around me and walked me back to the bathroom. She turned on a faucet; I looked down and realized I was quite a sight. My hands and lap were covered in blood; my blouse was torn and my face was red and swollen from crying.

"I'd better take a shower," I said.

"Okay, you go ahead," she said. "I'm going to fix you something warm to drink. Your skin is as cold as ice." She started up the shower for me as I peeled out of my clothes.

I stood in the shower, feeling the hot water pelt against me, watching the pinkish water from my skin go down the drain. Finally, I came alive a little and made myself start to scrub.

By the time I had dried off and dressed in a pair of jeans and a warm sweater, Bea was in the living room, a thermos waiting for me. "Take this with you," she said. I looked over at the kitchen.

"You washed all the dishes."

She ignored that. "Steven will be okay," she said. She turned to Frank, who was sitting on the couch, looking at me with concern. "Franklin, get the lead out. Irene is worried about that boy."

"What about you?" I asked.

"I'm fine. I'll just wait here for you to get back. Don't worry, I can manage."

"Thank you," I said, and meant it.

WE WERE SITTING IN THE WAITING ROOM AT ST. ANNE'S EMERGENCY Room before I opened the thermos. Just breathing in the aroma of the hot coffee made me feel better. I took a sip and realized it was laced with brandy.

I offered some to Frank, who took a sip, then made a face. "Wasn't expecting that. You go ahead and drink it. I'm driving."

I drank a half a cup and felt myself steadying a bit. I got up and went over to a pay phone and called the paper. They had already picked up the first police calls on the scanner. I gave them what I could on the story; we were past deadline, so the nightside staff was busy rearranging the front page for the morning edition. "I'm at the hospital now," I told the man on the City Desk. "I'll call again if I hear anything more on Kincaid's condition."

I sat back down next to Frank and drank more coffee. The waiting room chairs were apparently designed by the set decorator for the Spanish Inquisition. I would get up every few minutes and walk by the reception desk, which made everyone at the desk get very busy with things that made them face the other way. They were getting tired of telling me that they'd let me know about Steven as soon as they heard anything from the doctor.

It was a busy night, and I became uneasy watching the incoming stream of the injured and their worried friends and relatives. Frank finally coaxed me into putting my head on his shoulder for a while, and I fell into a restless sleep.

A voice was calling to me, and I awoke with a start. It was Frank, whose tousled hair told me he had dozed off as well. A weary doctor stood in front of us and told us she would take us back to see Steven, but only for a few minutes.

"Your friend is very, very lucky," she said. Her manner was calm and sympathetic and I felt myself unwind a fraction as we followed her down the hallway. "He has a hairline fracture of the skull. The blow caused a concussion, but if it had been a little harder, it might have damaged brain tissue, or caused problems with fluid build up. The CAT scan didn't show anything like that. We will want to keep an eye on him to make sure he doesn't have other problems. He's conscious now, but groggy. He's experiencing some pain, but when a patient has a head injury, it's unwise to medicate him for pain relief." She stopped outside the door to a room. "I realize you've been anxious about him and have waited out there a long time. But promise you'll think of his best interests—don't stay too long, all right?"

We agreed and walked into the room. It brought back all of my hospital memories, and Frank put a steadying arm around me. Steven was still ghostly pale, but they had cleaned him up. He had a white bandage around his head. He opened his eyes when we came up to the bed.

Steven could wake up and look at us. I felt a tremendous sense of relief just being able to see that for myself.

"Hi, Steven," Frank said. "Good to see you're still with us."

"Yeah."

"Frank speaks from experience," I said. "He banged his head up about six months ago. You look better than he did. But you still scared the hell out of us." I stopped. It occurred to me that I had been talking a mile a minute.

Faint smile.

"Did you see who hit you?" Frank asked.

"No. What happened?" His speech was thick.

"You were hit by a rock."

"I don't remember." He closed his eyes.

"Remember being on the beach?"

"Sort of."

He was tiring and it was obvious that questions were confusing to him. "Good night, Steven," I said. "I'll come back tomorrow."

He opened his eyes and said, "I heard you."

"Heard me what?"

"Crying. Praying, I think."

"Both. You apparently weren't the only one who heard me. Get some sleep."

He closed his eyes again and we left.

IT HAD STARTED TO DRIZZLE BY THE TIME WE WALKED BACK OUT TO the car. We sat in the front seat for a moment. I looked over at the man next to me, and something in me gave way. This happens every so often; some barrier within me suddenly crumbles, some barrier I haven't even realized was there. I reached over and pulled him closer, stretching up to kiss him. He didn't balk at it, and returned the kiss enthusiastically. "What was that for?" he asked.

"For—I don't know—standing by me, I suppose."

He smiled and kept his arm around me. We didn't say anything more to one another that night, just crawled into bed when we got home and held on to one another. That said all that needed saying.

# 25

I AWOKE WITH A START IN THE middle of the night, scared. I had been having a nightmare, one in which I went to the hospital, only to be told that Steven had died unexpectedly during the night. I must have made a noise or something, because Frank woke up and pulled me closer, so that my head was on his chest. "You okay?" he asked in a drowsy voice.

"Yes," I lied, wanting nothing more than to pick up the phone, to call the hospital to confirm that I wasn't having some psychic experience, a prescient dream. Eventually, the sounds of rain falling outside and Frank's breathing lulled me back to sleep.

Frank had already gone to work when I awoke the next morning. Bea was up and had hot coffee waiting for me. It was a gray day outside, and I had a gray mood to match it, but Bea was full of energy. I tried not to dampen her spirits. She had let the dogs in the house, and seeming to understand their luck, they were on their best behavior. Cody had started training them not to mess with him—each of them had felt the claws of Wild Bill.

Frank had filled his mother in on the news about Steven, and she asked me a few questions about what had happened out on the beach. "I'm so sorry all of this happened," she said. "I was hoping we could have a belated Christmas together."

"If you don't mind hanging around in Las Piernas for another day, we can celebrate it tonight."

"If you two don't mind my being here—"

"Not at all. It was a nice surprise. You helped me cope with last night—I appreciate it."

She was pleased by this, and I left her in a good mood.

I MADE MY WAY THROUGH LAS PIERNAS'S RAIN-WASHED STREETS AT AN irritating snail's pace. Traffic was at a crawl. I listened to the noisy staccato of rain pummeling the cloth top of my Karmann Ghia while my windows fogged up. I tightened my grip on the wheel in impatience.

As soon as I got to work, I called St. Anne's to check up on Steven. Not wanting to wake him if he was sleeping, I asked for a friend of mine on the staff there, Sister Theresa. She was happy to hear from me. I explained why I was calling.

"Mr. Kincaid, is it? Well, he's doing much better."

"You already know who he is?"

She laughed. "There's a constant stream of nurses in and out of that poor boy's room. He's quite handsome, you know. I only hope it doesn't cause him to be denied his rest. Detective Harriman had a guard placed at his door, and I'm beginning to think it was to protect the young man from our staff. I have looked in on him, and I must say he does look like a sleeping angel."

"Don't go forgetting your vows, Sister. He likes older women."

She found this highly amusing. She encouraged me to say hello to her if I stopped by to see him.

I worked on a follow-up story based on what Louisa Parker had told us. I called Pete Baird and found out that they were still waiting for a court order to look for adoption records.

"Sorry to hear about that kid getting hurt last night," he said. "I like him."

"Me too."

"You know about the slingshot?"

"Slingshot?"

"Yeah, they found a hunter's slingshot on the pier last night—the lab guys say it might have been used to launch that rock. They make these super-slingshots now—kids carry them around; they're a real pain in the ass as far as we're concerned. Lots of property damage. More accurate than the old-forked-twig-and-rubber-band routine we used when I was a kid. The lucky thing is, only a few places in town sell them, so if he bought it locally, we may be able to track down the buyer."

"He left it on the pier?"

"He may not have left it. Probably dropped it when he ran off. There's a partial print on it, but we can't tie it to anyone with a sheet."

"Somehow I get the feeling that this is Thanatos' first and only crime spree."

"For an amateur, he's doing a bang-up job of it."

"Yeah, well, he's had almost fifty years to plan it."

"So you're convinced it's this Grant kid?"

"Think about it," I said. "Some bully picks on you every day. One day while he's punching on you, your mom comes along and sends him flying into a wall. But what should be the most glorious day of your life becomes the beginning of hell on earth. The other kids, who've never treated you right, all point the finger at your mother. Your mother is taken from you, and after being bounced around like a bad check, you end up under the thumb of the bully's mother. Maybe you wait around praying for your mother to be released from prison, to come and rescue you. But instead she's murdered. You never see her again. She's murdered serving a prison sentence for protecting you from a bully."

"Yeah, I guess that isn't so hard to buy. But why wait until now? Why not try this when you're a younger man?"

"I don't know, Pete. I don't know." I switched to a lighter subject. "What's Rachel up to these days?"

"She's getting ready to move here. Can you believe it? She's actually going to be here all the time. I'm a lucky bastard."

I agreed with him. We said good-bye and I went back to work. I wrote up what I could, filling out some of the details and providing follow-up to previous stories. I spent a lot of time staring at the computer screen. I stopped by Mark Baker's desk for a couple of minutes and filled him in on the slingshot development. He had heard of them, having already done a story on some kids being injured by them.

The rain was still coming down at noon, so I was reluctant to go out anywhere to eat. I didn't want to endure the long lines in the cafeteria, so I bought a crummy lunch from a vending machine down in the basement. At least I got a chance to watch them run the presses and to shoot the breeze with Danny Coburn for a while. He pulled out a new assortment of pictures of his grandchildren. "Suzanne's going to have to buy a bigger wallet for you, Danny," I told him. He grinned. Talking to him was a pleasant distraction from all that had happened in the last few days.

That afternoon, scratching a mental itch I had about things that had been said to me over the last few days, I started doing some double-checking. I verified that Don Edgerton was an instructor at Las Piernas College, gathered the dates of his employment there, and asked about his teaching schedule. I called the Dodgers and verified what he had told us about being with the team.

I called Las Piernas School District, and was told that Howard Parker did indeed retire after teaching for more than thirty years. "He taught math," the woman on the other end of the phone said. "He won awards for teaching. We were very disappointed when he left, but he said that after his wife died, his heart wasn't in it. She taught for us, also—computer science. Lovely woman."

Justin Davis, I learned, had designed security systems of one type or another for almost every government entity and major business in Las Piernas, including Mercury Aircraft itself. His company was highly regarded, and he had a reputation for personally following up on any job they took on, making certain his customers remained satisfied.

I called Fielding's Nursing Home, where Peggy Davis was indeed a patient. The lady who answered the phone had a honeyed voice that made me want to ask if she had ever considered a career in radio. She gave me polite attention, which is more than you can say for a lot of people who answer business phones.

"Let's see, Peggy Davis—here she is. Mrs. Margaret Davis. She's fairly new here. That would be in Mrs. Madison's group. Would you mind holding for a moment?"

My God, *asked* if I would hold the line—and she waited for my answer! "Not at all," I said, finding myself lowering the pitch of my own voice to match hers.

Mrs. Madison's voice and manner provided a stark contrast. "Yeah, Madison," she answered. "Who is this?"

"Irene Kelly with the *Las Piernas News Express*. I was wondering if I could arrange to talk to Mrs. Davis."

"No."

"No?"

"No. Look lady, Mrs. Davis is a vacant lot, if you know what I mean. These old birds in here can't hold a conversation, unless you count being asked the same question ninety times an hour a conversation. Old Mrs. Davis doesn't even know who she is. She doesn't recognize her own son. And she doesn't hear so good, either. So no way is she going to talk to some newspaper reporter."

There was a click. "Thank you so very much," I said to the dial tone.

"STORM DAMAGE" WAS LIKELY TO BUMP THE THANATOS STORIES OUT of the lead position on A-1 by the time I was signing off the computer for the day. We had been getting calls on accidents, a roof collapsing, and road closures. Flood control channels, Southern California's deep and wide concrete-lined river beds, were filling up. The nearly stagnant trickles one usually found in them changed into shallow but dangerous rapids within a matter of minutes whenever it rained hard. Every year, it seems we write at least one story about someone who decides to go rafting in a channel and drowns. Amateurs misjudge the speed of the water and the amount of debris that comes rocketing along with it.

As evening fell, I decided I'd better hurry up and get over to the hospital to see Steven. I wanted to get home to Bea, also. I felt a twinge of guilt about leaving her alone.

I was packing up when Mark Baker hurried over. "Guess what! They've taken Don Edgerton in for questioning."

"Why?"

"They asked around at the sporting goods stores. Figured the clerks might remember someone older buying a slingshot. Turns out one clerk remembered him."

"A clerk knew him by name?"

"No. He just remembered that he sold a slingshot to a customer of his who also bought a lot of archery equipment. The detectives remembered that Edgerton taught archery at the college. They brought out a set of photos and the clerk pointed to Edgerton in nothing flat. They got search warrants for his house and office. Guess what they found in his desk drawer at the school?"

"The hammer that killed Edna Blaylock?"

"No. One of those synthesizers for disguising a voice over the phone."

"Good Lord." I sat down again, trembling. But as I thought about what he had said, something puzzled me. "Why would Edgerton keep those things in an office? Why not at home, where he has two Dobermans to stand watch?"

"I don't know. Could be he doesn't think the house is all that secure, even with the dogs. But his office at the college is very secure. And it has one of those special electronic locks on it."

Pete had told me about the electronic locks on the campus. It occurred to me that I had seen that type of lock several times in recent days.

"He's got all kinds of sports equipment stored there," Mark went on, "including a lot of his own personal equipment."

"Wait a minute! Now that you mention it, I realize we never saw bows and arrows or fencing gear at his house. Just the photos and the computer." I shuddered. "Maybe that's what he was doing with the computer—wiping out some records at Mercury that would have told us more."

"Maybe. But we didn't see the whole house. Besides, the damning evidence is the slingshot and the synthesizer, not the computer. Lots of people have access to a computer. Even Howard Parker, right?"

"I guess it doesn't matter now. Don Edgerton. That sonofabitch. When I think of what he's done . . ." I drew a deep breath and tried to calm down. "So now the problem is finding the link. The why."

"I'm going down to police headquarters and see if they'll let me talk to him. Want to come along?"

The phone rang before I could answer his question.

"Kelly," I answered.

"Cassandra."

Mark took one look at my face and picked up the extension. I couldn't make myself answer. I couldn't even see the room. All I could see was Steven Kincaid's bleeding face.

"Why so quiet, my love?" the voice said. "Surely Hyacinthus didn't mean so much to you?"

I tried to will my own voice to be steady and calm. "You're blowing it, Thanatos. You're either screwing up an effort to pin something on someone else or you're wasting your phone call from jail—"

He laughed. "Believe me, I'm not calling from jail. I just needed to keep your friends busy for a while."

"You screwed up anyway. You missed with Icarus. And you didn't do such a great job on Hyacinthus, either. He isn't dead."

"Not yet."

I felt a white-hot fury rising in me. "You're going to be the first to go. I swear you will."

"Not likely. I say Kincaid, Harriman, and then—well, who knows?"

"I'm Cassandra, remember? And I say it's going to be you. You're getting sloppy. You're forcing it now—going to extremes—like this business with the Mercury computers." I glanced over at Mark, who was frantically shaking his head at me.

"That was not at all difficult for me," Thanatos said. "Keep that in mind."

"Like I said, I'm Cassandra. It doesn't matter if you believe me or not. It will happen. You're next."

He laughed, then stopped suddenly. When he spoke, his voice was menacing. "You disappoint me."

"Pauline would have been disappointed in you, Jimmy."

"You—" he hissed angrily. "You're no better than the others!" He hung up.

Mark Baker looked like he was in shock. "Do you think that was wise?"

I was shaking. "No, it wasn't."

He came over and put a hand on my shoulder. "Look, I'm sorry. You've had a lot to cope with lately."

I didn't say anything.

"We better call Harriman."

I still didn't say anything, so he dialed the number and asked for Frank. I sat and listened while he told Frank about the conversation. Mark was quiet on his end for a while, then said, "Look, Frank—" but was apparently interrupted. He reluctantly handed the phone to me. "He wants to talk to you."

I took it from him. "Yeah?"

"Irene? What the hell has gotten into you? Goddamn it, do you think you're invincible? You drive me nuts when you pull shit like this!"

"Good-bye, Frank. Call me back when you cool off." I hung up. Mark looked like he was going to be ill. "Frank and I will be fine, Mark. It happens all the time."

He didn't look convinced. My phone started ringing again. I didn't want to talk to Thanatos or anyone else. It was probably Frank, but I knew he hadn't had enough time to get back under control yet. I ignored it and left. I needed some air.

ST. ANNE'S IS A SHORT WALK FROM THE PAPER, BUT I GOT SOAKED anyway. I didn't have any trouble getting past the guard at Steven's door. When I came in, Steven was sleeping. He roused himself a little, looked at me, and smiled. "Hi."

"Hello. How are you feeling?"

"Better."

He had a smaller bandage on now, and his forehead had a large, dark bruise on it. The edges of stitches showed, making me wince.

"Irene? Would you call my parents?"

"Sure. You want me to call them now?"

"If you wouldn't mind. Maybe you could do most of the talking. Don't scare them, okay?" He was still pretty out of it, but apparently this had been troubling him. I reassured him and dialed the number he gave me.

"What are their names?" I asked as it rang.

"Mike and Margaret Kincaid."

A man answered the phone. I explained that I was one of Steven's friends and that I was calling at his request. "Steven has suffered a head injury. He wants me to assure you that he's okay, but he's in the hospital recovering. He wants to talk to you to let you know that he's all right."

"The hospital?" There was a second of silence, and then he yelled, "Maggie! Pick up the extension! Excuse me, Miss—?"

"Kelly."

"Miss Kelly." There was a click of the other phone being picked up. "Miss Kelly, would you please repeat that for Steven's mother?"

I did. After he calmed his wife a little, Mike Kincaid asked me to put Steven on.

I listened to Steven's half of the conversation. He reached up and took my hand when I started to move away to allow him some privacy.

"No, Mom, don't cry. I'm fine."

He listened.

"It's okay, Mom . . . Look, I'm going to let Irene talk to you . . . No, no, she's not. She's a friend."

He handed the phone over and I reassured them once again that he was recovering and would be fine. "He just tires easily. . . . Travel out here to see him?" Steven looked a little panicked and shook his head no. "No, I wouldn't come out just yet." He relaxed. "Yes, he'll call again soon." I said good-bye and hung up.

"Thank you," he said.

"No problem."

A nurse came in and saw us holding hands and gave me one of the dirtiest looks I've had in some time. Steven looked at me knowingly and smiled a little. I couldn't resist. I bent over and gave him a kiss on the cheek. "Good-bye, darling. Get some rest. I can't wait to meet your parents."

Steven's smile widened a bit and he squeezed my hand. He closed his eyes, still smiling, and said sleepily, "I'll dream about you."

God, how I enjoyed that.

I was striding down the hall, feeling my oats, when I happened to look up in one of those round mirrors that are sometimes placed at the intersection of two hallways. I saw the reflection of one very angry Frank Harriman making his way purposefully in my direction. I was fairly certain he hadn't seen me yet, and I didn't feel like facing his wrath. I looked to my left and saw a door marked "Chapel." I ducked inside.

It was dark and quiet in the small room. There were about six short pews and an altar with a large flower arrangement on it. Beyond the altar, a section of the wall held a large, stained glass crucifix, which was illuminated by a lamp of some kind behind it. To one side was a statue of St. Anne, Mary's mother, a set of votive candles flickering below it. I lit one for old times' sake, or perhaps for the comfort of ritual. I strolled over to the altar and read the tag on the flowers: Donated by Bettina Anderson. I'd have to tell Barbara about this.

*Hey, Barbara-Babs-Kelly-O'Connor, I just happened to see Lizzy-Betty-Bettina-Zanowyk-Anderson's flowers while I was cowering in the chapel at St. Anne's.*

That's one thing about being an Irene, I thought. They can sing that old song to you every time they say good night, but Irene is Irene. Sort of elemental. Not like Bettina-Elizabeth or, say, like Steven's mom, Peggy—no, Maggie-Margaret.

Something nagged at me then, and it wasn't just guilt over the fact that I was hiding from my fiancé. I sat down.

Was it something I had heard earlier in the day? Or in the conversation with Steven's parents? But when I started thinking of the Kincaids, I grew distracted, wondering if they would fly out to California anyway. A stranger's reassurance that Steven was all right probably wouldn't count for much against a mother's worry.

I sat stewing over that and Thanatos and Frank and—well, yes, religion. I can't go into a church or chapel without trying to pin myself down on exactly where I stand on the subject. I'm not an atheist. Being an atheist takes more faith than I'll ever have in any religion. It was also too late to make a good agnostic out of me—too much faith for that. And I wasn't sure I could really count myself in or out as a Catholic. I wasn't much at home in Catholicism anymore.

But when you grow up in a religion that allows a day to honor someone named "St. Christina the Astonishing," it's just not easy to make yourself feel at home any other place, either. I thought of all the Greek mythology I had been reading. Were there lapsed pagans in those days? Did they falter in their faith? Maybe faith was based on something different in ancient Greece and Rome.

If one could base one's faith on gratitude for unexpected help, appreciation for all life's narrow misses and a sense that too much undeserved good had come your way, I supposed that I did have faith.

"Hello, Cassandra," a voice said behind me.

And it was going to be tested immediately.

# 26

"HELLO, JIMMY," I SAID WITHOUT turning around. I made myself stare at St. Anne's beatific plaster smile; focused on that while I talked myself into not showing him how afraid I really felt.

He reached up and touched my hair. I felt a shudder pass through me, but suppressed any other reaction. I thought of Edna Blaylock and Rosie Thayer and Alex Havens. I thought of Steven Kincaid and Johnny Smith and Rita Havens.

He moved closer to me and whispered into my ear, speaking too low for me to recognize his unsynthesized voice. "I'm almost sorry that it has come to this, Cassandra. I had other ideas. You are the daughter of a champion of justice, and for his sake, I wanted more for you."

I was trying to think of how he had decided that I was the daughter of a champion of justice, when he solved it for me. "Oh, I know you weren't his daughter by birth, but you might as well have been, you know. Your tributes to him—the articles you wrote about him after he was murdered—it was clear to me that no one else loved him as you did. I so appreciated it when you avenged Mr. O'Connor's death. You really are Irene O'Connor, in some ways. That's why I thought you'd understand."

"What was O'Connor to you?"

"Oh, so you don't know everything after all, do you, Cassandra?"

I didn't answer. He laughed.

"One of his very first stories was about my mother's murder. Unlike those who just reported a 'killing of a female inmate,' he told her story. He knew how unfair it had all been. I saved it." I heard a rustling sound and a fragile, yellow clipping was extended over my shoulder. It had O'Connor's byline on it, all right. I couldn't resist taking it from him. I read it, feeling Thanatos' eyes on me as I did.

He must have been very young when he wrote it, but O'Connor had owned a moving style of writing from the day he first walked on the job. He painted Pauline Grant as a young woman to whom fate had been overly harsh. "Somewhere a young boy has been praying for the day when his mother will come back home to him. Who will explain to him what has become of her? As he grows to manhood, what faith will he have in justice and mercy?"

O'Connor, I thought to myself, you were the real Cassandra. You saw this coming, and no one paid heed. I handed the clipping back over my shoulder. I set aside the kind of aching longing I could so easily feel for O'Connor; I set aside a fleeting sense of hopelessness.

But as if he knew what I was feeling, he said, "Ah, you do miss him still. I understand. Time doesn't heal every wound. Not the loss of a mother to a son or a father to a daughter."

His daughter. I was chosen for Cassandra because Jimmy Grant thought of me as Irene O'Connor. "I happen to be proud of the man who gave me the Kelly name," I said. "But what's in a name?"

Saying it made me realize what had nagged at me about the conversation with Steven's parents. Margaret-Maggie. Margaret-Peggy. I had heard the same names from the women at Fielding's Nursing Home.

Margaret Robinson—Peggy Davis. Margaret Robinson whose profile at Mercury didn't quite match the others. Who lost a child and then took another as a repayment. And whose journey to the River Lethe had, perhaps, allowed her adopted son to begin his long-awaited revenge.

"Did I tell you my father was a war hero?" the voice behind me was saying. He was speaking louder now; I was sure I already knew who he was. "I want you to understand. My mother loved my father. He was killed at Pearl Harbor. He was trapped in the hold of one of those ships, but he helped other men escape before he died. My mother was only nineteen when I was born, and she was widowed by the time I was five. But she was the best mother in the world."

We heard sounds out in the hallway. "It's time to go," he said. "Look at me."

I kept my gaze straight ahead. "Aren't you afraid to take Cassandra from a sanctuary?"

"What are you talking about?"

"Oh, come now. You read your mythology. A man by the name of Ajax dragged Cassandra from Athena's temple—a sacred place—and killed her. But the gods punished Ajax for his irreverence."

"This is my game, Miss Kelly. You don't make the rules. I do. Now turn around and look at me."

"I know who you are. I don't care to look at your face."

I felt the cold, sharp tip of a knife laid up beneath my chin. I swallowed. "All right."

He laughed and moved the knife. I slowly turned around and looked into the face I knew would be there.

"Is this better, Justin?"

"Don't ever call me that again," he said angrily. He grabbed my right arm and yanked me out into the aisle between the pews. I struggled to free myself but he knocked me to the floor. He sat on my back and pulled my right arm up behind me. He laid the knife against my face.

Since someone had yanked that same arm out of its socket not three months before, I own up to being something of a wimp about my arm being pulled up behind my back in that particular manner. The pain of the first injury was by no means a distant memory. I felt queasy. Nothing less than pure, unadulterated fear coursed through me.

"We're going to go outside now," he said. "We're going to walk out to the parking lot as if we were lovers. I have this knife, but I also have a gun. And if you cause trouble, I'll empty the gun into as many bystanders as I can shoot. And I'm an excellent shot. You'll watch them die before I stab you in the heart. You'll die knowing that you caused their deaths. Do we understand one another?"

I nodded.

He pressed the knife into my cheek.

"Yes, I understand!"

"Good." He pulled me to my feet. "Take your jacket off and put it over your shoulders. Keep your arms out of the sleeves."

I did as he asked. He grabbed my arm again, but hidden beneath my jacket, it would look as if he had an arm around me in an affectionate manner. He moved to my left side. "The gun is here in my jacket. In case your busy little mind should wonder, it will not be a problem for me to fire a gun with my left hand."

He took me out into the hall. I prayed I could keep my face a mask, that no one would notice anything wrong. It was the start of evening visiting hours, and there were people everywhere. If he began shooting, he'd have no shortage of targets.

My knees were shaking. I glanced up in the same hallway mirror I had seen Frank in; now I saw him again, in the distance, coming out of Steven's room. I looked down, not wanting Justin Davis to see him, hoping Frank did not see me. I knew that if Davis saw Frank, he would shoot him. And Frank didn't know that Justin Davis was Thanatos, so he wouldn't be ready to defend himself.

I caught my reflection in some glass along the hallway, and realized I looked anything but natural. I was too scared to carry it off.

Suddenly, down the hall, I saw one of the last people I wanted to see at that moment. She stopped and briefly studied me, then came walking towards us, smiling.

"Do you know her?" Davis asked, tightening his grip on my wrist.

I nodded.

"If you don't want her to die, you'd better give a star performance."

"Hello, Sister Theresa," I said as naturally as I could.

"Irene! You've got a new haircut. And who is this?"

"This is my friend—Jimmy."

"Pleased to meet you," she said with a nod, and I thanked God that she hadn't tried to get him to shake hands.

"Well, I've got to rush," she said. "So much going on here at St. Anne's tonight—but let me see here—" She reached into her habit. I could feel the tension in my captor and watched him reach into his left-hand jacket pocket.

*Please God, no—please God, no—please.*

I was on the verge of screaming a warning when she brought her hand back out with—of all things—a holy card. I stared at it dumbly and she pushed it into my left hand. A holy card of St. Jude. I wanted to break into hysterics.

"Thank you, Sister," I croaked out.

"You do know your saints, don't you, Irene?"

"Yes, Sister." She nodded and went on down the hall.

SEVEN PEOPLE KILLED BECAUSE OF HOLY CARD. What a headline that would make. HOLY CARD BLAMED IN HOSPITAL MASSACRE. ST. JUDE SHOOTING SPREE.

I had to inwardly shout at myself to get myself to pull it back together.

We walked outside and through the cold, heavy rain as if it were not falling. He opened the passenger door to a blue van. He pulled the gun out and said, "Get in."

He climbed in behind me, poking me in the ribs with the gun. "You drive."

As I crawled into the driver's seat, I noticed something like a backpack in the back of the van. There was only one.

"Get going. Head out to Dunleavy Road."

I did as he said. I started to reconsider the backpack notion. Dunleavy Road led out to a private airstrip. It was about six miles out of town, up in the hills.

"Doing some parachuting?" I asked.

"You'll be dead by the time I do."

"Nasty weather for it."

"That's merely a reprieve for you. But the storm is letting up, and by tomorrow, when we take off, the skies should be that glorious blue that only rain or a Santa Ana wind can bring to Southern California."

"This storm doesn't look like it's letting up."

"Oh, but it is. This is just the tail end of it. I've monitored this storm quite closely. You'll see. Before long, it will hardly be drizzling."

We fell into silence as I made the series of turns that would take us out to Dunleavy. Once or twice I thought someone was following us. My hopes would soar, then be dashed at the next intersection.

"I know your mother was killed," I said. "But why blame people who were only children? Why not go after people who were adults at the time?"

"Ah, so your curiosity is still alive. Good, good. It will make these last hours of yours pass more pleasantly." He didn't say anything for a while, then answered. "They set themselves up as gods. The Olympus Center and its little gods. It was time for them to fall from Olympus."

"But they were *children*."

"Children are the most cruel beings on earth."

"They didn't even remember the incident."

"Exactly. The most painful, awful time of my life. And to them? Nothing. They caused my mother's death. They blamed her. They were wrong."

"She did lose her temper."

"No. They said she lost her temper, but she didn't. You see, they were false judges. None of them saw what happened very clearly. But they took advantage of us. We were poor. My mother couldn't afford the kind of attorney that could have saved her life."

"She didn't deny hurting the boy."

"Don't you see? She was trying to protect me. I shoved that miserable sonofabitch into the wall. *I did!* The little bastard was choking me to death. She ran over, she tried to pull him off me, but I was the one who shoved him into that wall! They were liars! They were all liars! They hated me and they lied!" He was shouting, and scaring the hell out of me. His eyes were wild and angry, and I berated myself for bringing the whole subject up.

He grew quiet, then said, "She was the best mother in the world."

I looked over at him. He was crying.

We turned onto Dunleavy. There's about a five mile strip of it that runs along a flood control channel. As he had said it would, the rain had lightened to a drizzle, but the road was slick and muddy from rain and road construction. Bulldozers and graders sat idle on the right shoulder.

I glanced into the side mirror and felt knots forming in my stomach. We were being followed. I was fairly sure it was Frank's car. I realized it would be much harder for him to stay out of sight on this dark, deserted road.

Jimmy looked into the mirror on his side.

"What about Maggie Robinson?" I asked, trying to distract him. "She was a good mother, wasn't she?"

He turned to glare at me. "She was a rotten bitch who did nothing but punish me for her son's death for years. She was a little worried at first, afraid the Social Service people would come around, check on her. Afraid they hadn't made me disappear."

"What do you mean?"

"Don't pretend you don't know. Your detective friend was looking into it. You know what he learned. I was just so much lost paperwork. When my stepmother began to realize that she and J.D. had pulled it off, she started beating me. She used to tie me up and burn me with cigarettes. Look!" He pulled back a sleeve. There were rounded scars all along the inside of his arm. "I'd scream bloody murder, but did anyone ever help me? No. I was that poor Mrs. Davis's problem child."

He was silent for a moment, brooding. "I learned from her, though. I learned how to be invisible. It was the only way to be safe. I learned how to avoid attracting attention. She needed attention—couldn't get enough of it. I didn't. It made me stronger than her. No one knew what I was thinking, what I was feeling."

"Why didn't you just kill *her*?"

"I thought about it," he said. "Especially after my mother died. Peggy wouldn't let me grieve for my own mother. She'd tell me over and over how glad she was that my mother was dead. 'Now we're even,' she'd say. But I didn't let her know what I felt. It didn't matter. She didn't matter. She was mean, she was greedy, she was selfish—but she wasn't the one who caused the problem in the first place. The little liars caused it. Not her. Peggy Davis. Pathetic. She wasn't any more real than I was. She made sure I wasn't. Made me change my name. My name! My father was a war hero and I couldn't use his name!"

"So Margaret Robinson became Margaret Davis," I said softly, trying to get him to lower his own voice, to calm down. "It took me a while to make the connection between the nicknames for Margaret; she just changed from Maggie to Peggy. And you became Justin Davis."

He was looking in the mirror again and didn't answer me.

"Jimmy," I asked, trying to get his attention away from it, "why now? Why did you wait all these years?"

He looked back at me. "She would have told on me."

"Who, Edna?"

"No, no. Peggy. I used to be afraid of her. Not now. Not now . . . but before, before I learned that she was weak, she knew how to scare me. She was in control. That's what it's all about, you know. Being in control. She knew about me, so she was in charge. The person in control has to know everything. That's why I'm in control now. I know you. I've studied you. I know your secrets. Peggy . . . she knew all kinds of things. We had . . ." his eyes darted away from me for a moment. "We had secrets," he said, watching me again, as if looking for some reaction. When I said nothing, he went on. "But then the funniest thing happened. She forgot! She forgot everything! I thought it was one of her tricks at first, but it wasn't. She couldn't tell anyone anything. Nothing at all! Isn't that funny?"

He smiled at me. It was the first time I had ever seen him smile for more than a few seconds. A big, gentle smile. It transformed him somehow, and oddly, for a brief moment, he wasn't so frightening. There was a small boy there, an eight-year-old, perhaps. *What kind of monster wouldn't pity Jimmy Grant?* he once asked me. There was a killer beneath his smile, yes—but I wondered who he might have become if someone as monstrous as Peggy Davis hadn't been allowed to raise him.

He looked over at the side mirror.

The smile was gone.

"You bitch! You had us followed. It's your boyfriend, isn't it? Step on it—go on, speed up!"

"The road is muddy here—"

"Goddamn it! I said speed up!"

I stepped down on the accelerator. It was all I could do to keep the van under control.

"Damn you! Why did you have to ruin everything! It could have been so wonderful! I would have been good to you, you know." He rolled down his window and leaned out with the gun. "Say good-bye to Mr. Harriman. He's about to die, Cassandra."

Suddenly I didn't care what Jimmy Grant might do to me. I only knew that I wouldn't let him kill Frank. I used the only weapon I had on hand. I jerked the steering wheel hard to the right.

# 27

For a few seconds, it was dreamlike; an unreal combination of motion and time that didn't fit in the usual order of either. The van went into a spin, the mud from the construction removing all friction from beneath the wheels. We glided along at an amazing speed. With a deafening bang, we tore through a chain-link fence, then suddenly there was a sensation of moving though space. Which, of course, is exactly what we were doing.

For an instant I saw the concrete walls of the flood control channel sailing by in the headlights. Then all too soon, a bone-jarring impact, an explosion of sound, blackness.

I don't know how long I was out. When I came to, I thought for a moment that I had been blinded—it was pitch black. I hurt like hell all over—but my right side was killing me. The left side of my head throbbed, and I couldn't even figure out what I had hit it on. I could hear the roar of water rushing by me. Jimmy Grant was groaning and pleading for help. I had no idea where he was. I had no idea where I was. I had never felt such an utterly complete sense of disorientation.

My eyes began adjusting to the darkness—no, not adjusting. The moon was coming out. But my perspective on my surroundings seemed odd to me. Gradually, I realized that the van had landed on its side in the channel, blowing out the windows and headlights with the impact. I was covered with bits of glass, suspended above the water by my seat belt, which was pressing painfully into my right hip and my chest. I felt for and found the steering wheel, gripping it to ease some of the pressure from the belt. I straightened my legs, bracing my feet against the floorboard to help as well.

It was then that I got my first look at Jimmy Grant. His face was a bloody mess, and it was the only part of him that was above water. A mask, eyes wide with fright. "Help me," he said. I was still dazed, and couldn't figure out at first what was wrong. Then I saw that he was being pressed against the seat by the force of the current, and that he had somehow tangled himself in his seat belt. The moon went behind a cloud, and I lost sight of him.

I tried reaching down to him with my right hand. He must have somehow worked a hand free, because I felt his left hand grasp on to mine, skin chilled and wet. "Help," he said again, as if he expected none.

I pulled him up a little farther. The water was cold, and he had heavier clothes on than I did. They were weighing him down. Debris from the channel, sticks and old beer cans and small stones were coming in through the windshield, striking hard against him.

"I can't," he said weakly. "I can't hang on."

The moon came out again and I took another look at him. With horror, I saw that his right arm was almost completely severed. He had to be losing a lot of blood from it. His grip was weakening, and I knew I wouldn't be able to hold him by myself. Panic filled his face. Suddenly a large dark object rocketed against him; there was a loud cracking sound as it rammed into his head with an awful force. A tree limb, I realized, as it spun back out into the current. He suddenly released his grip and fell back into the water, his head at an odd angle.

There was a creaking sound, and I felt the van move. Every few minutes, objects from the channel would bang against it. Fearing the kind of blow I had just seen kill Jimmy Grant, I used every ounce of strength I had to pull myself back up away from the water. I had to get out.

The driver's-side window above me was broken, but jagged edges made me loath to try to go through it. I tried opening the door. It wouldn't budge. I'd have better luck with the window. I took my jacket off slowly, afraid that if I moved too much I'd end up in the water with Jimmy Grant.

Finally it was off. I covered my arm with it, awkwardly bracing myself as best I could, and smashed out the remaining pieces of glass. For a moment, I thought I heard a voice, but it was lost in the roar of the water. I shouted back, hoping someone could hear me over the noise.

Now I faced a dilemma. If I loosened the seat belt, and didn't have the strength to pull myself out, I'd fall into the channel. If I didn't, the belt would continue to hold me to the seat, but I'd never be able to crawl out of the window.

I gripped the edge of the window sill with one arm, and loosened the belt. My legs braced me for a moment, and I put the other hand up. I tried to push myself up. I slipped. In one arm-wrenching motion, I was left hanging, my arms above me, my legs in the cold water, the rest of me getting splashed with it. My headache was suddenly galloping through my skull. There was something soft beneath my feet. With alarm, I realized it was Jimmy Grant.

The horror of standing on him brought a surge of energy to me. I used my legs to scramble up on to the console between the seats and out of the water. I rested a moment, then straightened my legs. Gradually, pulling with my arms and pushing with my feet, I managed to get myself through the window. Sick and dizzy, I crawled out on to the side of the van.

I lay there shivering, utterly exhausted. I heard my name.

"Irene!" I rolled on to my side and looked over at the bank. Frank was standing there.

I waved a tired arm at him.

"Are you okay?" he shouted.

"I'm okay!" I shouted back, even though it made my head hurt.

"Stay there, help is coming."

Stay there. I wanted to laugh. I guess he thought I would try swimming ashore. I could barely move. Even if I had the strength, I knew not to try it.

Frank was pacing the bank like a tiger in a cage. I could tell he wanted to do something, was frustrated.

"Relax!" I shouted.

I could hear him laugh. A nice sound.

Soon I also heard sirens. Red lights pulsed as police and emergency vehicles pulled up. Spotlights were turned on and aimed at the van.

A helicopter arrived. They lowered a man down, who wrapped me in the welcome warmth of a big blanket. He helped me into a harness, and I was taken up into the hovering helicopter.

I was a little pissed off that my first helicopter ride was such a short one, but I was anxious to reach Frank and reassure him. Paramedics stepped in before I could do much along those lines. They talked about taking me to the hospital, but I managed to convince them that I wasn't suffering anything worse than bruises and a headache.

The rescue workers had warmed me up again with more blankets and warm liquids. I was battered but lucid, no longer suffering the worst part of the cold-water soaking. Eventually I answered questions from some of Frank's coworkers. They seemed to believe they'd know where to find me if they had more questions. I didn't want to stick around to watch Jimmy being taken from the water.

I knew Frank was really shaken, because he didn't talk much while all of this was going on; he just took my hand between his and held onto it for a long time. Finally, someone said I could go home. We were both ready for that.

We crawled into bed together and he rubbed my sore muscles while we told each other stories about our evenings. He had been walking away from Steven Kincaid's room when a nun came running up to him and told him I was in danger. Good old Sister Theresa. She hadn't missed a thing. Jimmy Grant just didn't know what he was up against. The holy card hadn't just been a stalling tactic, she told me later. St. Jude is the patron saint of hopeless causes.

EVEN THOUGH WE WERE BOTH WORN OUT, FRANK AND I TALKED FOR A long time that night. We fell asleep spooning, and all things considered, I'll take spooning with Frank over a helicopter ride any old day.

THE NEXT DAY, THE *EXPRESS* RAN A STORY ON THE DEATH OF DEATH, OR Thanatos. It provided details Mark Baker had worked hard to gather: Jimmy Grant/Justin Davis had rigged his own fuel mix in an attempt to draw suspicion away from himself. As Justin Davis, he had provided software for some of the computer security for Mercury Aircraft, and made sure he had access to it as long as he needed it. As the police were already learning by the time he abducted me, Davis had also done work for Las Piernas College, including providing a card key system for employee access. It wasn't difficult for him to get into Edna Blaylock's and Don Edgerton's offices. He planted the voice synthesizer in Edgerton's office.

While Edgerton was the buyer of a hunter's slingshot, the police suspected that during the time Jimmy Grant was stalking his intended victims, he learned of the purchase. He obtained a similar one.

Edgerton, it turned out, was trying to write a baseball book on the rise and fall of the Pacific Coast League, a strong minor league that had boasted the likes of Joe DiMaggio in the days before the Dodgers or the Giants moved west. Edgerton, self-conscious about his writing, had become nervous when he saw me getting near his manuscript. He later hired Mark Baker to help him write the book.

THREE DAYS AFTER MY HELICOPTER RIDE, STEVEN KINCAID CAME HOME from the hospital, worried about a scar that only made his handsome looks more dashing. Bea Harriman was looking in on him for me.

I told Bea about a young woman named Helen, from a sporting goods store, who had agreed to help out with Steven during his recovery. Bea promised to make sure they at least laid eyes on one another.

Jack was taking care of the dogs, and Barbara, who seemed to be worried about a decline in Jack's attentions, was stopping by to feed Cody. She had insisted.

AS FOR ME, I WAS DRIVING THE VOLVO HOME FROM LAS VEGAS. THE desert air was warm, the windows down, and from the tapedeck, Duke Ellington provided a delicious rendition of "All the Things You Are." Mr. and Mrs. Pete Baird were cuddled up in the backseat together, snoring in unison. On the seat next to me, my husband slept with a smile on his face.